For Troy —

THE SIRENS OF M

# The Sirens of Ming Hai

## John Williamson

The Verona Press, Inc.

The Verona Press, Inc.

Richmond, Virginia

Copyright (c) 2000 by John Williamson

Printed in the United States of America

First printing: October, 2000

This is a work of fiction. All of the characters, incidents, and dialogue are imaginary.

All rights reserved. No part of this book may be reproduced in any form or by any electronic or mechanical means, including information storage and retrieval systems, without permission in writing from the publisher, except by a reviewer who may quote brief passages in a review.

Excerpts from "The Laogai Archipelago" by David Aikman, September 29, 1997, used with permission of *The Weekly Standard*. Copyright News America Incorporated.

Publisher's Cataloging in Publication:
   (Provided by Quality Books, Inc.)
Williamson, John Lutz
      The sirens of Ming Hai / John Williamson. –
   1st ed.
      p. cm.
   LCCN: 00-190536
   ISBN: 0-9700144-0-6

   1. Spies—Fiction. 2. Chinese reunification question, 1949- —Fiction. I. Title.
   PS3545.I5575S57 2000 813.6
                  QBI00-403

*Remembering the prisoners of conscience who, desiring freedom for all of China, are denied their own.*

# Acknowledgements

I would like first to thank the manuscript readers:

Jim Boykin  Suzanne Wendelken-Ries  V. Lee Bailey  Benjamin Butler, Esquire  Paul and Anna Bojanowski  Christopher A. Lewis  Bobby and Julie Williamson  Suzanne Bojanowski  Vicki Yerly  Jim and Carol Rose  Jerry Creehan  Lisa Bain  Jessica Schesventer  Judy Katzen  Cathy Ratner  Peggy Prezioso  Charles and Betty Schesventer

I would like to express immense gratitude to Ms. Vikki Ball, Community Relations Coordinator for Border's Books and Music in Richmond, for the interest shown in the present volume and for her advice and assistance, so freely and so patiently given.

I would like to salute Lieutenant Commander Eric Cheney, United States Navy, who flew the A6E off the *USS America*, for supplying basic information on naval aviation terminology and weapons systems. The responsibility for any creative misapplication of his instruction rests solely with the author.

I would like to thank Cabell Harris and the staff of the Richmond advertising agency Work, Inc. for the concept and planning of the cover art. David Waraksa, Designer; Wynn Cole, Administrative Assistant.

Dean Hawthorne of Hawthorne Studios was the cover photographer. John Gerber was the assistant photographer. The cover model was Su Thongpan.

I would also like to acknowledge advice and assistance received from June Stephenson, Community Relations Manager, Barnes & Noble in Richmond, and from Charlie Finley, Verbatim Editing.

I would like to thank Lewis Creative Technologies, the printers and Chris Lewis, president, in particular.

There are others who have helped along the way whom I would like to mention: Donald and Stephana Hipsman, Troy and Tammy Henion, Steve and Mary Wilson, Tina Bailey, Captain Timothy J. Moriarty, USMC (Ret.), Doctor Gary M. and Kathy Hadfield, Robert and Mary Ann Williamson, George

Lewis, Buddy Jones, Richard Burns, Brian Moyer, Katie Bawell, Oliver Overby, Charles Chitty, Mike Hightower, Charles Barsavage, Sidney Richardson, Martina Slater, Robert Shanks, Susan Laverty, Bruce Redman, Don Engiles, Norma Jaramillo, Peggy Prezioso, Jessica Schesventer, Nova Lee Dickerson, David Smitherman, Jim and Penny Cottrell, Martha Anderson, Ron and Patsy Cottrell, the Right Learned Mr. Linwood W. Davis and the mysterious Madame Who?

Catering by Cuisine a la Carte.

Finally, I would like to thank the many musicians who provided the music to write by: L. van Beethoven, Sir Edward Elgar, J. Sibelius, S. Rachmaninoff, The Doors, F. Mendelssohn, The Eroica Trio, J.S. Bach, Aerosmith, G. Gershwin, G. Verdi, Virgil Fox, S. Brightman, G.F. Handel, Sheryl Crow, W.A. Mozart, C. Church and, of course, the world's greatest rock and roll band – ladies and gentlemen...The Rolling Stones.

# The Sirens of Ming Hai

## CHAPTER 1

On a mild and sunny day in March, Jennifer Jiang stood on the sidewalk in front of the Los Angeles Industrial Trade Building and stared almost straight up. Twenty stories tall, the outer walls comprised of vast sheets of dark glass, it was the most forbidding building she had ever seen; she hated to go in there.

It was not that she harbored any particular sentiment regarding issues of industrial trade – that could hardly be the case; rather it was that, housed on the penthouse floor of the trade building was a suite of offices which reminded her of the fact that, although she lived in America, she could never be free.

But because she was the niece of a fairly high-ranking Chinese government official, Jennifer was required to meet with the West Coast-based Chinese consul general each year, just prior to the renewal of her visa. In the past it had been a mere formality, her visit prompted by a reminder postcard sent through the mail.

This year, however, was different. Ji Wan Li, the consul general himself, had called and left a message, asking her to visit today at two o'clock.

She looked at her watch. It was five minutes before the hour; she could delay no longer. She stepped out of the Southern

California sunlight and into the dark, cavernous lobby of the building.

As she walked through the doors, she immediately felt a sick feeling in her stomach. She wanted to turn and run back to her car. She could telephone from her apartment and tell them she wasn't feeling well.

She knew how they would react to that: if she did not show up today, they would come to her apartment. To inquire after her health. To see that all was well, and to reschedule the appointment.

No, this was better. Go in, find out what they wanted and get it over with. She approached the lobby receptionist. "The consulate, please."

She was directed to a special elevator which went directly to the penthouse floor. When the elevator opened on the twentieth floor, she stepped into an exotic, yet familiar world. The walls were darkly paneled. The floors were covered in Chinese silk rugs.

She felt the eye of a dozen cameras, hidden in walls, watching her every move. A woman sat behind a vast desk and watched as she approached. "I have an appointment to see Ji Wan Li, please."

"Miss Jiang?" said the receptionist. "Yes, he was expecting you. I'll advise the consul general you're here. If you would like to wait in the gallery..."

Jennifer strolled around the spacious art gallery. There were gorgeous sculptures of Chinese dragons as well as warriors from the Han Dynasty. There were portraits of the greatest figures in Chinese history – emperors, scholars, the great Mao Zedong, as well as the current premier of the People's Republic. She found the objets d'art to be at once both beautiful and almost frightening in the sense of power they conveyed.

And then she heard his voice. "Jiang Ou."

She turned, startled. It was Ji Wan Li, standing in the doorway of his office, framed in the blinding light which came from that room. He was tall and imposing and powerfully built; she had always feared him.

He had called her by her Chinese name; on the three occasions they had previously met, he never called her by her Americanized name. He was known to despise the practice of Chinese nationals who adopted Western names; he considered it a kind of disloyalty.

"Come in," he said, speaking to her in Mandarin Chinese. She followed him into his large, elegantly furnished office. "Please sit down. Tea?"

She started to decline, as an American might do in similar circumstances, but then she remembered that, for the time that she was in this building, in this room, she was not in America; she was in a part of China, and in China it would be considered rude to decline a social offering from an important government official.

"You are doing well in school?" he inquired as he poured the tea.

"Very well, thank you, Honorable Consul General," she replied, following his lead and speaking in Chinese.

"I have your grades from UCLA," he mentioned casually as he picked up her file and leafed through it. "If you were a typical American student, I might commend you; however, for a Chinese student studying in America, this is not a particularly distinguishing record. You're studying hard, at least, I hope?"

"I do work hard at my studies, Honorable Consul General."

He placed several photos on the table. "These pictures tell a different story." He picked up the one on top and held it out to her. It was she, sitting in a crowded Beverly Hills nightclub; she was in the company of several television actors and appeared to be enjoying herself immensely. "And here you are again," he said, showing her a photo of herself in the company of a well-known talk show host whom she had met on the beaches of Malibu. "This is you, is it not?"

There were still more photos – of Jennifer in famous restaurants, Jennifer at extravagant Bel Air parties, Jennifer aboard a yacht, Jennifer at Lake Tahoe, Jennifer at a movie premiere in Hollywood.

Jennifer Jiang, it seemed, was everywhere – everywhere but in the library of UCLA, in the classroom, or in the lecture hall.

"I didn't choose a monastic existence when I came to America," she said defensively. "I was never told that I couldn't enjoy myself; I am a student, after all."

Ji Wan Li was contemplative. "Jiang Ou, how old are you now?"

"Twenty-one," she replied. "As I'm sure your records will clearly show," she added pointedly.

He set her file to the side. "Let me come to the point. You have spent more than a sufficient amount of time in the United States; it's time for you to return to China."

"But I haven't received my degree!"

"You have completed all of your course work, and are merely biding time. At any rate, I believe you have all the education you need in order to be the wife of a rising party official. Have you forgotten the man to whom you are engaged?"

She was jolted by that question. She hardly ever thought of her formal engagement, made years before, to Du Ming.

"I called you here today," Ji announced sternly, "to inform you that you are to return to Beijing on a flight that leaves Los Angeles tomorrow."

"Tomorrow?" She stood, her knees a little wobbly. "That's out of the question."

"Sit down, please, Jiang Ou."

"But…I don't love Du Ming," she protested. "I can't marry him."

"Love!" Ji scoffed. "Yes, you have definitely been here too long. You're starting to sound like an American…or to think like one, which is even worse.

"You must understand the political situation, Jiang Ou," he added coldly. "Your uncle Song Bei has been promoted once again. He will soon be looked at as a possible minister in the State Council. And yet he's still young; who knows how high he might ultimately go?"

She shuddered quietly at the mention of her uncle's name.

She had no doubt of his rise to power. She knew him well enough to know that he would stop at nothing to further his ambitions; if he were being considered for the State Council then he was already approaching the highest rungs of power in the Chinese central government. "I've always known that Song Bei would succeed," she admitted quietly.

"Indeed," said the consul. "Therefore you must understand that your continued presence here is starting to be of some concern. How would it look for a high-ranking official to have a family member who frequents nightclubs, strolls half-clothed along the beaches of Malibu and leads a typically decadent American existence? Not good, not good at all. A decent propagandist working against our interests might get the impression that you somehow...approved of the American way of life. You don't approve of the American way of life, do you, Little Jiang?"

"I think..." she said quietly, "I think it has a few advantages."

"I see; well, in that case, you've definitely been here too long."

"But what if I refuse to marry Du Ming?" she said defiantly. "Even in China, one is not forced to marry someone that one has no feelings for."

"For the ordinary citizen, that may be true," Ji conceded. "However, in cases where there are political considerations at stake...well, Du Ming is a strong supporter and valued ally of your uncle; his feelings must be considered. I'm sorry, Jiang Ou, but the decision has been made."

"I have every right to be here."

Ji merely laughed. "With one telephone call to the Americans, your visa authorization will be removed from the renewal list. It's a courtesy they'll extend to us without hesitation. And don't even think about disappearing into the vast expanses of the American Northwest, or some such romantic notion; such a move would be futile. Besides, such an action would hurt your family very deeply: your young brother and your seven cousins, all still in school, all still full of bright hopes for their own futures. You wouldn't wish to jeopardize their prospects, now would you, Jiang Ou?"

"This is unfair, Honorable Consul General."

"Unfair?" he said with a laugh. "Spare me, Jiang Ou. You've had advantages far greater than those of almost any of your contemporaries; even in your expectations and your complaints, you've become Americanized."

She knew it would be useless to try to persuade him. "May I go, then?"

"Any time you like," he replied. "And here I have your ticket," he added, holding it out for her. "The government will pay for your return home."

She stood and walked across the vast office but, just as she opened the door, she heard him speak. "Although..." he said quietly. "Perhaps there is a solution..."

She stopped and turned and looked at him. "I'm sorry?"

"There are alternatives," he said, rising from his chair and approaching her. He took her hand and led her back into the room. "Reasonable alternatives. If you wish to remain in the United States, perhaps you might choose to be of value to your own country."

"What are you saying, Honorable Consul General?"

"Have you ever considered the possibility of using your talents to serve China?"

"To serve China? In what way?"

"As an observer of the American political scene."

"An observer...? I'm sorry, I don't understand..."

"Oh, come now, Jiang Ou; don't be so obtuse. As an agent."

It took her a moment to understand what he was saying. "A *spy*? No, I couldn't possibly do that. What talents do I have? I have no training in those areas."

"Formal training isn't everything," he noted. "When trying to enter the highest circles of a foreign government, far more than ordinary training is required."

He circled her slowly, pointing out the obvious. "You are quite beautiful...young, poised, well-educated in the arts. But you are no mere adornment; you are tough-minded, intelligent.

Oh, yes, we have observed a great deal about you. You have the ability to vault into any social circle; that's quite clear from these photos."

He picked them up and held them out to her. "You could be of value to us and, as for your engagement to Du Ming, he would be told that you are performing a very valuable function and that he must sacrifice as well. No doubt he will understand; and perhaps...if your service is valuable enough, your engagement to Du Ming could be annulled. The premier himself can play a role in all of this, particularly if your service to your country is exemplary. There now, might you consider our idea just a little?"

The chance to stay in the United States and to be free of past entanglements was a temptation which deserved a fair hearing. Jennifer's silence was interpreted by Ji Wan Li as her willingness to listen.

They both sat back down. Ji pressed a buzzer and, within a few moments, a side door was opened. A tall, thin, bespectacled man walked into the room.

"This is Wei Gang," said the consul general, introducing a member of his staff. "He will explain the plan we have for you."

Wei Gang nodded his greeting to Jennifer, placed a large photograph on a stand and began speaking in rapid Mandarin. "This is the residence at 625 Q Street, Washington, D.C.," he said. "In this apartment building lives an American by the name of Ellen Conley. Recently divorced, she has a six year old son named Gregory; she works on Capitol Hill as a staff assistant in the office of Senator Joseph Callahan of the state of Maine.

"Currently living with her is He Nan Lin," continued Wei Gang, "a Chinese national who began sharing the apartment with Ms. Conley over a year ago. We asked Nan Lin to help us in the same way that we are now asking you. We were hoping that she and Ellen would become close friends, and that Ellen could introduce her into certain exclusive social and political circles in Washington. Unfortunately, He Nan Lin did not have the social skills which would permit her to succeed."

"It's most unfortunate that this opportunity was wasted on someone of such limited ability," interrupted Ji, "but I blame myself for that."

"I don't understand how…"

"During the time she was going through her divorce," continued Wei Gang, "Ellen Conley made the acquaintance of a young American naval pilot by the name of Lieutenant Nicholas Ferguson. Does the name Ferguson mean anything to you?"

Jennifer thought for a moment. "Well, there's just the vice president of the…" She looked up, a stunned expression on her face.

"Exactly; *that* Lieutenant Nicholas Ferguson – the son of Mark Ferguson, the vice president of the United States."

"So they are seeing one another then, Lieutenant Ferguson and Miss Conley?" she inquired. "Then I don't understand what my role would be."

"According to He Nan Lin," continued Wei Gang, "the lieutenant and Ms. Conley are no longer lovers, merely friends. Miss Conley is now considering marriage to a wealthy New York manufacturer. And yet Nicholas continues to visit Ellen Conley, mainly because of his affection for young Gregory.

"Ms. Conley approves of this continued visitation," he continued, "perhaps because her ex-husband doesn't pay much attention to the boy; or perhaps because she still holds out hope for a last minute reconciliation with Nicholas. Who can know these things? Now then, as we have planned it, you will take the place of He Nan Lin. She will be ordered to move out of the apartment immediately. She will advise Ellen that she has a friend who's moving to Washington from Los Angeles and would be most willing to take over the sublease rental agreement."

"Who knows?" added the consul general. "Perhaps you'll get to know young Nicholas when he returns from his current sea cruise; undoubtedly he'll find you to be quite attractive."

Jennifer was not completely convinced. "How do you know Lieutenant Ferguson would be interested in a Chinese woman?"

"We know quite a bit about the young man," answered Wei Gang. "When he was stationed at Iwakuni Naval Base in Japan, he practically lived with a young Japanese woman. He has no racial prejudices as far as we can tell; he loves women of every nationality."

"Young Ferguson is quite a dandy," added the consul general. "Handsome, brash, charming. If he likes you, he'll introduce you to many people; and there's never a shortage of important people in Washington who would be delighted to get to know the son of the vice president and whoever she is that he happens to be dating."

"And if I were to do this..." Jennifer asked tentatively. "What do you expect from me?"

"We want information," said the consul general. "Information at the highest levels. We want to know the attitudes that American officials have toward us. We want to know if their public statements match their private sentiments. We're not asking you to break into buildings or steal military secrets. Keep your relationships purely social; just meet people, go to parties, make friends, listen carefully, and tell us what you hear. This is a particularly vital time, especially with the American presidential elections this fall."

"But I am a Chinese national...and my uncle...I can't..."

"The Americans will not know that Song Bei is your uncle," said Wei Gang. "Song Bei and your father are stepbrothers – with different family names. Even the famed Secret Service will have no reason to take an interest in your background; after all, your father is a museum curator in Nanjing, and you are a student of the arts. You will be in Washington looking for work as an interpreter – all perfectly innocent. And besides, any important official who takes an interest in you will find a way to shield your identity. Those in positions of power will always have ways of keeping someone like you out of the public eye."

"So I'm to use Nicholas Ferguson as a stepping stone, then?"

"We want you to go to the highest level you can," said Ji. "Certainly Nicholas will introduce you to the vice president – whose wife died two years ago, I might add; you may well befriend him; or - who knows? - perhaps you can be introduced at the White House; you may become known to the president himself."

"The president! Why that's...the president is a married

man!"

"Technically, you are correct," said Wei Gang. "However, it's an open secret that the president's wife works as a book editor in New York during the week and that she sees the president only on weekends. And sometimes not even then – they each have separate cabins at Camp David. Sometimes Mrs. Billingsley arrives from New York on Friday afternoon with a young male editorial assistant in her company, and sometimes the president arrives with a female staff assistant."

"Of course, if you were to become the friend of the president himself," said the consul general, "you would exceed all of our wildest expectations; but it is not necessary to pressure yourself with these matters; you can do us some good at almost any level."

"You expect me to become a concubine, then?"

"We have no expectations other than that you succeed," said the consul general. "How far you choose to go in making available your considerable…charms is entirely your decision. Is there a problem, Jiang Ou? Is there some other man in your life?"

She stiffened; she could not even consider answering that question. "No," she said quickly. "No, of course there's no one else."

"Good," he said with a smile. "Now then, you hold in your hand a one-way ticket to Beijing; it leaves Los Angeles tomorrow night. If you like, you may trade it for *this* one-way ticket to Washington, D.C; that flight leaves at ten a.m. tomorrow. If you choose the one to Washington, you will be contacted by our embassy soon after you arrive. Pack only what you need right away; the movers will send the rest within a day or two.

"Now then, Little Jiang," said the consul general. "The time has come for you to make a decision. You may spend the next few months – perhaps a year – in Washington; or you may return to Beijing; it's your choice."

"Do you need to know my answer now?"

"Yes, Little Jiang. You must choose now."

There was no mistaking the vice president of the United States: at six feet three inches, with a square-cut jaw, he still possessed the bearing and imposing presence of a four star admiral, the rank which he had held prior to being chosen for the vice presidency.

As he walked side by side with President Edward Billingsley into the ceremonial area of the Rose Garden on the South Lawn of the White House, the vice president was greeted with a perfervid round of applause from the White House staff as well as from various congressional, military and corporate guests.

The navy band struck up and, in deference to the vice president, played *Anchors Aweigh* rather than *Hail to the Chief*.

The ceremony was brief, but poignant. Television cameras recorded the entire scene, to be broadcast nationally that evening.

A senior naval officer read the inscription which accompanied the award. It described how Mark Ferguson, Jr., the older of the vice president's two sons, had been killed nearly ten years before, during a training accident at Naval Flight School in Pensacola, Florida. Ensign Ferguson's jet engine had cut out on him and he had been unable to recover power.

The plane had been in too close proximity to navy housing for him to consider ejecting. Ensign Ferguson had stayed with the plane, choosing to ride it into the beach just past a section of densely populated enlisted quarters.

The funeral had been attended not only by hundreds of his fellow officers – which was expected, but by more than half of the enlisted population of the Pensacola Naval Air Station – which was not.

One of the pallbearers at the ensign's funeral was his younger brother Nicholas, who would later follow his brother to Annapolis, to Pensacola, and out into the fleet, where he was now assigned to the carrier *USS Andrew Jackson* as a lieutenant-pilot.

"...for conspicuous gallantry, above and beyond the call of duty; for placing the safety of his fellow servicemen and their families above his own, the self-sacrificial actions of the late Ensign Ferguson are hereby honored as being fully in keeping with the highest traditions of the United States Naval Services."

The president stepped forward and presented the vice president with the Distinguished Flying Cross, posthumously awarded, encased in a frame. The navy band played the national anthem, and then it was over.

After receiving the admiring wishes of the many guests present, the vice president made his way to his limousine, where he was joined by Paul Blake, his chief-of-staff, and Eric Whitford, his senior political adviser.

"Well, that was terrific," said Blake as the limo pulled away. "Sir, it looks like the president is going to pull out all the stops to make sure you stay on the ticket with him. Birthday party for you at the White House held last month, special high visibility duties assigned to you, and now this: a long overdue medal for your son presented in a Rose Garden ceremony. Give the man credit; he's trying."

"The president knows what's good for him," added Whitford. "The polls that came out this morning show that, without the admiral in the second spot, Billingsley loses the general election."

"That's not the worst of it," said Blake. "Polls are now starting to show that the party would do better in November if the vice president were at the top of the ticket. Sir, are you sure you don't want to come out and declare for the presidency yourself? I know you've said that you weren't going to do that, but look at these numbers."

The vice president's thoughts were a million miles away. He glanced at the newspaper for an instant, and then returned to his view through the window of the limousine.

"Gentlemen," he said at last, as he watched some boys playing football in a small city park, "I know as well as the two of you what it was that motivated the president to do what he did today. I wasn't born yesterday; but the simple fact is that Mark is dead and the fact is he did deserve the medal. So if it's all the same to you fellows, I'd just as soon not talk about politics for the duration of the day."

The three men rode in silence the rest of the way to the office.

BY SEVEN P.M., the westering sun had long since slipped below the horizon as the *USS Andrew Jackson* sat in the choppy waters of the Western Atlantic, five hundred miles off the coast of Georgia. Lit up like a Christmas tree, the flight deck of the huge Nimitz-class carrier was a beehive of activity as the crew pushed through a third harrowing evening of night operations.

From a distance of five miles out and an altitude of five thousand feet, the pilot of Ranger Flight Twenty approached the carrier at a descent rate of seven hundred feet per minute and requested clearance to land.

"Roger, Ranger Flight Two Oh," came the reply from the tower of the great carrier. "You are cleared for Case Three VFR recovery, approach time seven-oh-six and thirty seconds Zulu; over."

"Roger." Lieutenant Nicholas Ferguson lowered his airspeed to two hundred fifty knots, dropped his tailhook, put his speed brakes out, and let his landing gear down. He lowered his flaps and brought his F/A-18E Super Hornet down sweet and steady, never veering from his approach to the groove, keeping the plane's nose up and the wings horizontal.

With a deafening roar, the plane dropped almost even with the deck and caught the steel arresting cable stretched across the deck. He hit the "wire" perfectly and stretched it hard as the plane came to a rolling stop and then started to roll backwards as the hydraulic cable system recoiled.

When the plane had taxied into position, a crew came out to take control. Lieutenant Ferguson popped his canopy, unbuckled his harness and began the process of climbing down to the deck.

Steady on his feet, he now removed his flight helmet. Walking across the deck, he was approached by his chief flight technician, Petty Officer First Class F.T. Mullins.

"Great flight, sir."

"Thanks, F.T.," Ferguson replied to the petty officer. "Listen, I need to talk to Krumbein ASAP."

"Krumbein, sir?" said the chief tech. "Is something wrong?"

"Look, just get hold of him and have him meet me at the shack in one hour," replied the pilot, referring to the odd-parts storage room located at the aft end of the hangar deck. "Got that?"

"Yes, sir. I'll see that he's there."

The lieutenant left the deck, walked through the hatch and down the ladder to the squadron ready room for the required debriefing.

The debriefing completed, he walked hurriedly back out of the squadron room and made his way down to the Snake Pit, which was the term the enlisted men used to refer to the junior officers' staterooms located along the starboard-side corridor of the third deck. Walking through the hatch of his cabin, Ferguson was greeted by Russell "The Salivator" DiSalvo, his cabin mate, flight teammate, and closest friend aboard the carrier.

Lt. DiSalvo had flown earlier in the evening and had already changed and dressed for dinner. He was now lying on his bed, perusing a well-worn copy of *Playboy* magazine. "Evening, Flight Leader," said DiSalvo. "Word is you had a good flight."

"Scuttlebutt travels fast around here," replied Nick as he began tearing through his gear locker.

"Speaking of scuttlebutt," said DiSalvo, "did you hear your old man's announcement about whether he was going to run for president? I picked it up on short wave about an hour ago."

"He won't run," said Ferguson, as he stepped away from his locker and began to ponder intently. At age twenty-seven, he was a younger, but fairly exact copy of his father: six feet two, slender; hard, sinewy muscles; a square jaw and handsome face. The main difference was a complete dearth of silver in his carefully cut dark hair.

"Why do you say he won't run?" asked the Salivator.

"'Cause he already said he wouldn't," said Ferguson absently. "End of story."

"Oh, really? So rather than strike out on his own, you think he'd just prefer to risk going down with a sinking ship, is that it?"

"That's the old family tradition," Nick said quietly.

"Well, don't you even want to know what he said?" asked DiSalvo in frustration.

"Nope. Change subject."

"Man doesn't even want to know if his old man's running for prez. All right, subject changed. Think you're ready for tomorrow night?" asked DiSalvo, referring to the final evening of night operations, when Ferguson's Ranger Flight would test its skills against those of rival Tyrant Force in a special carrier defense exercise called Operation Keepaway.

"I'm ready," he replied as he began to change out of his flight suit and into his duty uniform. He glanced over at his pal, who seemed to be absorbed in his reading. "Salivator, why do you torture yourself with stuff like that?"

"I just read *Playboy* for the articles," said DiSalvo.

"Don't give me that tired old line."

"It's a fact," DiSalvo insisted, unfurling the centerfold. "I particularly enjoy the articles about naked women."

"About ready to hit the mess hall, Flight Leader?" said DiSalvo a few minutes later.

"I'm right on your six, Ace."

DiSalvo went on ahead, but Ferguson stopped suddenly at the cabin hatch and, without warning, turned back. Now he remembered where he had left it.

He retrieved a small bottle of liquid from his shaving gear and squirted its contents into his ear. He turned his head to the side and pounded the flat of his hand on the side of his head, forcing the medicine deep into his ear canal. He stood still, head cocked to the side, and waited, counting to one hundred.

While he counted, Lieutenant DiSalvo had come back to see what was keeping his wingman. "Something wrong with your ear, Loo-ten-ant?"

"It's nothing," he said, stepping through the hatch and into the corridor.

"You don't need to see a doc or nothing, do you?"

Ferguson laughed. "No, Mother. I'll be fine."

"Hey, don't be making fun of my nurturing instincts, Nicko," DiSalvo retorted. "Somebody's gotta look out for you. This ain't like shoreside, where you got those professional babysitters that watch your every move."

Ferguson threw his arm around his best friend and kissed him on the top of his head. "Salivator, if you weren't already married, I'd marry you myself."

"You been out to sea way too long," DiSalvo said, pushing him away. "You need to get back home to that girlfriend of yours. Do you even remember her name?"

Nick Ferguson laughed. "Sure I remember her name. Lucinda Something-or-other."

"I thought her name was Ellen."

"Ellen? I do remember an Ellen – vaguely, that is."

DiSalvo shook his head. "Pathetic. Man's got so many women after him he can't keep their names straight."

After a very fast visit to the mess hall, Ferguson made his way down to the odd parts shack. The fastest way to get there was to cut through the hangar deck just past VMFA-232. Here the fighter-attack squadron's twelve F-16's were standing in two rows. The planes had been through a maintenance cycle and were now refueled and ready to fly.

Ferguson walked briskly past the perfectly aligned noses of the fighters. The only other person in the entire area was a lone marine rifleman, whose task it was to keep watch over the squadron of planes. As Ferguson passed by, the marine raised his rifle and rendered a crisp salute. "Evening, sir."

Ferguson returned the salute. "Evening, PFC. Don't let anybody steal one."

"They'll live to regret it, sir!"

"That's the attitude."

Ferguson slipped through a door at the far end of the hangar area, and entered the small, unsecured room which was cold and poorly lit. On the other side of the room stood Krumbein. "We've got to stop meeting like this, sir," said the young medic.

"Krumbein, I need your help," said Ferguson. "Did you bring your magic kit?"

"I always have my kit," said Krumbein. "What seems to be the problem, Lieutenant?"

"My ear," he replied, pointing. "My right ear."

"Let me take a look. Have a seat, sir."

Krumbein rustled around in his bag and came up with an otoscope. He placed it in the officer's ear and took a good look. "Gosh, sir, it looks bad; pretty swollen. Any dizziness?"

"None."

"Are you sure, sir? Because with swelling like that you could have an infection of your inner ear."

"No dizziness, corpsman," the lieutenant said firmly. "I made a textbook three-point night landing tonight, just in case you happened to miss it; dizziness there was none."

"Right, sir. Still, if the lieutenant would place his hand over his left ear, I'd like to test your hearing on the right one."

"Suit yourself," said Ferguson, as he did what he was asked.

Krumbein leaned close to the lieutenant and whispered quietly, "Your mother swims after troopships and your sister's in love with a camel."

There was no discernable reaction from the officer. "Any time, corpsman."

"You didn't hear me, did you, Lieutenant?"

"I'm waiting for you to test my hearing, Krumbein."

Krumbein straightened up and moved around to where he could speak directly to the patient. "I don't know, sir. I don't think you better do any flying for a while."

"I didn't ask you for your advice, Krumbein."

"Well, that's...sort of what I do, Lieutenant," said the corpsman. "I dispense advice from time to time; some of it is even medically sound."

"I know what I need, Krumbein. I want an antibiotic, the strongest you got. I've been using some ear drops but they're not doing the job."

"Look, Lieutenant," said the corpsman, shaking his head, "if you want drugs you'll have to get an authorization from one of the docs at sick bay. These aren't combat conditions we're under; otherwise, I could help you."

"I'm not convinced you grasp the delicacy of the situation, Krumbein," said the frustrated pilot. "My squadron is trying to win a tactical competition; in order to win, it's very important that I lead my flight team tomorrow night. Now, if I go to sick bay with an ear problem, they're going to clip my wings; they have no discretion in the matter. You, on the other hand, have a great deal of discretion, if you gather my drift."

"Sir, sometimes you sirs are just too competitive for your own good," Krumbein sighed as he silently contemplated the officer's difficulty. "Well, all right. I think I have a small supply of penicillin that I keep handy," he said at last, fumbling through his medical bag. "I'll let you have a few, enough to take care of your problem; but you didn't get them from me, sir. Are we in agreement on that, Lieutenant?"

The taxicab rolled to a stop in front of 625 Q Street in Georgetown and a well-dressed man got out of the front passenger side. He removed a large box from the back seat of the cab and then paid the driver, giving him a generous tip.

The man picked the box up from the sidewalk and staggered with it as he attempted to carry it up to the third floor. When he at last arrived on the third floor landing, he put the box down and rang the doorbell.

Ellen Conley walked across the living room and opened the door to Apartment 3A.

"Oh, Tom!" she exclaimed, seeing what he had with him. "Let me help you. You shouldn't have carried this up here all by yourself."

Together they lifted the box, staggered into the room with it, and set it down as carefully as they could. Tom stood up, rubbed his lower back and, as he caught his breath, looked around.

The apartment was very spacious, with high ceilings, wooden floors, a fireplace, huge windows, a walk-out balcony and large airy rooms. It was of pre-World War II construction, and it was meticulously preserved.

Ellen looked across the living room and called to her son. "Gregory, can you come over here and say hello to Tom?"

But Greg Conley was in a world of his own. He was holding a plastic model of a navy F/A-18E fighter plane. Clearly the plastic toy had seen much use; it had been taped on the fuselage, on the tail, the rudder, and on the cockpit; even the wings were held in place by tape.

The condition of the toy, however, seemed to make no difference to the boy, who rushed around the room, holding the plane high over his head, and then swooping it downward to the floor. "It's Lieutenant Nicko Ferguson, in the battle of his life!" he exclaimed. "Attacked on seven sides by Russians, Germans, and Japanese! It's twenty-seven planes against one! There's no way out for Nicko!"

"Greg?" said Ellen. "Greg! Could you stop for just a moment?"

He turned and looked at her. "I'm not Greg. I'm Ace Fighter Pilot Nicko Ferguson, United States Navy."

"OK, Ace," said his mother. "I need you to stop for a minute, now, OK, honey?"

"Fighter pilots don't talk to girls." He zoomed away at mach two.

Ellen laughed. "I can well assure you that they do. Now, can you say hello to Tom? And then you can help Mommy open up this big box so we can see what's inside, OK? I have a funny feeling all this is for you."

"I don't want it," he answered, tearing around the room, defending it against all enemies, foreign and domestic.

"Of course you want it, dear," Ellen replied. "Didn't I tell you that Tom was bringing you a huge box filled with toys? They were all made by his company, and none of these toys will be in the stores until next Christmas, so you'll be the only one in your school to have them; isn't that wonderful?"

"Fighter pilots don't play with toys." He rejoined the battle in progress.

"Well, let's take a look anyway." She retrieved a knife from the kitchen and, with Tom's help, began to remove the wrapping. "Oh, look, Gregory!" she exclaimed as she opened the box and examined its contents. "It's Captain Amazing, and RoboMan, and Battleship America, and...what else?" She named at least a dozen more items as she emptied the box and set the toys on the floor.

Greg walked over, took a quick look at the toys and then tore off down the hallway with his model plane. "It's Nicko Ferguson going it alone!"

"Well, it looks like Lieutenant Ferguson has quite an admirer," said Tom, trying to mask his disappointment in the young boy's reaction.

"I'm very sorry, Tom," said Ellen sympathetically. "He gets like this sometimes. Especially when he knows that Nick is coming back into port. He should be here in a day or so; maybe then things will settle down."

"You know," Tom mused, "I never thought that, as the owner of a toy company, I would be ignored quite like this. I mean...I could understand if I made cough syrup or something like that...spinach, maybe..."

"Tom, it's not your fault," Ellen insisted. "He's just at that age."

The toy manufacturer was philosophical. "Well, Greg's excitement at seeing Nick Ferguson is quite understandable, I suppose; just as long as his mother doesn't feel the same way."

"Don't worry," she replied, as she put her arms around him and gave him a reassuring hug. "I got over Nick Ferguson a long time ago."

Tom was quiet for a moment; he pulled away from Ellen. "What are all those boxes piled in the corner?"

Ellen turned and looked. "Oh, those are Nan Lin's things. She's in the process of moving out."

Tom was surprised. "Didn't she give you any notice?"

Ellen shrugged. "Well, not really, but she says she has someone perfect to take her place; someone coming in from Los Angeles tomorrow who needs a place immediately. I could hardly say no to the situation; after all, Nan Lin is letting me keep her deposit – which is quite generous of her."

Tom Yancey was contemplative. "But you don't know anything about the new one?" he asked.

"She's from China; her last name is Jiang, but she goes by Jennifer. She left a message for me here while I was at work. She left the names of six or seven faculty members at UCLA who she said would give her excellent references. I called one of them – a Professor Kirk – who told me that Jennifer is very fun-loving and quite popular, and that she would be very considerate. And besides, the girl is a mere student; what harm could she possibly do?"

THE FLIGHT from Los Angeles was tiring for Jennifer, and it was just after four in the afternoon when the 757 began its descent to Ronald Reagan Washington National Airport.

Ji Wan Li had offered to have a car waiting for her at the airport, but she had properly declined, stating that a good spy would never draw attention to herself unnecessarily. She would deal with the encumbrances of travel as though she were any other tourist or businessperson. The consul general had been impressed with her instincts but, of course, he was completely unaware of the fact that she had an ulterior motive for wishing to remain unescorted upon her arrival in Washington.

After she disembarked from the plane, she made her way through to the baggage area, retrieved her luggage, stored it in a locker, and hailed a cab. Just in case she were being trailed, she made an obvious show of going to the tourist information counter, loading herself down with all the maps and disposable cameras she could carry, as well as a pair of sunglasses and a straw hat, to shield herself from the sun. She would look and play to perfection the role of a tourist.

She took the Washington Metro from the airport, heading northwest to the mall area, where most of the national museums and monuments were located.

She exited the subway at the National Gallery of Art, and entered its modern, triangular West Wing. She walked about the galleries, was in and out of the gift shop, took the people mover over to the cafeteria and then back again, went up and down the elevator and got off at various floors.

When she was certain that no one was following her, she ducked into a small lecture hall which visiting scholars used in order to give public lectures. She closed the door, walked down the left aisle of the semi-darkened room, stopped at the sixth row, and scooted sideways over to the tenth seat, where she sat down.

She found herself sitting next to a man in a light gray overcoat; she and he were the only two people in the room. She looked at her watch; it was precisely five o'clock.

"Your name is Jiang Ou," said the man, who spoke without introducing himself and who continued to look straight ahead, seeming to admire the several works of art placed on the stage in front of them. "Although you call yourself Jennifer. Now then, how can I help you? Or rather, how can you help us?"

She chose not to be coy. She told him everything about her background and family in China, her student days at UCLA, and her most recent meeting with the consul general, Ji Wan Li, in Los Angeles.

She told him about the swift and disconcerting choice she had had to make, about her engagement to Du Ming, about the apartment in Georgetown, about Ellen Conley, and Nicholas Ferguson, about the vice president and the situation at Camp David. She told him about the role she was expected to play, and how it could benefit China.

She told him everything that she knew and, when she was finished, she waited quietly for him to speak.

"So, then, Jiang Ou," said he, "it sounds to me as though this latest move is a very good deal for you. You already have had the advantage of a good education in the United States; and now you have the opportunity to spend more time socializing here in Washington; and then you are freed from your marital engagement. It sounds as though you couldn't ask for anything more. So why did you contact the Taiwan Trade Office at the World Trade Center in New York yesterday? And why did they send you to talk to me?"

She knew that he already knew the answer to that question. "Because I want to make a deal with a representative of the government of Taiwan."

"What kind of deal?"

"The information which I obtain for the benefit of China," she said, "I will share with you; or rather, I will give China just enough information to be minimally useful, but anything of real value I will give to Taiwan."

"I see," said he. "You realize, of course, that you are asking to become a double agent. May I know the reason why?"

"Because I want you to do something for me in return."

"Go on."

"Several years ago, before I left China, I was in love with a young man. This young man – his name is Jin Yi-bo – was everything to me; he was a poor student, but very intelligent and very, very self-confident. He had no fear – of anything. He was a member of the pro-democracy movement; in fact, he was a leader in it."

"And you didn't know?"

"I found out very late. I believe that he was intentionally keeping this information from me, perhaps because my background was quite privileged in comparison to his and he feared I would disapprove of his activities."

"Or perhaps because he wished to protect you," suggested the man.

"Yes, that could be it," she admitted. "But eventually I did find out. Four years ago, not long before I came to America, there was a major pro-democracy demonstration and worker strike in the city of Nanjing. It was quite bloody but this time, unlike at Tien An Men, the Western press knew nothing of it. Many were arrested – among them was Jin Yi-bo. In a secret trial, he was sentenced to twenty years in prison.

"Soon thereafter," she continued, "I was told by one of his friends that Jin Yi-bo had died not long after entering prison. Although I was terribly saddened to hear this, in some ways I felt he was better off dead; at least his suffering was over.

"Only recently," she continued, "after I had come to America, did I receive information that leads me to believe that Jin Yi-bo is still alive. I believe he is in the lao gai outside Harbin," she added, referring to the political labor camps in which were imprisoned some six million Chinese political dissenters.

"Why had the friend told you that he was dead?"

"I now believe that this friend wanted me to forget about Jin Yi-bo," she replied. "He wanted to become my lover, and so he lied; but I never wanted to believe that Jin Yi-bo was dead, and so I held onto hope."

"And your engagement to Du Ming?" he asked. "Why did you consent to that?"

"I was forced into that in order to be allowed to study in America," she replied. "My parents felt that such a commitment on my part would cause me to concentrate on my studies. I have not been involved with any American men until now, not because of my engagement to Du Ming, but because I feel as though Jin Yi-bo and I are inseparable.

"When I thought that he was dead, I felt this way; now that I have reason to hope he is alive, I can feel no differently. I think about him every day, and how cold and hungry he must be and how they must surely treat him like an animal." As she spoke, her voice wavered and tears came to her eyes, not in pity for herself, but for the treatment which she knew Jin Yi-bo was forced to endure.

"Yes," the man replied, placing his hand on her arm in a comforting gesture, "life in the lao gai can be difficult; but is it possible he could be released in some sort of political amnesty?"

"Even if I were to return to China," she said quietly, "there is no hope for us. If he were to be set free, I could never associate with him in any way, because of my uncle."

"That is a quite realistic assessment," said he. "And so what is this deal you had in mind?"

"Very simple," she said. "I will provide as much valuable information for you as I can; and you will rescue Jin Yi-bo from the lao gai, and get him out of China. I assume you have operatives working on the mainland."

He neither confirmed nor denied her assumption. "Do you realize what you are asking of me? Men could die in such an effort."

"I do realize that," she admitted. "But keep in mind that Jin Yi-bo is important not only to me; his leadership is important to the freedom of my country, and therefore of yours."

The man was contemplative. "There are many working in the effort to bring about democracy in China," he said at last. "Therefore the life of a student languishing in the lao gai could hardly be worth the sacrifice of others. You must understand that we would not consider a rescue effort unless the information you could provide us were of vital importance to us. We don't consider gossip to be of any value, nor hearsay, nor speculation, nor rumor; the only thing we care about is hard information which relates to the security of Taiwan; for that we are willing to risk lives. Do you understand?"

"I do," she replied soberly.

"Very well. Then you must also think about the fact that Jin Yi-bo may be killed in the rescue effort, or in the effort to get him to the coast."

She was quiet as she considered that possibility.

"You need to think about yourself as well," he added. "You are playing a very dangerous game. I'm sure you know what will happen to you if the Chinese find out what you are doing. You will simply disappear from the earth; yes, right here in the middle of the freest country in the world, you will vanish. The Americans will not care what happens to you, and we will never know."

"I have given these risks considerable thought," she said quietly. "But as things now stand, I may well spend the rest of my life without Jin Yi-bo. Under such circumstances, how can death make much of a difference to me? As far as the risk to him, I believe that he feels he can do no good in prison, and would rather risk death by trying to get out."

The man was silent for a considerable time. "Very well. We, too, must give this matter considerable thought; I hope that such a delay does not disconcert you."

"To the contrary," she replied. "I would interpret an immediate agreement on your part as a sign of insincerity."

"An astute observation," he noted. "You have the makings of a very good agent, I believe. When do you move into the Georgetown apartment?"

"I will be meeting with Ellen Conley this evening," she answered. "I expect to move in immediately."

"Very good," he replied, standing up. "You will be contacted."

He left through the stage door; she left through the gallery door. She noted on the way back to the Metro that, despite her intimate and involved conversation with the man, she had no idea what he looked like.

## Chapter 4

By the time the briefing for Operation Keepaway had ended, the sun had slipped below the horizon. By means of the runway lights, the pilots from VFA-72 made their way along the ready deck and approached their waiting planes.

One by one, the F/A18E Super Hornets began taking off from the carrier deck. When Nick's turn came, he wiped out the controls, checked the indicator bank for fuel, temperature and power, checked movable surfaces left and right, throttled his engines up to ear-deafening levels, braced himself for the incredible take-off acceleration he would experience, and saluted the shooter. The catapult flung the aircraft off the end of the carrier deck, hurling him forward, out over the black sea and up into the winter sky.

Nick knew the attack plan cold. He would lead Ranger Flight against a flight of four aircraft, called Tyrant Force, which would be simulating an attack against the carrier.

Ranger Flight's journey to Juniper Sector took ten minutes and covered a distance of one hundred miles. They were flying IFR – Instrument Flight Rules – for the darkness did not permit them to see much more than the sun's fading glow in the western sky and a few of the brightest stars to the east.

After they had gotten away from the carrier and had achieved flight level, the two pilots engaged in their usual banter. "Say Nick," began the Salivator, "I've noticed a distinct absence of cigarettes in our stateroom in recent days. Have you by chance given up smoking?"

"That was my New Year's resolution," replied Nick.

"Really? So you quit, just like that; that's remarkable."

"Just like that; and what was your New Year's resolution?" asked Nick.

"Me? Why, I resolved to tell no more jokes involving the planet Uranus."

"Really?" asked Nick. "And how's that effort going?"

"Well…I made it all the way to January sixth."

"January sixth, you say? Very impressive."

"January sixth; my grandmother's birthday, in fact."

"No kidding; and how old was Granny this time around?"

"One hundred ten years young," declared the Salivator.

"One hundred ten! That's incredible. What's her secret?"

"Secret…?"

"Secret to living such a long life."

"Life? Hell, she's been dead for twenty years."

"I thought you said…"

"Hey, you don't stop aging just because you die," said the Salivator. "Now you take Alexander the Great; man must be twenty three hundred years old. No, sir; you just keep right on going."

"I suppose you're right: I never looked at it that way."

Upon their arrival on station, Lieutenants Ferguson and DiSalvo leveled out at twenty-two thousand feet and began a slow series of lazy eights, with two thousand feet of altitudinal separation between them. They expected to wait only a minute or two before Tyrant Force One would sweep into the sector. Nick kept a steady eye on his radarscope, ever watchful for the expected intruders.

They were not to be disappointed. Within five minutes, the radio began to crackle. "Ranger One, this is Mammoth." It was the CIC – the Command Information Center, calling directly from the carrier.

"Go ahead, Mammoth," replied Ferguson.

"You have two Tyrant bogies at three-four-five, distance eighty-two miles, bearing one-seven-five, angels twenty-six, speed seven-fifty."

"Roger, copy." Nick came out of his starboard turn, and began searching the skies. Within seconds the Tyrant aircraft appeared on his screen. "Judy!" he called, signaling to the CIC that he had achieved a radar sighting and would call his own movements. He throttled forward. As previously rehearsed, he would attempt a frontal intercept maneuver. "Salivator, you see 'em?"

"Affirmative."

"Let's knock 'em out. You swing left, I'll go right."

Georgetown, in the District of Columbia. The doorbell rang at precisely seven-thirty, which was the time the new roommate had said she would be there. Ellen walked quickly across the room and opened the door.

The young woman who stood in the doorway seemed slight and fragile. She was also quite beautiful. She had black, shoulder-length hair. Her face was marked by fine, delicate cheekbones, and her eyes were like black almonds.

Ellen had always considered He Nan Lin to be an attractive woman, but the one who stood in the doorway now was in a class by herself. "You are Jennifer, I assume?" Ellen said. "Please come in."

The woman bowed ever-so-slightly and then stepped into the room.

IN THE PITCH DARKNESS, the pilots depended entirely on their radarscopes to tell them what they needed to do. Ranger Flight was closing with the first wave of the Tyrant Force at a combined rate of speed of fourteen hundred miles per hour. The separation was only ten miles – a distance that would be covered in less than thirty seconds.

DiSalvo called out to his wingman. "I've got a lock; ready to fire. Nicko?"

"Lost him."

"What do you mean? What's wrong?"

Nick was wrestling with his controls. "Don't know. Electronics...I've lost radar contact. Proceed. I'll recover."

DiSalvo maintained his lock on his target and called a "kill." With his wingman out of the picture, DiSalvo was forced to attempt a rear intercept in order to try and overtake the second bogie. It took him nearly a minute to get into position but by that time it was too late. The second Tyrant roared past them, exited Juniper Sector and was vectoring straight-on for the carrier.

DiSalvo radioed the CIC and warned them of the incoming aggressor.

ELLEN SHOWED HER new roommate about the apartment. Jennifer was quite pleased with it and they seemed to be completely comfortable with one another within minutes.

Jennifer had brought a small airplane for Greg, and he shyly took it from her hands. Ellen noted with interest the fact that he did not hesitate to take the gift from Jennifer, a complete stranger. There was something about Jennifer that Greg seemed to like.

Of course, that merely begged the question – what was it about Tom Yancey that Greg didn't like?

"Are you from China?" Greg asked Jennifer as they carried her luggage into her new room.

"Yes, I am."

"Is Jennifer your real first name?"

"Why no, it's not. My *real* first name is Ou," she replied. "It rhymes with 'grow.'"

"That's a funny name; what's it mean?"

"It means seagull."

"You were named after a bird? That's strange."

"Haven't you ever known anyone named Robin?"

LIEUTENANT DISALVO had not heard from his wingman for several minutes. "Nicko, you all right?"

"Still got a problem with my electronics," Ferguson announced coolly, searching his indicator bank, trying his best to find a cause for his problem. "Comes and goes. Seems all right now. Sorry."

"Don't worry about it, Nick. Just stay with me for the second wave."

Moments later, Tyrant Force Two arrived on scene. This time there were four of them; but Ranger Flight was prepared for this situation. They had a plan of attack already in place.

This time it was DiSalvo's turn to give the commands. "Heads up, Nicko. We got company. Forward intercept at thirty miles. You take Bogie One, I'll take Four. Then roll outside and swing back for rear intercept. I'll take Three, you take Two. Copy?"

"Roger. Got 'em on my 'scope."

This time he wouldn't fail, Nick vowed; this time he would nail it cold. He peeled off to the port side and headed directly into his first target. He was approaching max velocity, closing at fifteen hundred with a distance of eighteen miles.

And then it happened again. His indicators started to flicker, and he was having difficulty maintaining flight direction. Suddenly the aircraft started to rotate on its axis, and it seemed to have a mind of its own. Nick dropped his altitude and tried to regain control of the craft. He cut back his power. Nothing he did seemed to work. The plane was spiraling out of control.

There was no longer any choice: he would have to bail out. His voice went out over the emergency channel. "Ranger One to Mammoth Base. Mayday! Mayday! Mayday! I am out of action. Repeat, out of action due to mech failure. All directional control capabilities lost. Altitude sixteen. Bailing out at this time. Out."

He reached high over his head and grasped the canopy release handle with both hands. He jerked straight down, and hard. In an instant the canopy flew off and he was propelled, cockpit seat and all – straight up and out of the now useless aircraft.

After a three second upward trajectory, the seat fell away, the parachute deployed, and Nick began to drift downward toward the cold, black sea.

He watched helplessly as his plane continued falling – its engines still flaming – and saw it hit the ocean a mile below. There was a huge, explosive splash, and then the aircraft disappeared below the surface of the Atlantic.

Ferguson continued to drift downward. As he got closer to the ocean surface, he could hear the sound of the waves, but he could see nothing.

He hit the water hard, and felt the cold envelop him.

THE CIC WENT into Uproar Mode; there were ten sailors and officers talking at once. Captain Ernest Rutherford, the commanding officer of the *USS Andrew Jackson*, was on the bridge when he got a call from the watch officer. "Sir, this is Commander Updike. Aircraft down in Juniper. Sir, Lieutenant Ferguson has jettisoned."

The captain winced. "Christ; anybody but Ferguson. All right, Updike, notify Search and Rescue. Send all – I repeat all – SAR units. Priority one. Notify CINCLANT, as well as the National Command Center."

"Yes, sir."

"Oh...and Updike?"

"Yes, sir?"

"Notify the White House as well; the president will want to know about this."

Captain Rutherford felt a nauseous sensation in the pit of his stomach. The loss of any pilot was bad enough, but the loss of the son of the vice president was going to be a nightmare.

Three Seahawk search and rescue helos left the carrier within two minutes and headed to the last charted location of the downed Super Hornet. Twenty-five minutes later they arrived on location.

From his station in the CIC, Commander Updike radioed

the lead SAR pilot. "No signal as of this time," he advised, referring to the intermittent signal that would have been sent out from Nick's personal emergency transponder and would have been picked up by a satellite and relayed to the carrier. They would use the signal to locate the position of the pilot.

"If he's anywhere on the surface, we're ready to pick him up," said the chopper pilot.

"Roger," said Updike on the come-back. "You should be on his last-known position in about five minutes. If he sees you he should be popping a flare."

The lead Seahawk pilot responded a few minutes later. "No joy at this time, sir."

"Well, keep looking. He bailed out; we know that much. So he's gotta be out there somewhere."

THE NEWS HIT official Washington like a lightning bolt. Every agency involved in any way with national security was put on notice that it might be called to assist.

The White House held the news for an hour, and then decided they could not keep the story quiet for much longer. All of the major networks interrupted their prime time scheduling in order to carry the announcement.

Greg Conley was sitting in his mother's bedroom watching television when he saw the picture of Nick flash on the screen. He wandered into the living room, where Ellen was still talking with Jennifer. "Mommy, did something happen to Nicko?"

"Why do you say that, dear?"

"His plane," the little boy said. "It fell in the water."

"Oh, Greg, where did you hear that?"

"From TV," he replied. "You left it on in your room."

Ellen excused herself and flipped on the television in the living room. Whatever programming it was that had been interrupted had already resumed. Ellen switched over to one of the all-news channels, where the story was still on the air. It was true; Lieutenant Nick Ferguson, USN, had bailed out somewhere over the Atlantic and rescue helicopters were on the scene.

Ellen quickly explained to Jennifer who Nick was but, of course, Jennifer already knew. Ellen turned and picked her son up and held him in her arms. "I'm sure Nick will be perfectly fine," she said with forced assurance. "He just had a little accident with his plane, that's all."

"Can't he tape it up?"

Ellen had to smile. "Yes, that's one thing about Nick; he always carries plenty of tape with him wherever he goes."

"Are you sure, Mom?" asked Greg. "Nicko isn't going to die, is he?"

The three stared at the television set for several minutes more. Finally, Ellen set her son down and stood up. "I need to make a phone call."

Jennifer thought that it would be a good time to unpack and get comfortable in her room. Greg stayed and watched television.

Ellen walked into her bedroom and closed the door. In seconds, she was on the phone to the Secret Service. "I want to speak to Agent Haraldsen." Ellen knew Agent Conrad Haraldsen from his work as the deputy leader of the Secret Service's vice presidential detail.

He came on the line almost immediately. "Ellen? Listen, I meant to call you earlier but things have been pretty hectic around here tonight."

"I understand, Conrad," she replied. "I just have one favor to ask of you. If the news is bad – the news about Nick – I don't want to have to hear about it on TV."

"Ellen, if the news is bad, I'm sure that the vice president will call you. He always had a very high regard for you and still thinks Nick screwed up bad by not working things out with you."

After hanging up, Ellen sat on her bed and stared at the television. After a short while she saw her door being pushed open. She was not surprised to see Greg walking into her room. "Mom, can I stay with you?" he asked softly.

"Yes, of course you can, honey."

Greg got into the bed and helped her keep vigil. He was

quiet for a long time before he spoke. "Mom...?"

"Yes, sweetheart."

"I'm a little worried about Nick; his luck may have run out this time."

Ellen felt bad about ignoring Jennifer, and so she invited her to come and sit in the bedroom and watch the news channel with them. Ellen, of course, could not have known that Jennifer was intensely interested in the news, as everything she wanted to accomplish depended on her ability to get to know Nick Ferguson. Indeed, if Nick were to die, she might never be able to get Jin Yi-bo out of China.

At nine thirty-seven the phone rang. Ellen stared at it, fearing to pick it up. Her heart was beating wildly as she finally did so. "Hello?"

"Ellen?" said the friendly voice at the other end. "Tom."

"Oh, Tom," she exclaimed. "I'm so glad it's you."

"I like the sound of that; I hope I'm not calling too late."

"We're wide awake," she said. "Although I was expecting another call."

"Won't keep you but a minute," said he, apparently oblivious to Nick's situation. "I was working late and I just wanted to call and see how your son liked the toys."

"My son?" She wished Tom would call Greg by his name. "You mean Greg. Why he loved them, of course, when he finally got around to looking at them. Thank you."

"Any one of them in particular?"

"What?" she asked with some annoyance. "No, I mean he liked them all. Why do you ask?"

"Oh, I was hoping to get a feel for his reaction," he explained. "I guess that's just the test marketer in me."

"I'm sorry, Tom," she replied with a tinge of irritation in her voice. "I just thought you sent them because you wanted him to have them."

At that moment a news bulletin flashed across the screen. It was news about Nicholas Ferguson. Ellen stared at the screen.

He was safe! Nick was safe!

Ellen dropped the phone and hugged Greg. They both began jumping up and down on the bed, delirious with joy.

Jennifer hid the fact that she was just as relieved as they were. She laughed at the two of them, and then picked the phone up off the floor, introduced herself to Tom, and explained to him what had happened.

# Chapter 5

The crowd was growing larger by the minute. More and more people were crowding into the Square of the People's Enlightenment, and yet the crowd remained orderly.

The purpose of the assembly in the middle of the great city of Nanjing was to protest wage constraints and working conditions which had been placed on certain municipal workers, workers who had been promised much better terms by the local party officials.

Their cause was just; however, after the uprising and massacre at Tien An Men, all party officials were anxious to defuse any such public demonstrations as quickly as possible.

Their approach was to look for the slightest infraction by the demonstrators, and to use that as an excuse to break up the crowd and send everyone home. However, on this particular day, the police seemed to be looking for infractions which had not occurred. They handled the crowd roughly, shoving unnecessarily and seeming to want to provoke fights with unarmed citizens.

Jin Yi-bo was standing with the speakers, who were aware of the threatening situation.

Jin Yi-bo stepped forward and began to denounce the conduct of the police and, with his fearless presence and with his words, he whipped up the spirits of the crowd, which began to rally to his words, and then began to openly confront the police.

But the police had marked Jin Yi-bo as a principal target, and plainclothed officers materialized from several points around him; before he realized what was happening, they had come up onto the speaker's stand and immobilized him.

His friends tried desperately to prevent the arrest. "Don't let them get him!" they shouted as the police dragged him down the steps of the stand, but it was already too late. The police had him in their grasp, and they began to beat him and wrestle him toward their van. Jin Yi-bo's followers, including Jennifer, tried to wrestle him out of the grasp of the police, but more police crowded in and began to grapple with them as well.

They dragged Jin Yi-bo away, along with several of his supporters, and shoved them into the back of an unmarked van. The van surged forward through the crowd. Jennifer tried to break away and follow, but her friends held her back.

And then he was gone.

She screamed, and screamed.

And then she opened her eyes and tried to remember where she was.

A few moments later, there came a knock on the door. "Jennifer? Are you OK?"

Hearing Ellen's voice, Jennifer rose and walked to the door. "Just a little nightmare, that's all," she said, putting on her robe. "I'm terribly sorry; did I awaken Gregory?"

Ellen turned on the hall light. "He could sleep through a hurricane," she said with a smile. "Listen, why don't you let me fix you something to drink, something that will help you sleep?"

Jennifer followed Ellen into the kitchen, where they sat together for an hour, talking quietly. It was nearly three a.m. when she made her way back to her room, but she never got back to sleep. The nightmare brought back a flood of memories.

The months after Jin Yi-bo's arrest were the most painful time in her life. He was detained in prison for three months, after which he was put on trial for crimes against the people. Although she could not attend the trial, Jennifer was able to learn what was happening by reading the local newspapers, which in fact did a fairly good job of relating the complete mockery of justice which passed for the Chinese judicial system, particularly in cases having to do with matters of dissidence and internal security.

Ultimately, it was her uncle who had so much to do with the outcome. Song Bei was a rising star in Nanjing's communist party, and he intended to use the incident to further his own political ambitions. A strong proponent of law and order, he intended to send a message that anyone who chose to oppose the existing order would be dealt with in the harshest manner.

Still, she did her best to try to influence the course of events. Of course, she could never disclose to her uncle her relationship with the young man on trial. The notion that his own niece was so closely connected to the leader of the demonstration would have been personally intolerable to a man of his stature, as well as a tremendous threat to his political advance. Knowing of such a relationship, he would have simply ordered Jin Yi-bo to be taken off in the middle of the night and executed.

"And why is my niece so interested in the fate of these criminals?" he asked her one evening when she visited him in his grand house.

She could never reveal the real reason for her concern. "It's not the prisoners I care so much about," she answered deftly. "It's the fate of China. How can we ever make progress if opposing opinions are not heard?"

To which her uncle answered in his simple, but infuriating way, "You must remember, Little Ou, that the people know best."

Of course, by the word "people" he did not mean "the people" in the democratic sense; he meant the small, elitist band of party officials who acted however they saw fit in order to preserve their own power base at the expense of the people.

The word finally came to her that Jin Yi-bo had been given

twenty years in the lao gai. A lifetime.

Her hatred of Song Bei had begun from that moment; but, of course, he was unaware of her feelings, and he would never know. At any rate, Beijing had already taken notice of his role in the disposition of the case and before long he was on his way to a position in the central government.

Jiang Ou had not seen her uncle since those days, nor had she seen Jin Yi-bo; but they were both constantly in her thoughts. Toward the one she felt nothing but concern and compassion; toward the other she felt the most scathing form of hatred.

## CHAPTER 6

Nick Ferguson awakened slowly. As he became cognizant of his surroundings, he realized that he was not in his familiar Snake Pit stateroom. "Where am I?" he said to no one in particular as he sat up in the bed.

"You're in sick bay, Lieutenant," came the reply from the far side of the room. "I'm Commander Michaels, chief of the ship's medical section."

Nick glanced at the regulation navy clock on the wall. "I slept 'til eleven?"

"I gave you a mild sedative last night," said Michaels. "You seemed a little traumatized by your experience when you came aboard last night, so I thought a few extra hours of sleep would help."

"Actually, I feel fine." He sat up and swung his feet over the side of the bed, and tried to step down. When he put weight on his foot, he winced. "Except my foot hurts."

"It should," said the medical officer, approaching his ward. "You banged it up pretty bad jumping out of your ride; and what about that ear? Looks pretty swollen; have you been taking any medication recently?"

Nick paused. "Medication...why do you ask, sir?"

"Well, Lieutenant, I'm a doctor," came the physician's reply as he inserted an otoscope into Nick's ear. "There's nothing I love more than to waste people's time asking stupid questions."

"I was using some ear drops," Nick offered.

"Anything else?"

Nick mumbled his reply.

"What was that?" said the doctor.

"Uh...just a little penicillin."

When Commander Michaels had finished the aural exam he pulled up a stool and sat down, facing Nick. "Lieutenant, do you remember stumbling last night after you got off the helicopter?"

"Uh...no, sir; did I stumble?"

"I was told that you did," said Michaels. "Are you experiencing any dizziness right now?"

"No, not really; nothing major."

The doctor was unconvinced. "Let's run a little test," he said. "I want you to stand up, close your eyes and reach above your head with both arms."

Nick did as he was instructed, and almost as soon as his arms were in the air he began to sway and had to reach out and grab the bed rail.

"That's what I thought," said Michaels. "Do you mind telling me where you got the penicillin?"

"I'd rather not say, Commander."

"Lieutenant, you do understand I'm obligated to report this matter to the captain?"

Nick said nothing. The medical officer finished up his report and directed him to stay where he was until the ship's commander was ready to see him.

Nick sat quietly for over an hour, reading a magazine, and just after noon he was pleasantly surprised to see his stateroom mate standing in the doorway. "Gee, last time I talked to you I was falling out of the sky," said Nick to Lt. Russell DiSalvo.

The Salivator sauntered into the room and made himself at home. "I would have brought you flowers but the florist shop was all out of forget-me-nots. How you feeling, Bunkie?"

"Like I had my horse shot out from under me."

"Understandable," said DiSalvo, walking over and closing the door. "Completely understandable. The doc find out about the penicillin?" he asked in a low voice.

"He asked me and I told him that I had taken some."

"You tell him where you got it?"

"I'm leaving Krumbein out of this," said Nick. "Still, the ear is irrelevant. It wasn't a medical problem that knocked me out of the sky; there was something wrong with the avionics."

"I sure hope so, flyboy."

"Well, hell's bells, Salivator, you heard me on the squawkbox last night," Nick exclaimed with exasperation. "Didn't you hear me saying that the controls weren't working? I know they heard it in the CIC; they hear everything we say."

"Look, Nicko, I'm no board-certified neurologist but...if your brain is going haywire from a serious ear infection you might think it's your instruments that are going bad..."

"Baloney, Salivator! I know it was my instruments! Don't you believe me?"

"Nicko, I hope you're right," said DiSalvo. "I really do; I hope the problem was somewhere in the avionics. Unfortunately for the home team, however, the evidence is lying on the bottom of the ocean. And face it – the way the brass is going to see it, you're the one that took the chance in going up when you knew you weren't one hundred percent. Who knows how these minor health problems can affect your mental perceptions? Nicko, you're talking about flying a plane doing six hundred at very limited visibility. The mind plays tricks."

Nick was subdued; the Salivator's motives were beyond reproach; he could be counted on to dish out the straight scoop.

"By the way, the Secret Service is here."

"Are we in port already?"

"We're seventy-five miles off the coast," DiSalvo explained. "They flew a chopper over from Norfolk at dawn. They're conducting a full-blown investigation and we're all invited."

Nick was summoned to the captain's quarters at fourteen hundred hours. When he entered the captain's stateroom, he cut his eyes to the side and saw that several members of the Jackson's senior staff were seated along the paneled bulkhead. He approached the captain's desk, halted smartly, and saluted. "Sir, Lieutenant Ferguson reporting as ordered."

Captain Rutherford did not offer the lieutenant the opportunity to stand at ease; nor did he offer the customary pleasantries. "Lieutenant Ferguson, Ranger Flight left my flight deck at nineteen-fifteen hours last night with four Fighter Attack Eighteen single-seater fixed-wing aircraft in formation and yet – to my amazement – only three came back. At thirty million dollars a copy, I was just wondering if you would care to explain where that fourth little number might be."

"My guess would be the bottom of the North Atlantic Ocean, sir."

"Oh, I'm so relieved," said Captain Rutherford. "I would never have been able to figure that one out on my own."

"Glad to help where I can, sir; go navy."

"OK, Lieutenant, let's cut the clowning," said the captain sternly, "Why don't you explain how that hardware got where it is."

"Malfunction in the controls, sir," said Ferguson matter-of-factly. "The avionics went south on me."

"The avionics," said the senior officer. "I see…Care to be more specific on that point?"

"Well, sir, each time I went into attack mode I experienced one or more uncommanded banking angles." Unbidden, he departed from his position of attention, and illustrated his speech with precise yet lively hand movements.

"I'm listening; and what airspeed was that, Lieutenant?"

"Sir, at about point eight Mach; and that was at a fairly high angle of attack. Seemed like the wing just dropped out from under me."

The captain listened quietly, asked no more questions, and waited for the lieutenant to finish before he addressed him. "Lieutenant Ferguson, I have been advised that you experienced dizziness this morning during a physical exam; that you stumbled last night while departing the SAR helo; that your ear is badly swollen, and that you have been taking penicillin without benefit of a doctor's examination or a visit to sickbay. Please fit all of those facts into a cohesive framework so as to explain what you were doing flying my hardware around in the nighttime sky."

"Sir, I was experiencing no vertigo when I was flying," Ferguson said adamantly. "None whatsoever. My rather minor ear condition was worsened by being in the water for a good hour and made even worse by flying in a well-ventilated SAR helo in the winter air; in other words, it didn't bother me until I got back to the ship."

"I see," said the captain, mulling over the response. "Lieutenant, where did you get the penicillin?"

"I'd rather not say, sir."

"That wasn't an optional question."

"Sir, with all due respect, I see no need to damage the career of a good sailor who was simply trying to do me a favor."

"Lieutenant, you will answer my question or you will face the consequences."

"Sir, I would ask that the captain reconsider his directive."

"Are you refusing a direct order to answer my question?"

"I'd like some time to think about it, sir."

"I'll give you all the time you want," said the captain. "You will be confined to quarters until further notice. Furthermore, this ship will not dock in Norfolk until such time as you reveal the name of the sailor who gave you the penicillin. I'm willing to wait as long as it takes, Ferguson. Meanwhile, you think about this: four thousand enlisted men, away from home for six months, all waiting on you to answer my question, growing angrier by the minute. All I can say is, it's a good thing you have a Secret Service detail aboard to protect you, and I strongly suggest you not attempt to leave your quarters. Master Chief!"

The ship's master chief petty officer stepped forward. "Sir!"

"Please conduct Lieutenant Ferguson to his quarters. The

lieutenant is to remain in his stateroom until further notice, and you will station a marine guard outside to ensure that he does. And you can pass along the word as to why this ship is not heading in to Norfolk."

"Aye, aye, sir."

And with that, Nick Ferguson saluted his commander, backpaced twice, and faced about. He followed the master chief out of the ship's HQ and made his way down to the Snake Pit.

## CHAPTER 7

Beijing, China. Lou Jian Ren found the message buried deep inside a routine report which had come from Shanghai. The message had been received through a Taiwanese agent operating in the great coastal city, and had been passed along by another worker – also sympathetic to the plight of political prisoners in China – who worked in the administration of the vast prison system.

Lo carefully made a copy of the encoded language and took it home with him that evening. In his tiny room, he worked late into the night, turning the cryptic text into understandable language. "Confirm the existence of Jin Yi-bo," it said, "a prisoner in Harbin. Ascertain first if he is still alive. Following that, determine his general health and assess his ability to travel.

"After that you will explore the possibility of a transfer to Shi Men Prison."

Lou Jian Ren stood and walked over to his map of China. After a moment he found the location of the prison at Shi Men. It was quite close to the coast by the Sea of Japan, in the little wedge of Chinese territory that lay between North Korea and Russia.

Clearly some consideration was being given to a prisoner

extraction. Such rescues were extremely rare and risky and would have been authorized only in cases where the prisoner was of great importance. Lou Jian Ren did not know the name Jin Yi-bo. He was not one of the more famous dissenters, known to the West. So who was it, then, who cared about his life, and why was his life worth risking that of others in order to get him out of China?

He would send a message to his contact in Harbin and provide the answers, when they came, to Shanghai.

## CHAPTER 8

The next morning, the vice president of the United States sat in his office and received a report from the Secret Service. "What's the latest?"

"The *Andrew Jackson* is now ten miles off the coast," said Conrad Haraldsen, deputy chief of his security detail. "Nick is fine."

"And the investigation?"

"They've looked at all the maintenance records, sir. They're still in the process of interviewing anybody and everybody who got near that plane anytime in the last forty-eight hours. So far there doesn't seem to be anything that points to a problem with the plane."

Ferguson contemplated the news. "So they're saying the problem was with his inner ear? Is that right?"

"That's what they believe, sir. The medical reports tend to back that up. However, the Secret Service detachment interviewed him yesterday and he swears he was experiencing no vertigo or other physiological problems during flight."

Ferguson shook his head. "I can see where this is heading. Well, by now I would assume they're wrapping things up. When do they plan to dock in Norfolk?"

"Well, that's one thing that's a little crazy," said Haraldsen. "Captain Rutherford is keeping the *Andrew Jackson* at sea; he won't let them dock."

"What? Why not?"

"Officially, it's because they say the investigation is still ongoing; but the fact is they're just about done out there; it's just a matter of completing the paper work, but they can do that in port if they want to.

"The real reason they're sitting out there," continued the agent, "is because of Nick. He refuses to reveal the name of the man who gave him the penicillin. Ernie Rutherford says they'll stay right there – practically within sight of shore – until Nick comes clean."

"So that means the enlisted men are going crazy, right?" said Paul Blake, Ferguson's chief-of-staff, who was listening to the conversation.

"Well, that's pretty much what Rutherford was expecting to happen," came the reply. "Unfortunately, it didn't turn out quite that way. Rutherford has never been very well-liked by the men of the *Andrew Jackson*. He's something of a tyrant, and so naturally the sailors are quite delighted that a junior officer is protecting one of them.

"Morale couldn't be higher at the moment. They're scrubbing the ship, saluting the officers…hell, the ship's bakery has been delivering pastry to all the junior officers every hour on the hour. It's an absolute lovefest out there on the water; I've never heard anything quite like it."

"So Rutherford's little ruse backfired…" said Ferguson. "Old Ernie served in my command years ago; he wasn't a very good tactician back then either."

"He's made a fool of himself," said Eric Whitford, Ferguson's political adviser, "backing himself into a corner like that."

"Well, maybe the fleet commander could order him into port," suggested Ferguson. "That would end the standoff."

"I don't see that happening, sir," said Haraldsen. "From what I hear, Admiral Stagg despises Rutherford; he won't bail him out."

"So now they're stuck out there," said Blake. "Every ship commander in the fleet must be laughing his head off."

"Unfortunately, it's not a laughing matter," said the vice president. "What are they charging Nick with?"

Haraldsen referred to his notes. "Dereliction, destruction, conduct unbecoming, and failure to obey. I know this can't be a happy day for you, sir."

"No, I suppose it's not," said Ferguson with a sigh. "But at least he's alive."

A moment later, the phone rang; a secretary announced the call. "It's the president, sir."

Ferguson picked up the line. "Good morning, Ed."

The president was in the Oval Office; he had been joined by his national security adviser and the chief of naval operations.

"Admiral," said the president, who, like many others, often addressed the vice president by his naval rank, "I have just been advised that your son is involved in a little standoff aboard one of our ships in the fleet. Now, the last thing we need is for this incident to turn into a national joke; so I want to know what you're going to do about it."

Ferguson paused for a moment before he responded. "What would you *like* for me to do about it, Mister President?"

"Well...I'd...I'd like for you to order your son to provide the information that has been requested from him by his commanding officer."

"Unfortunately, sir, I'm not in his chain-of-command," he replied, winking at Agent Haraldsen. "They tell me I'm not even in the navy any more. I don't think I can order him to do a damn thing."

"I see," said Billingsley. "I see; well...I am in his chain-of-command. I'm his commander-in-chief, by Jenkins."

"So why don't you just have the CNO order the ship to come ashore, sir?"

"My Pentagon advisers are telling me that I should not personally intervene; it would make us look ridiculous for the White House – for the *president* – to get involved in this already ridiculous situation."

"But you want *me* to intervene."

"All I'm asking is that you get a message to that son of yours. Tell him he's embarrassing the chain of command, embarrassing the navy, embarrassing the White House and, quite frankly, if the media finds out about this, it will be a major embarrassment to the reelection campaign."

"I'll be happy to do that, sir, although I must be honest and tell you that I don't hold out much hope for any influence I might have. I understand that Nick made a promise that he would protect the identity of the enlisted man who gave him the penicillin, and I just don't see him going back on a promise like that."

"Your *son*," said the president with a harrumph, "needs to learn that sometimes there are promises you need to just forget you made."

"Maybe you could have a little heart-to-heart with him when he gets back, Mister President," said Ferguson coolly, "Clear it right up for him; Lord knows I've done my best."

"Well, no offense to you, Admiral," said the president, oblivious to Ferguson's sarcasm, "but I hope they throw the book at your son."

"Yes, sir. I'm sure they will; is there anything else?"

"As a matter of fact, there is," Billingsley replied, his tone of voice lightening considerably. "I need you to fly down to the Caribbean sometime in the next day or two and meet with Osuka and Munez. I understand you know them somewhat – is that correct? From your days with the Pacific Fleet?"

"I believe I may have met them both on occasion," said Ferguson with characteristic modesty. "I spent quite a bit of time in both Japan and the Philippines."

"That's what I thought. Well, it seems they're ready to talk about the open market trade treaty and they want to be sure that the United States is going to uphold its end of the bargain. I told them I might not be available to meet with them and I suggested you go in my place."

The vice president smiled. He suspected that what had really happened was that the two Asian heads of state had specifically requested his involvement as a condition of the treaty's being signed.

Foreign Secretary Osuka of Japan and Trade Minister Munez of the Philippines knew Ferguson quite well from the days when he served in the historic and hallowed command position known to American sailors around the world simply as "CINCPAC" – commander-in-chief of all American forces in the Pacific; his command had extended from the west coast of the United States to the coastal waters of China, and he had met with Asian leaders on many occasions. He considered many of them to be old friends, and his word was known among them to be his bond.

"Mister President," replied the admiral in response to the request. "I'll be more than happy to meet with the gentlemen."

The business at hand now taken care of, the president seemed almost jovial. "Admiral, I'm sorry about all this folderol with your son. I sure hope it blows over soon; but don't worry, I'm sticking by you as far as the campaign. No matter what happens, you've still got a place on the team."

Another disingenuous remark; Nick could have sunk the whole damn carrier, and the president would have kept Mark Ferguson on the ticket.

"Thank you, sir. Means a lot."

## Chapter 9

Harbin, China. The horn sounded at precisely eight a.m. and the prisoners began trudging out of their cell blocks and lining up in the courtyard. It took twenty minutes for the three hundred members of Section Six to get there and, as they waited on the slower moving ones – the lame and the sick – they had no choice but to stand quietly in their designated places.

Finally, accompanied by a dozen armed guards, Chen Wei Dong arrived. He was the commander of Section Six of the People's Rehabilitation and Reeducation Camp Number 216, located outside the city of Harbin.

The prisoners were quiet. Standing in front of his charges, Chen Wei Dong held up a pair of chicken feet as well as the head and neck of the same species. "Who stole my chickens?" he bellowed.

There was complete silence in the courtyard.

"Who stole my chickens?" he shouted again, but received no response. He paced back and forth, fuming madly over his chickens. He stopped and pivoted, and cursed the men who stood shivering in the cool air.

"Six chickens – gone," he wailed dramatically. "How can I eat when my own family steals from my table? My own children disgrace me in this fashion. Do I not treat you well? Do I not concern myself with your every need? Am I not a kindly old man, suffering the abuses of ingratitude on a daily basis?"

There was silence among the prisoners; mockery was a punishment they would gladly endure; it left no wounds for flies to feed on.

"I am glad that some of you have enjoyed a fine chicken dinner at my expense," he bellowed with a merry laugh. "As long as it provided happiness to a few of you, how can I complain? No one will confess? I thought as much." He pointed to a prisoner. "You there! Your stomach confesses for you – I see you are heavier than when I saw you last."

One of the guards yanked the man from the ranks. "No, Chen Wei Dong," the man muttered pleadingly. "I never took your chickens."

"Down on your knees," the man was commanded, and he did as ordered.

"Now, you will flap your wings and cluck like a chicken."

The man did so – moving his arms up and down and crowing like a rooster. Chen Wei Dong laughed and motioned for the prisoners to laugh as well. Three hundred voices, weakened by hunger and beatings and the cold late spring weather, laughed softly.

"Keep flapping," Chen Wei Dong commanded. "Keep crowing. Keep laughing."

This spectacle went on for several minutes, until the point when Chen Wei Dong stretched his arm out, a guard placed the handle of a short sword in his hand, and the commander swung it around and severed the man's head from his body. The laughter died as fast.

"Now then," said Chen Wei Dong. "Six chickens are missing; six chickens must be replaced. You have forty-eight hours to replace them or ten more of you will play the Chicken Game. Dismissed."

## Chapter 10

In the aftermath of Nick's crisis, Secret Service Agent Conrad Haraldsen had called several times to keep Ellen informed and, in the course of their several conversations, she happened to mention that she had a new roommate. As Nick would no doubt be visiting in the near future, Haraldsen thought it best to come out and interview Jennifer, so that she could be given clearance to be in Nick's company. Jennifer agreed to be available late in the morning, and she was waiting quietly with Ellen and Greg when the agent arrived at the Georgetown apartment.

Agent Haraldsen had her fill out the standard questionnaire; they all sat quietly as she spent nearly a half-hour doing so. When she was done, she handed it back and he looked it over. "You just came out from Los Angeles, I see," he noted casually.

"Just two days ago."

"And you are looking for work as an interpreter? Well, that shouldn't be too difficult to find in this town."

"Good. I hope you're right."

He smiled. "Just out of curiosity, how did you happen to know He Nan Lin – the previous tenant?"

She paused; the consul general's man, Wei Gang, was supposed to have explained that point on the way to the airport, but in the rush he had forgotten; she would have to ad lib. "Oh, well, we…uh…we took a class together."

The agent seemed puzzled. "You attended UCLA, I see. Funny, I thought He Nan Lin studied at USC. Well, who can remember all that? I talk to so many people. I'd have to check my notes."

"I believe she did study at USC," said Jennifer quickly. "It was just the one class we took together. It was a class given at USC."

"Right; I understand," said the agent with a smile. "You know, it's funny how a chance meeting – in a classroom or whatever – takes place and now look where you are? Sitting right here in Washington and being interviewed by the Secret Service."

Jennifer smiled. "Life can be funny that way."

"Well, I need to be going," said the agent, rising. "Jennifer, it was great to meet you. Ellen, Greg, wonderful to see you both again. And I'm sure I'll see you all when Nick gets back into town."

## CHAPTER 11

Corpsman Krumbein made his way down the passageway toward the Snake Pit. His passage was hindered somewhat by the unusual number of sailors who were in the area of the junior officers' quarters. The "era of good feeling" precipitated by Lieutenant Ferguson's standoff with the captain, as well as the fact that the six month cruise was ending, had led to a good deal of fraternizing among the ranks.

The entranceway to Ferguson's cabin was guarded on both sides by marine privates. Just inside the doorway were two Secret Service agents who, while they waited for their helicopter ride back to the coast, spent time chatting with the occupants.

Crowded into the room were a number of fellow pilots and members of the Super Hornet squadron; music was blaring loudly, and there was food and drink everywhere. Krumbein had to work hard to get into the room and make his presence known to Lieutenant Ferguson.

"Krumbein!" exclaimed the Salivator when he realized who it was. "Have a croissant; they're still hot. And what are you drinking? Vodka? Gin? Or may I recommend a very fine *vin blanc,* courtesy of the Petty Officer's Association, with their compliments. Despite its effete undertaste, the top notes are blowsy and carnal."

"I'd just like to talk to Lieutenant Ferguson, if that's OK, sir; in private."

It took several minutes to clear the room of all but Ferguson, DiSalvo, and Krumbein. "What's on your mind, Krumbein?" said Ferguson.

"Well, sir, I appreciate the fact that you've kept your word and all, and not ratted me out, but I think it's best if I turn myself in."

"Do you now? And why's that?"

"Well, sir, I just don't want to keep us all out to sea after the investigation ends, which it's getting ready to do. It's not fair to everybody else."

"You realize that you could get yourself keelhauled for this."

But the lieutenant could tell from the look in Krumbein's eyes that he wasn't terribly concerned about his fate. "OK, Krumbein. Let's go see the captain."

THE HEAD of the Secret Service detail that had been dispatched to the *USS Andrew Jackson* had just been ushered into the quarters of Captain Ernest Rutherford. "Sir, we'd like to give you a courtesy report of our investigation," said Agent Fairweather. "You understand, of course, that the investigation is not officially over until the navy and White House say that it is..."

"Of course," said the captain, whose ship was still held hostage to his stupid ultimatum and who was therefore in the foulest of moods. "Just give me the bottom line," he said gruffly.

"Yes, sir. Well, we've gone through all the maintenance records. We've interviewed everyone who even glanced at that plane."

"And...?"

"Nothing. That plane has been beautifully maintained from the day it was first assigned to this carrier."

The captain smiled for the first time all day. "And your assessment of the pilot's medical condition at the time of flight?"

"We're not medical experts, sir; however, I would say that the lieutenant was borderline at best."

"Well, then…"

At that moment the ship's executive officer, Commander Sutton, joined the conversation. "Sorry to interrupt, Captain, but Lieutenant Ferguson is here to see you."

"Lieutenant Ferguson! And what could be on *his* mind?"

"I believe he wants you to hear his confession."

"By all means; send him in."

Commander Sutton disappeared and returned momentarily with the lieutenant and the young naval enlisted man in tow. Both men approached the captain and saluted smartly.

"Well? What is it?"

"Sir, Corpsman Krumbein wishes to admit responsibility."

"Responsibility for what?"

"Well…uh…not for losing the plane, sir; just for providing Lieutenant Ferguson with penicillin."

"Correction on that, sir," said Ferguson. "I'm taking responsibility for the entire incident. I admit to unduly pressuring the corpsman into providing the medication."

"Well, you're both in hot water," said the captain. "Of course, Ferguson, being an officer, you're in it a lot deeper. Well, is that all you two have to say?"

"Yes, sir," came the reply from both.

"OK, Krumbein. Thank you for coming by. I want you to make a full written statement of this matter. Commander Sutton will give you pen and paper. In the meantime, you're suspended from duty until further notice. Dismissed."

"Aye, aye, sir."

Commander Sutton escorted the corpsman to a desk and put him to his task.

"As for you, Ferguson," said the captain. "You may well be facing a court-martial over all of this. So you can save your statements for your legal eagle, who will be assigned to you as soon as we arrive in port; and you are dismissed as well."

Rutherford turned to the men of the Secret Service. "Thank you, gentlemen. I commend you for your superb work."

He then turned to Sutton. "Now get my boat to Norfolk."

## 12

Six leaders among the prisoners were crowded together in a darkened cell. "How could any of us have stolen his chickens?" said one.

They all knew it was impossible; anyone who was caught stealing from a guard as vicious as Chen Wei Dong faced immediate execution and would bring ruination on the others. They began talking among one another, raising suspicion as to who could have betrayed them all by doing this.

After a minute of this, Jin Yi-bo spoke up. "No chickens were stolen."

They all turned to their leader. "This is a trap," he explained. "The only way to save ten lives is to replace the chickens. The only way to replace the chickens is to go to the village. The only way to get to the village is to leave the prison by the secret route. The guards are forcing us to use the secret route, and they will be waiting in the woods, watching to see where a prisoner comes out and goes back in. Chen Wei Dong doesn't care about his silly chickens; they want to plug the hole in the wall, if they can find it.

"Whoever they catch," he added, "will be killed." He paused and then grinned slyly. "But don't worry; I won't be caught."

"Why should you be the one to go, Jin Yi-bo?"

"Simple," he replied. "I know where to get the best chickens."

The prison guards must have been surprised to realize that there was a secret route leading out of Prison Camp 216. When a massive breakout had occurred the fall before, the prison commander assumed that the prisoners had taken advantage of the slight breach in the West Wall. The escapees had been caught, forced to repair the breach, and then, in front of a mass formation of all prisoners, had all been shot in the back of the head.

The guards never suspected the true means of escape. The route was in fact more of a discovered passage than the result of arduous work. A prisoner, now dead, who was by profession a university geologist, and whose crime against the people was his attendance at a demonstration in favor of academic freedom, had discovered long before he was imprisoned that the ground lying between Harbin Prison and the Sungari River contained a number of caves.

As a new prisoner, the ex-professor had volunteered to care for the sick, and his work carried him to every part of the prison. One night, looking for food supplies in an ancient storeroom, he discovered a section of flooring that had fallen through, revealing a narrow passageway. He had repaired the flooring but had hinged it in such a way that it could be lifted and the passageway accessed.

Enterprising prisoners had entered the passageway and mapped out a series of caves which led to the river.

After the failed breakout, the leaders among the prisoners now made sure that access to the escape passage was strictly controlled. It was to be used rarely, as in the winter, when they suffered the most, in order to get food and medicine. The few prisoners who had been trusted to go out had been extremely careful in remaining unseen, but obviously someone had been spotted on a recent excursion, and that was why Chen Wei Dong was now playing the Chicken Game.

It was from this maze of caves that Jin Yi-bo would emerge late the next night. He would crawl out near the Sungari River, far beyond the picket line of guards who would be waiting for him, and he would head along the river towards the village of Mao Yang.

## Chapter 13

Jennifer had left three urgent messages with the consul general in Los Angeles and was rather irritated by the time he finally did send a message to her electronic pager. As procedure required, she went to a nearby payphone and called him back. "Didn't you get my message?"

"I'm terribly sorry. I was out of town, Jiang Ou. What can I do for you?"

"Well, you were in such a hurry to get me on the plane," she said. "Isn't there something you forgot?"

His silence told her that he had no idea what she was talking about.

"Wasn't your man Wei Gang supposed to brief me about my relationship with He Nan Lin? Basic things like 'how I met her,' 'what she looks like,' and so forth?"

There was a long pause. "Is there a...problem, Jiang Ou?"

"Well, I can't say. There could be; the Secret Service came by to interview me yesterday. The agent wanted to know how I had come to meet He Nan Lin. I was supposed to be briefed about it on the way to the airport. I had a lot on my mind, and I happened to forget, but shouldn't your man have remembered?"

"I see...yes, that was rather careless of us."

"I should say so. If you expect me to risk my future for you, don't you think you should tell me everything I need to know in order to survive? You need to understand that any mistake I make can cost me everything."

"Of course, you're absolutely right; I do apologize. How did you explain it?"

"I told him that she and I had taken a class together."

"Fine," he said calmly. "We will arrange for you to have taken a class at USC with He Nan Lin."

"How can you do something like that?"

"Through the magic of computers," he replied, pulling up He Nan Lin's personnel file on his computer screen and looking for her college transcript. "Let's see, I've got her file right here. Now, what class would that be? You're an art student; know anything about eighteenth century Japanese art?"

"A little."

"Good, then eighteenth century Japanese art it is. Tell me, this agent – do you think he was suspicious?"

"He's in the Secret Service; he gets paid to be suspicious. Now I want everything on Nan Lin as soon as possible."

"Very well. We have all of her information in our file. You will be contacted by our Washington agent." *One* of our agents, he might well have said.

"I'll wait to hear," she replied. "Now, you won't forget, will you?"

After they ended the conversation, the consul general summoned his resident computer expert. "Chung, I need you to get into the student records computer at the University of Southern California. Create a file in their student database for Jiang Ou."

"I tried to get in the other night," said Chung. "They've got a new fire wall in place. It may take a while to break through."

"Very well. When you do, make an entry into her record to show that she took a course called History of Eighteenth Century Japanese Art...at the same time that He Nan Lin did." The consul general paused. "Oh, and I need for you to make it look like the computer file was created in January a year ago."

"That...can be a very difficult thing to do, Consul General."

The official was unmoved. "I believe it was the Romans who said, 'The *difficult* we do immediately; the *impossible* may take a little longer.'"

Diplomatically, Chung did not consider it his place to remind the consul general that Chinese civilization pre-dated the Roman Empire by two thousand years and had so far survived the Decline and Fall by fifteen hundred more.

"Just give me some time, Honorable Consul. I'll see what I can do."

## CHAPTER 14

That afternoon, Paul Blake popped in to inform the vice president of the latest news. He had with him Tony Phillips, the president's political adviser. "Sir, the *Andrew Jackson* is heading into port," Blake said. "And now Captain Rutherford is denying he ever gave Nick any ultimatum; he says it was all a lot of rumors which got out of hand. His staff is backing him up."

The vice president laughed. "Well, at least they're on the way back. I'd like to see Nick, but it looks like I'll be in the Carib for several days, depending on how long it takes to get things ironed out on this treaty. Anyway, I think Nick is going to be very busy over the next few days. Have they assigned him a lawyer yet?"

"Yes, sir," replied Blake. "Lieutenant Commander Jack Neely will handle the case. He's quite good, from what I understand. However, there is a problem I need to tell you about; actually, maybe it would be best if Tony explained."

"Go ahead, Tony. What is it?"

"Well, sir, the national reelection committee has been quietly putting pressure on the president to see that this whole incident doesn't blow up into a big publicity show. They think that Nick is…well…about the mechanical problems with the plane..."

"They think he's making it all up to cover for his screw-up with the penicillin," said Ferguson. "Is that it?"

"Yes, sir," replied Phillips. "Exactly. And they think he should admit he screwed up, take whatever he's got coming to him, and let this thing die quietly. The committee people don't want a media circus surrounding a navy court martial at the same time we're trying to win reelection. It's not good for the navy, it's not good for the country and, of course, it's not good for the campaign."

"What about Nick's career? Does that figure into any of this?"

Phillips seemed unprepared to respond to that question.

Ferguson moved on. "And so the president is going to want me to make Nick see the light on all of this, is that right?"

"I think that's what the president is hoping for," said Phillips. "Although he doesn't want to alienate you, of course. He wants you to understand that he is sympathetic."

"He sounded very sympathetic on the phone today – something about throwing the book at Nick..."

"The president regrets that remark," said Phillips. "Quite frankly, Admiral, the president is walking a tightrope and he's hoping you'll help get him through this."

Ferguson shook his head. "Tell the president that I will have a heart-to-heart talk with Nick just as soon as I get back. And, when I do, I'll ask him point blank if he there's any possibility he could be mistaken about the mechanical problems. If he's not one hundred percent sure, I'll certainly urge him to drop the matter."

"And if Nick still maintains that it was a mechanical failure...?" asked Phillips.

"Let me answer that question for you in a roundabout way," Ferguson replied as he walked over to the window and gazed out upon the perfectly manicured lawn. "It used to be, when I walked into my office every morning, there were about a hundred admirals who wanted to know what kind of mood I was in that day. I had four hundred ships and four hundred thousand men that I could move around the globe like pieces on a chessboard.

"Now, when I come to work, I have to decide whether I want to speak at a luncheon for some ladies' auxiliary group or whether I want to read to some kids at an inner city school – all very worthwhile activities, mind you, but it's not quite the same as commanding the world's greatest navy, now is it?

"My career is over, Mister Phillips. I enjoyed my thirty-six years with the navy, and when I resigned to become vice president it was like they put me in the old folks' home.

"So I think that Nick's career should take precedence over mine," he said quietly. "If Nick is absolutely certain that something happened to that plane up there, then I won't muzzle him." He turned and faced Phillips squarely. "And if the president wants to make an issue of it," he said with unmistakable firmness, "he can have my resignation any time he likes."

"Admiral, surely you wouldn't resign over this incident!" exclaimed Phillips.

"Just watch me. Gentlemen, I'd rather spend my time sitting at my son's court martial, giving him whatever moral support I can, than flying around the country trying to get reelected to a job that, quite frankly, bores the hell out of me. Now, does that answer your question?"

Phillips had never dealt face-to-face with Ferguson before; coming from the White House as he did, he found such directness to be unsettling. "Sir, I...I...I'm absolutely certain the president would not want you to even think about resigning. I'm sure I speak for everyone at the White House when I say that we need you on the team."

Ferguson smiled. "Just tell the president I'll do everything I can to see if there's a way out of this so that all parties are happy." He escorted Phillips to the door and opened it for him. "You have my word on it although, from what I hear, a sailor's word is not good for much these days."

"I'm sure the president will be very heartened by your cooperation, sir."

After Tony Phillips had gone, Ferguson glanced over at Paul

Blake, who seemed ill at ease. "What's eating you?"

He paused for a moment. "Sir, you remember how I used to start out a conversation by saying that I was just going to let my imagination roam and see where it led to?"

"Sure I remember; that's a practice of yours I'm quite familiar with. So, is the imagination roaming these days?"

"A little. Sir, don't you think that the timing of Nick's aerial mishap was somewhat coincidental?"

"Coincidental with what?"

"Coincidental with all this speculation that you might bolt the ticket and announce your own candidacy."

"I don't follow you," said Ferguson. "Or maybe I do…You're saying that Nick was deliberately knocked out of the sky in order to distract me from thinking about a presidential bid?"

"Bingo."

"That's lunacy."

"Oh, I agree that only a lunatic would do something like that."

"This sounds like another one of your well-known conspiracy theories, Paul; but go ahead, reason this out for me."

"Well, like any good criminal lawyer, one must consider both the means and the motive. Motive: the president desperately wants you on his ticket; but let's say he's sure you're going to bolt anyway…"

"I've issued numerous denials that I was going to run."

"Let's say the president is just slightly paranoid and he doesn't believe your denials. Let's say despite every effort to keep you in the fold – the birthday party, the Rose Garden ceremony, the high visibility assignments – he still thinks you're going to announce.

"He needs to create a distraction in your life, something that will destroy any thought of political ambition. What can he do? Your wife has been dead for two years, your oldest son Mark for ten; all that you have left is Nick."

"And you think…"

"Sir, I've been with you for over twenty years. I was with you when Mark was killed. I know what you went through. To the officers under your command, you were a little distant, a little distracted for a few months; but I saw you at the worst. I saw you in private; for a while there I didn't think you were going to pull through. If something happened to Nick..."

"OK, you've shown motive," said Ferguson curtly, clearly uncomfortable with the memory. "Let's move on. What about the means?"

"The means: the president is very close to Arnulf Kinder, the chairman of the board of Uniqraft, the largest airplane manufacturer in the United States – the manufacturer of the Super Hornet. As such, it would not be terribly difficult for a Uniqraft technician to do something to that plane; there are always a bunch of techs stationed aboard the carriers when they put to sea."

"Ah, but there's a major flaw in your argument," said Ferguson. "I made a firm and absolute public denial of any interest in running and I made it several hours before Nick fell out of the sky."

"Of course you did, sir, but you did it on the spur of the moment, without first consulting the White House. The president may have presumed that you were finally going to announce your candidacy. Let's say he panics and gives the order to set things in motion right at that moment: he picks up the phone, talks to Kinder, who sends a message to a shipboard tech. Something is done to Nick's plane – it might only take a few minutes. Then, of course, you make your final public denial but by the time Nick gets in his plane it's too late – for whatever reason – to reverse what was done."

"Very interesting ideas you have there; and have you told anyone else about this?"

"No one."

"Good. Let's deep-six this theory, Paul. The president may have his share of deficiencies, but he's not a cold-blooded murderer."

## 15

Jin Yi-bo found his chickens at the home of a sympathetic farmer half a mile from the village. He stuffed the birds in a burlap bag and, under the light of a crescent moon, made his way back to the caves.

His problems started when, walking on a riverside pathway, he spotted a troop of soldiers coming toward him. They were laughing, disorderly, apparently drunk – but they were armed. He quickly moved out of their way, but stumbled and fell. And then he heard a chicken squawk.

The soldiers heard it too and began laughing and shouting. Jin Yi-bo stood up and ran as fast as he could. He heard wild, undisciplined shooting, and then he felt a sharp sting in his side.

He made it back to the caves, through the maze and into the storeroom, where his comrades were waiting for him. They cheered his good luck, and then they saw the blood.

## 16

Conrad Haraldsen, the deputy detail leader of the United States Secret Service's Vice Presidential Protection Detail, was a meticulous and a diligent man. A thoroughly dedicated public servant, he prided himself on his conscientious approach to every aspect of his job, as well as on his oft-commended memory for details.

He liked for everything to check out; loose ends he did not appreciate. He never wanted to be in a position to have to say, "I should have looked into that; I should have been more suspicious." That was standard Secret Service doctrine; that was the code he lived by. That was the code he believed in.

It was, therefore, always important to question the motives of anyone who might be in contact with someone like Nick Ferguson on a regular basis, no matter how innocent-seeming he or she might be.

As an example, Jennifer Jiang had said that she and He Nan Lin had gone to school together. But Haraldsen's prodigious memory had told him that He Nan Lin had attended the University of Southern California, not the University of California at Los Angeles.

That slight little discrepancy was what he termed a loose

end. It might mean absolutely nothing – probably did mean absolutely nothing. Jennifer had explained the matter by saying that they had taken just the one course together at USC and that that was how they met. A perfectly reasonable explanation; and the best part was that it was easy enough to check out. Therefore, in order to satisfy his loose-ends-despising mind, he had asked the USC student records office for an electronic copy of the transcript of Jennifer Jiang.

He had been out of his office for a day, and when he got back he had on his desk the printouts of not one, but two separate replies from USC.

Reply Number One was almost twenty-four hours old. This reply said that there was no record of either a "Jennifer Jiang" or a "Jiang Ou" having ever attended a class at USC.

The second reply had come earlier that very morning. In it, there was information that she had indeed attended USC but had taken only one course: Eighteenth Century Japanese Art.

There was an elaborately-worded apology from the manager of the USC Student Records Office, along with his assurance that computer glitches of that type, though rare, were not unheard of.

Haraldsen compared the course number, instructor name, and time of the course with He Nan Lin's record: ART 307, check; Assistant Professor Kawagaki, check; 7:00 to 9:30 p.m., Monday and Wednesday, check; spring of the previous year, check. It all matched perfectly.

Still, despite the fact that these were all what he classified as Low Probability Anomalies, the situation nicked his conscience ever-so-slightly: a chance meeting in a classroom...two separate replies from USC...a rare computer glitch...a file which wasn't there one day but was there the next...

Perhaps it was his overactive imagination; even a series of LPAs did not necessarily mean anything. He remembered the basics of probability theory which *every* schoolboy knew: the probability of Event A had no bearing on the probability of unrelated Event B.

And yet, if he dropped the whole matter now, his conscience would not be one hundred per cent clear; and he *did* like for his conscience to be clear.

He sent a message back to the USC Student Records Office and asked them to check their computer's file creation log for her record and advise him of the date that the electronic file was created. In the same message he asked to be provided a means of contacting the instructor; perhaps Assistant Professor Kawagaki had kept his class records.

Perhaps all of this was overkill but, at least for Haraldsen, part of the fun of his job was the opportunity to be continually amazed at what he was able to ask for and get. Experience told him that if USC had the information, they would send it. He was vaguely aware that there were congressionally mandated privacy rules which protected the confidentiality of student records; anyone else would have to get the student's permission to obtain the information. But when dealing with the civilian world, the words "Secret Service" were magical. Bureaucratic obstinacies crumbled before him; legalistic spiderwebs vaporized in a flash. He had ways of making people talk. Just by being himself.

He looked over her brief record once more. "Eighteenth Century Japanese Art," he noted. "And she got an A. Very impressive – if she actually earned it."

There was one more little test he had in mind. Now that Nick was back in Washington and would almost certainly be dropping by to see Ellen Conley's kid, Haraldsen was sure that he would run into Miss Jiang again. He buzzed his secretary. "Mrs. Walters?"

She came right in. "Yes, Mr. Haraldsen?"

"Didn't you say you had a contact at the Library of Congress who knows how to find out almost anything on any topic?"

"Oh, yes, Mister Haraldsen," she replied. "Frank Coffey is wonderful."

"Get on the horn to old Frank, would you? Get me some basic information on a prominent Japanese artist of the eighteenth century: school, style of painting, influences, that sort of thing – a few catch phrases that I could memorize easily. Type them up on a three-by-five card and have the card on my desk sometime next week. No hurry."

"Yes, Mister Haraldsen," she replied, checking her shorthand. "Japanese artist – eighteenth century – basic information on style, school, influences – three-by-five – on your desk. And which artist was that again?"

"I told you. Prominent. Eighteenth century. Japanese. I don't care which one."

## CHAPTER 17

No prisoners had been seen or heard leaving or returning to the prison during the night. No villagers, upon being questioned, had any information regarding the sale of chickens during the night just ended.

No soldiers of the People's Liberation Army admitted going on a shooting spree and failing to kill a single defenseless chicken.

No explanation could be given as to how six chickens had miraculously come to appear in Chen Wei Dong's walled yard which adjoined the prison wall near Section Six. No prisoners were beheaded in anger, as Chen Wei Dong did not want to reveal his frustration at having been fowled once again.

No report could be presented to prison authorities regarding the severity of the wound which Jin Yi-bo had received. No explanation could be offered as to how the wound had come to be received. No surgical equipment was available to operate on the wound, no antibiotic to stop the infection, no anaesthetic to ease the pain.

One life for ten: that was the way a philosopher would see it; but the men of Section Six of the People's Rehabilitation and Reeducation Camp Number 216 were not philosophers; they were freedom fighters, and Jin Yi-bo was their leader.

## Chapter 18

"Can I help you with that, Lieutenant?"

The *USS Andrew Jackson* had finally arrived in port. There were thousands of family members jammed onto the naval base, waiting to pick up a friend or a loved one.

Lieutenant Ferguson left the ship in the company of his maintenance crew.

Every possession that Nick Ferguson had aboard the carrier was carried off voluntarily by the enlisted men of his squadron. They would have carried him as well if he had asked them to.

By his own request, Nick's Secret Service protection did not fall into place until he left a naval base and reentered a civilian environment. Thus, without the contingent of men in dark suits surrounding him, it took him nearly an hour to get away from the ship, as sailors were constantly coming up to him, wanting to introduce him to their mothers, their wives, or their unattached sisters. He left the dock area with about a dozen phone numbers stuffed in his pockets. He would file them with all the others.

After checking into the bachelor officer's quarters, Nick made his way to the offices of the judge advocate general. He had a five o'clock appointment with Commander Jack Neely, his legal defender.

The JAG building was nearly deserted as Nick made his way down the hallway to Room 27. The door was open; Nick tapped on the glass and addressed the officer who was hunched over his desk, seemingly hard at work. "Lieutenant Ferguson reporting as ordered, sir."

The officer acted as though he had known the lieutenant all his life. "Hi, Nick," he said, jumping around and offering his hand. "Jack Neely. What do you drink?"

"I beg your pardon, sir?"

"Name's Jack, not 'sir'," said the senior officer as he stepped to the other side of the cramped room and opened a small cabinet. "Bourbon, scotch, you name it. Have a seat, Nick, and would you please relax?"

"Uh, nothing for me," Nick said, moving some legal papers aside and making room to sit down. "Or just a soda. Anything's fine."

Jack Neely would have a bourbon. He handed Nick his soft drink and sat down on the leather couch, facing his new client. "Well, you've had an interesting week. Let's see: fell out of the sky, dropped a thirty million dollar jet into the drink, interrupted prime time TV in fifty million homes, held up newspaper printing all over the country, forced a Nimitz-class carrier to stand still in the water for twenty hours, caused a crisis in the Pentagon as well as the White House. And, gosh, here it is only Thursday..."

"I think you've summed things up quite nicely, Jack."

"Well, then, let's go over the charges: dereliction of duty, in which you failed to report to sick bay with an ear infection prior to flight, choosing instead to self-medicate.

"Destruction of government property, to the tune of twenty-nine million dollars and change.

"Conduct unbecoming an officer, in which you pressured an enlisted corpsman into providing unauthorized medical care.

"And finally, failure to obey a direct order, in which you refused to provide the name of one Corpsman Krumbein to your commanding officer when directed to do so. We've got an arraignment before the judge advocate tomorrow. How do wish to plead?"

"Well, if you look at it objectively," Nick replied soberly, "I guess I am pretty much guilty."

"Fine. You'll plead not guilty."

"Well, all right; whatever you say."

"Now, let's talk about strategy. The way I see it, if we can prove that there was a problem with the avionics, then it is always possible that the 'dereliction' and 'destruction' charges will be dropped. The 'conduct unbecoming' charge could be dropped if the prosecutor has a change of heart and decides you were just a little overzealous in your desire to compete. As far as the 'failure to obey...'"

"I was keeping a promise to Krumbein," Nick explained.

"Doesn't matter," said Neely. "You can't use that as a defense when it's part of a cover-up. You should never have entered into the agreement to cover up in the first place because what you were doing was non-regulation. Understand?"

"Right, sir...Jack."

"However, let's say that somebody knew there was a problem with the plane and they kept this information from you, thus endangering your life. The navy loves its public image and they definitely don't like the idea of people questioning the billions of dollars spent on a new weapons program. Thus, there might be a certain willingness to overlook your relatively minor infractions in exchange for your willingness not to go public with any detrimental information; that, of course, is assuming that we can find something to nail them with."

"You're talking about 'nailing the navy'? Aren't you a naval officer yourself?"

"Let me explain something to you, Nick. When it comes to defending my clients, I wear the uniform, and I follow navy regs, but I'm a lawyer first and foremost. Are we squared away on that, Nick?"

"Squared away, Jack."

"Good. Now then, I understand you've been given a new assignment..."

"Desk jockey in Washington. I guess they want to keep an eye on me – make sure I don't wander outside the sandbox."

"I'm sure; between the navy, the Secret Service, and the media watching every move you make, they might as well put you in the National Zoo."

"There's a thought. How's the food, I mean, in comparison to navy chow?"

"I think you'd like it. So, have you got a girl up in the D.C. area, Nick?"

"Well, I did have a particular favorite; but things took a bad turn."

"Oh? How's that?"

"Well, things were going along pretty well for a while there," Nick explained, "but she basically told me that she didn't feel I was quite ready to settle down to the responsibilities of marriage and step-fatherhood; said she thought I was still running a little too wild."

"Wild? You? I'm shocked."

"Well...you know...reckless..."

"Can't imagine where she got that idea, Nick. You ready for some bourbon in that drink? No, sir, I believe that girl has you all wrong."

## 19

They had no choice but to operate on Jin Yi-bo. For a scalpel they would use a knife stolen from the prison kitchen. For sutures, they would pull threads from their buttons. For needles, they sharpened one end of a wire and carefully notched the other. For anesthesia, they would fill him with rice wine. To pull the bullet out, they fashioned tweezers from a pair of ivory chopsticks stolen from the home of the prison commander.

They had a small lamp to see by, and blankets torn into strips to stop the bleeding. A bucket of water stood nearby to douse the wound as they worked. Four men were available to hold him down, and one would clamp his mouth in case he screamed.

To handle the operation, they would bring in two specialists: from Section Two, a middle-aged man who had once worked as an assistant to a doctor in Shanghai; and from Section Ten, a young man of twenty-one who used to drive an ambulance.

The operation started at two in the morning, and finished up at four-thirty. At the time they left his cell, he was still alive.

# CHAPTER 20

Air Force Two landed at the naval air base on the island of Vieques near the Commonwealth of Puerto Rico at just after noon. There were no media present, as none of the governments involved desired their presence. There was only a small welcoming party and a naval escort.

Those waiting to greet the American vice president consisted of Foreign Secretary Yurii Osuka of Japan and Trade Minister Antonio Munez of the Philippines, and a few of their aides. When the airliner rolled to a stop, Mark Ferguson made his way down to the tarmac and shook hands with his old friends. "It's great to see you again, Admiral," said Munez.

"Hello, Antonio. Great to see you, Yurii."

The three officials were driven to the officer's club in one limousine, and they spent the short drive renewing acquaintances. Upon their arrival at the O-club, they found that an outdoor terrace had been cordoned off for them, affording them a beautiful view overlooking the Caribbean Sea. White-coated waiters brought their lunch, poured tea, and stood quietly by for further instructions.

At the appropriate time, Munez, who had requested the meeting and had arranged the luncheon, thanked the staff.

"And now, we'd like to be left undisturbed for the next twenty minutes."

The doors leading from the main dining room were closed and thus it was just the three men, the soft, flowing wind, and the Caribbean Sea.

Ferguson was the first to speak. "Gentlemen, I know how important this meeting is to you. As far as the trade treaty, I have every assurance from Senator Morrison that our senate intends to comply with all of the recommendations in your final proposals."

Osuka and Munez traded glances and the latter was the first to speak. "Admiral, the trade treaty is not the real reason we're here."

Ferguson did not hide his surprise. "That's all you have to say? I was expecting a little more discussion." The face of the American clouded over. "What is the reason, then?"

"This has to do with you personally, Admiral," said Osuka. "We think we can make you an offer which, as you Americans say, you can't refuse."

The vice president put down his fork and sat back in his chair. "OK, I'm listening."

"The free nations of the Asia-Pacific region are looking to form a Pacific Free Trade Association," said the Japanese foreign secretary. "Similar to the European Economic Community, or the North American Free Trade Association."

"However, we want the West to understand that we are not doing this as an act of economic aggression," added Munez. "To that end, we need a spokesman who is respected in both hemispheres. You are highly regarded in every country of the Pacific region."

"Admiral," said the Japanese bluntly, "I'll come to the point. We would like you to consider co-chairing the association's board of directors."

"That sounds like a full time job," said the admiral.

"Indeed, it is a full time job," said the Japanese minister, "and it would require you to live in Tokyo."

The American looked at his friends with suspicion; he was quiet for a good long while. "I know perfectly well that you both know that I'm on the ticket for reelection," he said quietly. "So why now?"

Osuka smiled. "Well, like the rest of the world, we were waiting to see whether you were going to bolt and declare for yourself. Since that didn't happen…"

"Why didn't you do what everyone was hoping you would do?" asked Munez. "Why didn't you declare?"

"I just couldn't do that," said the Old Man. "It wouldn't be right."

"It's not the navy way?" offered Osuka. "Is that it?"

"Exactly." The admiral stood and walked over to the edge of the terrace, where he faced out to sea. "Gentlemen, I hardly know what to say. It would of course be great to be back in the Pacific once again…"

"Before you say no," said Osuka, "consider this: you would have the freedom to come and go as you please. You would in effect be a highly visible liaison between the developing nations of the East and the United States and Europe."

"And of course, the pay…" added Munez.

"Would be considerable. My personal view," added Osuka, standing up and joining the admiral by the terrace railing, "is that if you don't declare and run, then you will be out of office come next January. Of course, our offer will still be available to you then…"

"Quite frankly, we don't see much chance of the president's being reelected," said Munez. "President Billingsley is a very good party politician but the people seem indifferent to him."

The vice president listened quietly to their various points before he turned and countered them. "Gentlemen, with all due respect, I happen to disagree. I believe that the president will be reelected; narrowly, but reelected nonetheless."

"In which case you will have four more years in a job which cannot possibly be fulfilling to you," responded Osuka.

The admiral smiled. "Unfulfilling – perhaps – but Nick is stationed at Norfolk, and my fulfillment comes in keeping up with him. Anyway, I believe it was John Milton who said, 'They also serve who only stand and wait.'"

JENNIFER WAS instructed by the consul general's office in Los Angeles to meet her Washington contact under the rotunda of the Jefferson Memorial at nine o'clock at night.

The woman's name was Lily Zhang. She was a small, compactly-built woman, with a tightly-drawn face, and hard, black eyes. Immediately she seemed to know who Jennifer was. Wordlessly, they walked out of the rotunda and along the walkway which ran beside the reflecting pool.

Lily Zhang issued no greeting and made no small talk, but got down to business straightaway. "Here is everything we have on He Nan Lin," said Zhang, slipping an envelope to her.

"You have no idea of the scare you put me through," Jennifer said as she placed the envelope in her purse. "I thought you people were supposed to be well-organized."

"The Honorable Consul General expresses his sincere apology," said the agent with not the slightest trace of sincerity in her voice. "Now then, have you been enjoying your stay in Washington?"

"I haven't really had time. I'm still getting settled in and looking for work; as well as developing my contacts, of course."

"Have you met the naval lieutenant?"

"I understand he'll be arriving in a day or two; I'm looking forward to meeting him."

"Yes, it's very important that you make the best possible impression," said Zhang, lighting a cigarette. "How are you doing for money? College students generally don't have much money."

"I can get by."

Cigarette held tenuously in her lips, Lily reached into her purse. "Here. Go to the best shops in Georgetown. Buy some clothes; have your hair done, makeup…nails. You want to look your best." She took a long drag on her cigarette.

Jennifer felt funny taking money from this stranger, but

found it much easier when she simply thought of her as the enemy. "Thank you."

"Don't worry so much about things. You need to relax," advised Lily Zhang, perhaps the least relaxed human being on the planet. "You should get out and see the sights; have you been to the museum?"

Jennifer froze. "The museum? What museum?"

"The art museum." Another drag; she stared Jennifer in the eyes. "The National Gallery of Art."

Did they know that she had gone there as soon as she had arrived in Washington? Had they followed her there?

"You studied art, didn't you?" Lily asked, with just the slightest tone of impatience in her voice. Puff, puff.

"Yes, I did."

"Then you should go." Drag. "I highly recommend it." Puff. "I'm surprised you haven't been by now." Puff, puff, puff, puff, puff.

How should she respond to that? If they knew she had been there and she lied about it, she was finished; there was only one way to answer. "In fact," Jennifer said, "I was fortunate enough to be able to get there on my first day here. I just couldn't wait to see it, so I played tourist for a few hours." She paused and waited.

It seemed as though Lily were staring right through her. Long, agonizing drag. She blew out the smoke slowly, staring coldly at Jennifer. "A wise decision," she said at last. And then she turned and walked off, leaving Jennifer to watch her fade into the night.

A 'wise decision?' What did she mean by that? A 'wise decision' to go to the museum? Or a 'wise decision' to tell the truth? How much did they know?

Lily Zhang gave her the chills.

AIR FORCE TWO flew into Andrews Air Force Base at six o'clock in the evening. On the flight back from the Caribbean, Mark Ferguson had called the president and told him that the treaty was acceptable to all parties and that he was now free to announce an agreement.

He was sure that the president would do so and would of course never bother to bring up the vice president's perceived role, particularly now that the issues surrounding the ticket were settled. Now that he was securely on board with the president, that would be the end of the pampering and special assignments.

That was all right; it wasn't important. He would be busy enough over the next few months in the effort to win reelection as well as in his assumed role of advising Nick as needed. And then, after the election – win or lose – he would think seriously about taking up golf.

But for now, he was much more interested in the dinner guests who would be arriving at the Naval Observatory – now the vice presidential residence – within the hour. Paul Blake and Eric Whitford had been invited to the residence in order to discuss the campaign. And then Nick had called and left a message with his office and said that he would be arriving in Washington that evening.

Their reunion would be a happy one. With the deaths of Mrs. Ferguson and Mark, Jr., and the fact that both of them had lived most of their lives in transit, they understood that they had only each other now.

As it turned out, Nick arrived before the others and so he and the Old Man spent nearly an hour sipping their drinks and making small talk. They talked of life aboard a carrier…foreign ports…and the antics of the Salivator, whom the vice president had met and liked immensely. Ellen Conley came up briefly.

Finally Nick decided to broach The Topic. "Aren't you going to ask me?"

"Ask you what?"

"About the plane: whether there was anything really wrong with it or not?"

The vice president shrugged. "Why should I ask you that? You've stated to your superiors that there was a problem in the avionics. I've seen the Secret Service report."

"Well, it's been suggested – in one or two newspaper reports – that maybe I was using that as an excuse to cover up for my medical problem. And so I just thought that that possibility might be on a few people's minds."

"Not mine."

"Well, I just think you're entitled to know…"

"Thank you," said the admiral, signaling for a member of his staff to approach. "If I ever have any doubts as to your veracity, Nick, I'll be sure to let you know. Now then, you'll stay for dinner…"

The admiral left the room in order to speak with the cook. As he sat alone in the study, Nick was reminded of why so many sailors held the Old Man in such high regard. If he never had a reason to question someone's truthfulness, he wouldn't do it.

He had always instilled in Mark, Jr. and Nick the importance of dealing respectfully with those of lesser rank. The admiral had a high regard for enlisted men – thought they were valiant, capable and resourceful – and gave them a great deal of responsibility and credit for getting the job done.

The Old Man had illustrated this attitude toward subordinates by presenting a problem: "You have two shovels, two seamen first class, a chief petty officer, a sack of concrete, and a flagpole. How do you get the flagpole set up?"

Mark, Jr. and Nick knew the answer. "You say, 'Chief, raise the flagpole.'"

The Old Man was known to despise those of his fellows officers who manifested a distinctly superior attitude towards the lower ranks – the Prince-of-the-Church mentality, he liked to call it – and was always disgusted when those officers instilled in their wives and kids the same frightful attitude as well.

Ever since Nick was old enough to run around, he and his older brother Mark had wanted to be navy pilots. Those were the days when the admiral was still a relatively junior officer. They would all go down to the port in Norfolk or San Diego or any of the other half-dozen places they had lived, and they would wave goodbye as the Old Man trooped up the gangplank of a destroyer, or a battleship, or a carrier.

In his wildest imaginings Nick could not have dreamed that all these many years later Mark, Jr. and his mother would be dead, and his father would be roaming the corridors of power in Washington.

Since those early days, Mark Ferguson, Sr. had been promoted swiftly and placed in various important commands, including commander-in-chief of the Pacific forces. And then it had fallen upon the newly elected and popular President Lawrence Holdren to name a new CNO, or chief of naval operations. Holdren had elevated Admiral Ferguson to the leadership of the navy.

Admiral Ferguson's politics were unknown, but he had impressed many in the U.S. Senate when he had come to Capitol Hill in his first year in Washington in order to defend naval appropriations requests. He had become friends with many on Capitol Hill, and when Vice President Edward Billingsley was elevated to the White House upon the sudden death by cardiac arrest of President Holdren, the new president had formed a committee made up of party and congressional leaders in order to suggest possible nominees to fill the second post in government.

Several senators had mentioned Admiral Ferguson to the White House, and he had been approached and asked to submit to the nominating process. He had done so with extreme reluctance, loathe to leave behind the navy he had served with such devotion for over thirty-five years. When all was said and done, however, Mark Ferguson had easily emerged as the premier candidate for the vice-presidency, and had won quick senatorial approval.

A few minutes later, a car drove up. Two men got out and within moments were escorted into the sitting room by the vice president. "Nick, you know Paul Blake, my chief of staff."

"Nick, always great to see you."

"And Eric Whitford, my political adviser."

Dinner was served, and the range of conversation covered

everything but politics and Nick's troubles. As the plates were being cleared away, Blake spoke up. "Have you told him yet, sir?" he said, clearly indicating Nick.

Nick looked around. "Told me what? Is there something I'm supposed to be told?"

It was decided that they would retire to the library, where cigars and brandy were waiting for them. The vice president waited until all had been served, and then he closed the double doors, with instructions to be left undisturbed. "Go ahead, Paul; this was your idea."

"Well, Nick, there are some people who seem to think that your plane may have been sabotaged," said Blake. "Myself for one."

"You're kidding, right?" Nick said with a nervous laugh. He looked around the room, and checked for signs of levity; there were none. "And who might want to do something like that?"

Blake was ready with the answer. "Some people think...that is – *I* think – that the president is behind it."

"What!" exclaimed Nick. "Excuse me...This is a joke. Why would...?"

"To disable your father," answered Blake. "To drag him down, to keep him from bolting the ticket and declaring for the presidency."

Nick shook his head in bewilderment. "I don't believe that."

"To be honest with you, gentlemen," said the admiral. "I've never believed it for a minute. The more I think about it, the less sense it seems to make. Think about it this way: suppose things had turned out differently. Suppose that, instead of announcing that I were going to remain on the ticket, I had announced that I were going to run and then a few hours later Nick falls out of the sky – let's take it a step further and say that he doesn't make it.

"Well, what then? Don't you think that twenty million people wouldn't simultaneously get the same idea – that there was a connection between those two events? Look at all the conspiracy theorists – and not just you, Paul – who would make something out of that; they'd be crawling out of every cave and fill-ing the talk radio airwaves with nothing but this."

"On top of that," added Eric Whitford, buttressing the vice president's argument, "for someone to plan something like this, think about all the things that have to go right. And none of the people involved can ever breathe a word, ever again, for the rest of their lives; otherwise, it all falls apart. What incentive would these people have to keep this secret quiet for the rest of their lives?"

As Whitford spoke, Mark Ferguson turned and looked out of a window and in the direction of the White House. "Paul, the president has one finely-tuned ability that has served him very well over the years: he knows how to survive. He's the quintessential politician who would rather do nothing than make a decision. He doesn't take risks; he doesn't take the initiative. He likes the status quo just fine and he just wouldn't do something dumb that would mess things up for himself. That's how he got to be president and that's why I'm one of the few people who happens to think he'll win reelection. He's a safe choice, and sometimes the country is perfectly comfortable with a safe choice in the White House."

He turned and faced his audience of three. "Of course, I am open to counterargument if anyone sees things differently."

Paul Blake was not quite willing to concede the battle. "OK. Well, then consider this idea," he began. "Suppose it were just a coincidence...Suppose that the plane were in fact in the process of being sabotaged but it just happened to be by chance that you made your announcement when you did."

The vice president furrowed his brow. "So you're saying that someone intended to do this all along, and it just so happened by sheer coincidence that I made my announcement that very day?"

"But you still have the problem with the cover-up," argued Eric. "Look, we can speculate all day long about hypotheticals like this. The point is, we just don't know. How could we? We really don't have any hard evidence."

"If I may, sir, one more idea," said Blake, not quite ready to abandon the field. "Let me postulate an amendment to my own theory: it wasn't the president; it was a member of his staff. Let's say it was this staffer who's getting tired of waiting for you to make up your mind and so he meets with Arnulf Kinder and arranges to have this done."

"That's quite a limb for a subordinate to go out on," said the admiral. "And which staffer would you nominate for this role?"

"Tony Phillips, sir."

"The one who came to my office yesterday?" said Ferguson. "Seemed like a nice enough fellow; didn't look like a raving madman to me."

Whitford had by now grown impatient with Blake's ramblings. "Come on, Eric. You think he's close enough to Arnulf Kinder to pull something like that off?"

"I'd say he is; he's engaged to Kinder's daughter."

The room grew still; that particular fact seemed to come as a surprise to all present.

Paul Blake picked up his drink and swirled it around. "Still think it's outside the realm of possibility, gentlemen?"

## Chapter 21

The invitation had come by mail and there was an RSVP included. The seventh birthday party for Greg Conley was an event which promised an interesting evening. It was very kind of Ellen Conley to invite him personally, Conrad Haraldsen thought, as he examined the calligraphic handwriting on the envelope.

He had gotten to know Ellen and Greg during the time that Nick was a regular visitor to Ellen's residence. Ellen had always been thoughtful and kindhearted in this way.

Of course, he would expect to see Jennifer Jiang there as well.

Interestingly, the earlier suspicions he had about her seemed to have evaporated. He had received a reply from USC regarding her records: the electronic file of her transcript had been created nearly a year and a half before, at the time the course started. For Haraldsen, that pretty much settled the issue: Jennifer Jiang appeared to be hiding nothing.

USC had also informed him that Assistant Professor Kawagaki had been denied tenure at the end of the previous academic year and was believed to have returned to Japan. As a courtesy, USC had sent a message to Kawagaki's last known mailing address. Endlessly helpful, these civilians.

Perhaps it had been silly to suspect someone like Jennifer Jiang. Still, he felt good about the fact that he had done his job according to the rarified standard he had set for himself.

Conrad Haraldsen did not make a great deal of money in the service of his country, but he liked to believe that he earned all that he was paid.

THE REPRESENTATIVE from the Taiwan Trade Office in the World Trade Center in New York had contacted Jennifer and arranged for her to have a face-to-face meeting with her Washington contact.

They met in a tiny Moroccan restaurant in Northern Virginia in the middle of the afternoon. The rationale for meeting then and there was that if another Chinese person happened to come into a Moroccan restaurant while they were talking, the odds were extremely high that such a person would be an agent of the People's Republic.

As it was, it was just the two of them. Jennifer spotted him in the third booth, just as he had said. "Major Chen?"

Seeing him now for the first time face-to-face, she saw that he was a large, powerfully built man with an open, friendly expression. "Have a seat," said he. "First of all, I have some interesting news for you. We have located Jin Yi-bo."

At the sound of his name, her heart leaped up. "Yes…and …?"

"He's alive, but was recently shot; not a fatal wound, but there are complications."

"What do you mean? What happened?"

"I'm sorry," said the major. "I don't have details. He has friends who are doing everything they can to help him, but there is very little medical care in the lao gai, and political prisoners are generally treated pretty badly throughout China."

"Is it possible to get any medical help to him?"

"It's possible to get anything into the lao gai," said the major, "if one bribes the right people. The problem is that we can't diagnose his condition from a distance and so it's difficult to be sure we are doing the right thing."

"Of course; I understand."

"The thing that makes the most sense is for us to somehow get a doctor in there. There is a British unit of the International Red Cross that has recently received permission to visit some of the lao gai in Northern China. They will be traveling through Hong Kong in a week or so, and we can have someone contact them and try to persuade them to go to Harbin as soon as possible. If they can stabilize him, then he may have a chance of traveling."

"That would be wonderful," she said. "What about getting him to the coast?"

"There are two ways to accomplish that. Escape is one way. The Chinese don't like to admit it, but with six million prisoners, a few do manage to find their way into the mountainous areas of Western China. Of course, recapture means summary execution..."

They were both silent as they contemplated that possibility.

"The other way," continued the major, "is by some sort of interprison transfer. In this case, the goal would be to get him to the prison at Shi Men, which is in an isolated area near the Sea of Japan. However, with the injury, there are added complications. For one thing, he'll be traveling over some rough terrain and that could be hard on him. Secondly, his support network may have to be left behind at Harbin.

"I must be perfectly honest and tell you that we could lose him no matter what decision is made. You *must* understand that."

The thought of losing Jin Yi-bo hit Jennifer with the solidity of a brick wall. She realized that she was making decisions which affected the life of another human being, in this case one she cared deeply about.

It was one thing to fervently hope to see Jin Yi-bo again. It was quite another to set into motion events which would place him at risk and leave open the possibility of death. But she was sure, even more than she was sure of her own feelings, that that was what Jin Yi-bo would want. She nodded her understanding.

The major could see that this news, coming as it was all at once, was hitting Jennifer very hard. "Don't worry," he said. "We will do our best to get him out of there. So how's the life of a double agent?"

"Nerve-wracking," she said, trying her best to remain cheerful. "Tell me – do you have anyone following me?"

The major shrugged. "No, there's no reason to. Why? Do you think that someone is?"

"I can't be sure," she said. "The Chinese seemed to know that I went to the museum on my first day in town."

"Anything is possible...and you had a Secret Service background check, right? How do you think you did?"

"It was touch and go; I think I'm OK."

"It's not a bad idea to assume at all times that someone is tracking your whereabouts," said he. "Because if they're not now, just wait till you begin to associate with somebody really important."

"The consul general told me that men in power will protect me."

Major Chen laughed. "Didn't anyone ever tell you not to believe everything you were told? Let me give you the best advice you'll ever get: protect yourself, because nobody else will. That's the harsh reality of life here in Washington and the sooner you learn that the better off you'll be."

TOM YANCEY was sitting on the floor of Ellen Conley's apartment, wrestling with his company's latest creation, a toy called Roboticus. "OK, then, Greg," said Tom. "It looks like this part goes here and this goes here..."

Except that it didn't; despite the fact that he was one of the key players in the lucrative toy industry, Tom Yancey was mechanically inept. "Hey, I'm a finance guy," he explained jokingly to Ellen.

They had tried a dozen times but Roboticus was not going to come to life.

Luckily, there came a most welcome diversion in the form of a knock on the door. Ellen opened it, and all turned to see

Conrad Haraldsen, whom they all knew, along with Lieutenant and Mrs. Russell DiSalvo, whom they didn't.

And of course Nick. Greg Conley looked up and saw his hero, returned at last. "Nicko!" he exclaimed as he stood up and ran into the sailor's outstretched arms. Nick picked the boy up and swung him around.

"Gregory!" Ellen exclaimed. "Tom was just about finished showing you how…"

"Oh, it's all right, Ellen," said Tom, standing up and rubbing his back. "A living, breathing Nick Ferguson trumps a mere toy any day of the week."

"Nick," said Ellen, when Nick finally set Greg down. "I'd like for you to meet Tom Yancey."

"Hello, Tom," he said, pumping his rival's hand. "Well, should I say congratulations, or am I too early for that?"

"A bit premature," said Ellen and quickly changed the subject. "Nick, aren't you going to introduce your guests?"

"Of course. This is Lieutenant Russell DiSalvo, known throughout the fleet as 'The Salivator.'"

"Hello, Lieutenant DiSalvo," said Ellen. "I've heard so much about you. I hope you don't mind if I call you Russell instead?"

"Not at all," said he. "And this is my wife Jeannine." Jeannine DiSalvo looked to be about thirty months pregnant.

"Well, Jeannine, why don't you sit down?" Ellen quickly offered.

"Thank you," said Mrs. DiSalvo. "I try to stay off my feet as much as possible. When you're as big as a troop carrier…"

"I didn't say you were as big as a troop carrier," interjected her husband defensively. "Clearly you misheard me. What I said was that you are *like* a troop carrier in the sense that that particular type of ship carries people around inside it. I was making a nautical analogy that all naval personnel would understand and consider to be insightful and instructive."

"Salivator," said Nick, "the more you try to explain it, the worse it sounds." He glanced down and saw Greg looking at the toy. "Whatcha got there, Greg?"

"It's Roboticus," said the boy, "but it won't work right."

"Unfortunately, I think I brought a defective sample with me," said Tom.

"Mind if I take a look?" asked Nick. He examined the toy carefully, turning it over and holding the pieces at various angles. "Have you tried removing this clip?" he said as he removed the obstructive item and forced the recalcitrant parts into place.

"Well, I'll be..." said Tom, clearly impressed.

The perfect hostess, Ellen drew attention away from Tom's embarrassment. "And now – I'd like everybody to meet our new housemate, Jennifer Jiang."

Everybody turned to see the young woman who had just walked out of the kitchen carrying a platter. She was dressed in a stunning white outfit which set off her shoulder-length black hair. "Hello," said she, realizing that she had just become the center of attention.

"Jennifer has come to Washington to look for work as an interpreter in Chinese," Ellen explained. She then introduced the DiSalvos; Jennifer also greeted Haraldsen, whom she had already met.

And then she was introduced to Nick. "How do you do?" he said, taking her small hand in his and squeezing it gently. "Nick Ferguson."

The room grew quiet as all watched the reaction between Jennifer and Nick. Aware of the attention, their eyes held for a moment longer, and then they both turned away in order to diffuse the tension in the room and get the conversation started again.

Ellen served drinks and Jennifer set out the hors d'oeuvres, and everyone spent some time relaxing and commingling. The Salivator walked up beside Jennifer and checked out the raw vegetable platter she had just brought in. "Ah, your basic broccoli and celery," he said, sampling the goods. "I once dated a Chinese dietician," he then announced, crunching loudly. "Name was Lo Fat Chow."

Jennifer smiled politely and moved a step away.

"Her sister was a child bride," he added. "Name of Wei Tu-yung."

Jennifer could manage only to stare at him.

He tried a different tack. "An interpreter, eh? So...where'd you pick up your Chinese?"

"I was born there."

Salivator had to think about that. "Oh. So, then, it's like a total immersion approach," he speculated as Nick came up beside him and listened in. "I hear that's the best way to learn a foreign language."

"Well, it really wasn't a foreign language to me..." she replied slowly. "To me, it was my native language."

"OK, I'm with you now. Sure – of course; and so what did you study out there at UCLA, Jennifer?"

"Art history."

"Art history? Is that one of those interdepartmental degrees, where you study a little bit of art and a little bit of history?"

"Well...not exactly," she explained. "Art history is the history of art."

"I'm definitely with you now," said the Salivator. "Myself, I started out as a psychology-chemistry major..."

"Don't pay any attention to him," said Nick.

"...but then I decided to switch to remedial math-English; of course, I have trained extensively for a second career as a mattress tester."

"A *mattress* tester?"

"I wanted to have something to fall back on."

"Exit, stage left," Nick said as he grabbed his flight mate by the arm and steered him toward the kitchen. "Salivator, you've managed to reaffirm your standing as a world-class idiot. Come on, let's get something to drink."

"What did I say?"

The door swung closed behind them. "Total immersion? Are you *nuts?*"

"Well, when you think about it, everybody speaks a foreign language."

Special Agent Haraldsen had been eyeing Jennifer ever since he arrived. Professional considerations aside, he had to admit that he found her to be the most captivating person in the room. She was attractive and poised and seemed to become – and to effortlessly remain – the center of attention, like some bright light which compelled the gaze across a darkened sky.

Directly or otherwise, all of the men in the room – including Tom Yancey and Russell DiSalvo – seemed to be playing for her attention and yet, strangely, these actions seemed to create no sense of anxiety or jealousy on the part of the other women in the room.

Despite her attractiveness, her allure, and the air of mystery that surrounded her, Jennifer Jiang seemed to be not the slightest bit threatening to the other women. They seemed to like her as much as the men did.

It was as though the women could tell that she was merely amused by the antics of these men, and no more. Despite the fact that there was something of a competition to try to engage her in conversation, she seemed to be almost completely detached from the scene – serene, placid, at peace with herself – as though her thoughts were half a world away; which, of course, they were.

Agent Haraldsen would have given anything to know what was going on in that private little world of hers – what inhabited it, what made it spin.

Obviously, men like DiSalvo could only manage to make fools of themselves in front of her. As for the businessman Tom Yancey, he was purely a materialist – all wrong for someone as ethereal as she.

And he certainly saw no evidence that she was particularly enamored of Nick. That would have been understandable – Nick Ferguson was still quite immature in many ways. He would be fun to be around, but any mature woman would tire of him eventually. Witness Ellen Conley.

Perhaps a young woman such as Jennifer Jiang would appreciate the finer qualities of a more serious man – a man who was sober and clearheaded, one who knew the meaning of responsibility and purposefulness.

To say nothing of preparedness: he himself had taken the trouble to learn about a prominent eighteenth century Japanese artist – well, yes, for investigative purposes, admittedly, but that was beside the point; still, was there anyone else here tonight who could possibly be prepared to speak to her intelligently about her own field of interest?

And so why not use that as an icebreaker? Indeed, if the saying were true that "chance favored the prepared," then he had to admit that he liked his chances.

And he had his three-by-five with him, just in case he needed to refresh his memory. No, he felt that he didn't. He sauntered over to her and addressed her rather casually. "Hello again, Jennifer."

She smiled and tried to hide her nervousness. "Oh, hello, Agent Haraldsen; it's nice to see you here."

"Well, Ellen has made me feel at home quite often," he replied. "I almost feel as though I'm part of the family. And please, call me Conrad; I realize that the badge and gun and the whole presidential protection thing can be intimidating to some, but deep down we're all human beings – sensitive, feeling, caring, full of mystery in our own way – hard on the exterior, creative and perhaps artistic on the inside."

"You have an artistic bent, Conroy?"

"Conrad. Well, I've taken an amateur interest in art over the years; amateur, yes, but passionate all the same."

"Oh, really?"

"In fact, I've developed a particular interest in Japanese art," he said matter-of-factly. "Know anything about that subject?"

Jennifer felt a chill go down her back; her smile froze on her face.

The United States Secret Service was an extraordinary organization. Obviously, this agent had taken note of her assertion that she and He Nan Lin had met through a course taken at USC. Amazingly, he had gone to the trouble to find out the course she had "taken." And then he had researched the subject matter. It was astounding.

She was cornered; nevertheless, a challenge had been issued and it had to be answered. "I don't consider myself to be an expert in the field of Japanese art," she said quietly, giving no clue to him that he had rattled her to her core.

"Nor do I," said he. "But you know, I've developed a real affinity for the works of Keijo Surazawa. Are you familiar with his work?"

She paused; she was somewhat familiar with the artist. "Are you referring to the early period or the later works?"

He hesitated. There was nothing in Mrs. Walters' notes about any *early* or *late*. "Both..." he therefore replied with uncertainty. "Although I suppose I'm much more familiar with his later works."

"Well," she replied, "As you no doubt know, the prevailing view of the early period is that it's marked by the orthodoxy of the day."

"I quite agree," he replied, reciting his memorized opinions. "His landscapes in particular seem rather conventional. His later work, however, reflects an individualism which some consider to be presciently Western, suggesting the viewpoint of someone who was...who was in fact quite worldly."

Jennifer stood stock still, seemingly mesmerized by his erudition. Her silence encouraged him to keep going, and he did so, ad-libbing all the way. "My guess is that he traveled widely, possibly as a soldier or merchant; that would seem almost obvious. Don't you agree?"

She had a funny expression on her face. "That's strikes me as rather implausible," she replied, "particularly in view of the fact that Keijo Surazawa was a woman."

His jaw dropped. "He was? I mean..."

"She was indeed," Jennifer repeated. "In fact, she was crippled at age eighteen and took up painting as a way of overcoming her isolated existence. Surazawa never traveled fifty feet from the front door of her house. That's what makes her work so extraordinary and that's the main reason her work is studied to this day."

"I see," replied Haraldsen flatly, his tone of voice reflecting his complete and final disarmament. "Indeed. Well, we gain fresh perspectives every day, don't we?"

There was a strange silence between the two of them as they eyed one another. Haraldsen realized that the woman he was talking to was genuine in every respect – a person of true gravity and seriousness; indeed, a person not unlike himself in many respects. How silly it now seemed that he could ever have questioned her. Was it possible that fate itself had led him, through the mysteries of chance and irony, into the company of a woman who was in so many respects his very equal...?

...Jennifer, on the other hand, had come for the first time to understand what it meant to be tossed into shark-infested waters. If Agent Haraldsen were typical, then the people who were charged with protecting the VIPs of the United States government were the most amazingly disciplined people she had ever known.

As she sat in her room later that evening, she realized that the conversation with Haraldsen had rattled her harder than she would have thought possible.

What had she gotten herself into? The consul general had made it sound so simple – just go to parties, get to know people, listen and observe. Ji Wan Li was an incredibly naïve man, sitting up there in his tower in Los Angeles, thinking that it would all be so easy.

One misstep on her part – that was all it would take – and she would be finished. And the closer she got to the seat of power, the more the danger of her being discovered. And now, not only did she have to worry about the Secret Service's figuring out her game, but the Chinese were probably watching her as well.

It was almost too much to have to deal with – and yet she had no choice but to go forward. For if she wanted to be reunited with Jin Yi-bo, she would have to face all that the unfolding situation would demand of her, now and in the future.

## CHAPTER 22

Ellen noted that Gregory was very quiet all throughout breakfast. "What is it, honey?"

He didn't need to be asked twice. "I don't like Jennifer."

"Well, for goodness sakes, why not?"

"I think she likes Nick."

"Oh! Well, uh…How do you know that?"

He looked about the room, as though he were a spy on the lookout. "I saw them in the kitchen talking together last night," he confessed. "I could tell. She was very interested in everything he said, and she was laughing at his jokes; and his jokes weren't even funny."

This was *indeed* serious; Greg had never spoken ill of his hero in the past.

Ellen shrugged. "Well, there's nothing wrong with the two of them talking. They're both adults; if they happen to be attracted to one another, it's perfectly natural. Besides, I think they're just friends, that's all; now, is that all that's bothering you?"

The little guy was not finished pouring out his troubles. "I don't want Nick to marry Jennifer," he said quietly. "And I don't want *you* to marry Tom. I want you to marry *Nick*; and Jennifer can marry Tom if she wants to."

"You've got it all worked out, I see," said Ellen sympathetically. "Don't you like Tom?"

"He's all right, I guess."

"He treats you very nicely, and I think he likes you."

"Mom, do you like him just because he's rich?"

She was taken aback by that question. "No, not at all. Tom has many fine qualities. You'll see."

"He can't fly a fighter jet."

"Well, that's true, he can't," she admitted. "But regardless of how you feel about all of this, you can't be rude to Jennifer. Do you understand?"

He looked away.

"Greg-o-ry? Do you promise?"

"OK, Mom."

THE OLD MAN had called Nick and asked him to stop by the vice presidential residence after work. As soon as he arrived, they went into the library and closed the doors. "How are things coming along with Jack Neely?" asked the admiral.

"He's getting ready to request information on the avionics flight testing."

"I assumed that he would want to do that. However, I think you're going to run into a little problem. There's a high likelihood that the records you get will be heavily edited. Any problems with the avionics during the testing phase will have been looked over very thoroughly and possibly deleted before they give them out to you."

"That's navy policy?"

"Of course not. Navy policy is to give you every scrap of paper you ask for. What I'm describing is the real world, where some mid-grade officer gets the bright idea that making the navy look good is more important than your career, and so he goes through the records and gets rid of anything that's detrimental to the flight program in question. Remember, it's you against them now.

"However, there is a possibility you might want to look into.

Testing for the F-Eighteen was done at Naval Air Station Mayhew in South Carolina. Captain Rick Hewitt is commander of the base, and I know him very well. Officially, he can't lift a finger to help you...Unofficially, he'll do what he can. You want to take notes?"

Nick grabbed a pen and notepad and started copying.

"There is a building on the base – Building One Zero Two One Six – which contains extensive flight testing records. Your one chance is getting to those records first, before Lieutenant Commander Brightboy starts looking through them. It's restricted access; requires a top secret clearance, which there's no way you're going to get at this point.

"Now, here's what's going to happen: unofficially, two keys will be left under a painted rock five feet from the back door of said building."

"How are the keys getting there?"

"You don't need to know that. Officially, your lawyer can't know about this either; he'll have a conniption, because you're in enough hot water as it is.

"You'll be able to get in the back door. The window in Room Sixteen is blacked out but once you turn on the light you're going to need to go back outside and see that there is no light coming through the window. If there is, then you need to have some black paint with you so you can take care of it.

"You can take a scanner, video camera, whatever you need to record anything and everything that looks like it relates to your problem. You can't take anything out of there, of course. You can just look, that's all. Later on, when you officially request these documents you can compare and see that you got everything you requested.

"There is a guard that walks through the building every night. He checks every door, so by all means lock yourself in. You need to be out of there well before dawn, because early risers will be in the area by five or so. OK, that's it."

Nick finished writing, looked over his notes, and then shook his head. "I can't let you get involved like this."

"I've chosen to get involved."

"But if I get caught, your role may come out."

"That's my problem. If it comes out, I'll tell the truth and take the hit. I'll just say that during the course of my career I've known situations where records have mysteriously disappeared and I wanted you to have a fair shot.

"After thirty-six years in the navy, I have an awful lot of dirt on an awful lot of people; I've never used any of it to my own advantage, but I will if I have to. Don't worry, I'll be OK on this."

THE SALIVATOR was unconvinced. "Don't you think you should run this past your lawyer?"

"He's just going to tell me not to do it."

"Yeah, well...what happens if you get caught?"

"That's what I've got a lawyer for."

They drove all night to get to South Carolina. They spent the day in the little coastal town of Crumpton, South Carolina, and at just past five in the evening, when the rush hour traffic coming out of the base was the heaviest, they drove to the main gate and approached the guardhouse.

With the bright blue officer's sticker prominently displayed on the Salivator's bumper, they were waved onto Naval Air Station Mayhew by the marine sentry on duty, no questions asked. They drove to a desolate area of the base, near a firing range, got out of the car, and slept on the ground for several hours.

It was after eleven in the evening when they finally roused themselves, and they drove to Flightline Road, where dozens of aircraft maintenance and repair facilities were located. There was no place to park a civilian car in that area without its being noticed by a passing military police patrol, so they drove down a side road and hid the car on a dirt pathway which seemed to go nowhere.

They grabbed all of their gear and made their way back to Flightline Road. There they made their way along by walking in the shadows between the buildings and stopping every now and then to listen.

"That's the building," Nick said when they arrived at Building 10216. It was a long, one-story cinderblock building painted white, with a row of windows along the side and a door at the front and back. "Well, what do you think?"

"Just like the Old Man described. Let's go find the keys."

They hunted around in the vicinity of the back door, found the painted rock, lifted it, and retrieved the keys. By now it was close to midnight, when the last security check of the evening was normally made. They waited in the shadows for several minutes until they saw a jeep coming down Flightline Road. "And there he is now."

Every few yards the jeep would stop, and a naval military policeman would hop out and check the doors of each building, ensuring that all had been secured by any lingering late night workers. They made quick work of it.

"OK, let's go."

The key fit perfectly. The plan was for Nick to go in and take care of business, while DiSalvo would stay outside and act as a forward observer.

Nick used the flashlight to find Room Sixteen. The key did its work, and he locked himself in. He flipped on the light and then opened the window slightly so that he could talk to DiSalvo. "Do you see any light coming through?"

"Lots of tiny little scratches," said his partner as he opened his can of black paint and went to work, daubing and sweeping the brush. "It'll just take me a minute to take care of them all."

They had walkie-talkies with them, and Nick set his out on a table and turned the volume up. He then set up his video camera and started filming. He went at it methodically, along one row of bookshelves, and then down to the next, and then the next. It took no more than twenty minutes; he had the title of every book and set of records in the room.

The next step would take longer. He needed to find those volumes which pertained specifically to avionics and flight testing and to film their tables of contents, just so he would have a good idea of everything that these books contained. He worked methodically, but quickly, deciding in seconds whether a particular volume would have any value to him. When in doubt, he filmed.

At half past one, he heard the walkie-talkie squawk. "Nick! Incoming vehicle!"

Nick killed the light and DiSalvo dived behind a bush. The jeep passed by slowly and continued on down the road. DiSalvo watched it fade out of sight. "Coast is clear."

The final step was to go through each volume which looked particularly promising and to look for anything that might to relate to flight problems and discrepancies. He would sweep his hand-held scanner over any page that interested him, and he had a portable computer with him which allowed him to download continuously from the scanner.

He worked for over an hour before DiSalvo checked in. "How's it going?"

Silence.

"Nick? Are you there?"

"Yeah, I'm here."

"Well...anything?"

"Zilch," he said wearily. "I did find tons of info on the avionics. No relevant testing problems to speak of."

"Don't give up, Nick."

"I won't, but so far all the signs point to one spiffy little airplane and one naval pilot with extremely bad judgment."

At four a.m. DiSalvo came into the building and helped Nick pack up the gear. They made sure the room was in order, closed the door and locked it, went out the back door, replaced the key, and made their way back to the car.

## Chapter 23

Nick was fairly dejected about the state of the world – his world – and so he decided to cheer himself up. The following Sunday, he called Ellen, who was more than happy to let him take Greg and go kite flying for the afternoon. When he showed up in Georgetown an hour later, Jennifer seemed pleased to see him again, and so he spontaneously asked her to go along. She seemed pleased with that idea as well.

They found a site along the Potomac within sight of the Lincoln Memorial and within a few minutes they had a kite up and sailing high. Jennifer scored some points with Greg by explaining that kites had been invented thousands of years before in China, and that some had been built large enough to carry a man up in the air in order to observe the battlefield.

"You mean, like a spy?" Greg asked.

"Exactly," she replied, and immediately regretted bringing up the subject.

She noted that Nick seemed quiet, and was sure she knew why. "So what do you think you're going to do about your situation?" she asked gingerly as they walked along with the kite.

"I don't have any idea."

"Would you like my opinion?"

"Sure," he replied. "After all, you're the perfect disinterested party; you have no stake in all of this."

Jennifer could only smile; if only he knew what a huge stake she had in seeing him stay around town – preferably in and around official Washington – for as long as possible. She needed him to be his fun-loving, gregarious self – just long enough for her to meet the people she needed to meet. And so – could she give him objective advice? Never.

Could she give him good advice? Without a doubt. "I think it's never a good idea," she began thoughtfully, "to just – what's the expression? – cut and run. In fact, resigning may ultimately be the right decision for you, but it's far too early to say."

"What you say makes a lot of sense," he said. "It's always good to talk to someone who can stand a short distance away and look at things objectively."

With regard to Jennifer, he found himself coming to the same conclusion that Conrad Haraldsen had arrived at the other night: that she was a serious, sober person who weighed carefully what she had to say. He was starting to think that he liked her very much. "Listen, there's an event at the White House coming up on Saturday," he mentioned casually. "It's the reelection kickoff. If you'd like to get the inside view of things, you could go with me."

"To the White House?" she said with some excitement in her voice.

"Well, there'll be hundreds of people there," he explained. "It's not like a quiet, intimate evening with the First Family; but there should be plenty of business people there – big money campaign contributors. If you're looking for translation work, that should be the place."

"Well, yes, of course," she replied. "That would be perfect."

THAT EVENING, Jennifer was on the phone to Lily Zhang. Even though Jennifer was technically no longer on their side – appearances notwithstanding – she thought it prudent to ask for practical advice when it made sense to do so. And at this particular moment, it made a great deal of sense to do so. "I've been invited to the White House," she said calmly.

"This is very good news." Puff. Hack. "I congratulate you."

"It's for the reelection kickoff," she explained. "I'm going with Nick Ferguson and he says it will be a good opportunity to meet people."

"Indeed."

"But should I go?" Jennifer asked, desperate to understand the ramifications of such a public appearance. "I mean, there will be media all over the place. There's usually a certain amount of interest in anyone who is seen with Nick Ferguson, from what I understand."

"So what's the problem?"

"The problem," she explained carefully, "is – suppose my picture gets into the newspapers? Suppose someone tries to investigate my background? The Secret Service was suspicious about me once before; how do you think they'll feel when they find out Song Bei's niece is attending events at the White House?"

"Have you told anyone in the United States about this connection? Any of your American friends?"

"No. Never."

Drag. "And in China itself, how many know?" Puff.

"Outside my family, maybe two dozen friends."

"Submit a list to me of those individuals." Puff, puff, puff. "You will have nothing to worry about. No photograph of you will be allowed into China, and no one who knows of this will ever be contacted by foreign press. We will make sure that all of those details are firmly in hand."

ON SATURDAY, Nick put on his dress whites with all of his ribbons, and his two gold stripes on his shoulder boards. As he dressed, he had a strange feeling that this would be the final time he would wear his whites.

He had known about the newspaper column all day, but had been trying hard not to think about it. The column, which had appeared just that morning, was the nastiest piece of work he had read about himself since the Big Splash. Manfred Pelling of the New York *Mirror* had done quite a number on him.

Regarding his accident, most journalists were content to describe the known facts, speculate somewhat on possible outcomes, consider long and short term political ramifications for the president and the reelection effort and, in a few instances, speculate philosophically on whether the navy tended to encourage overly competitive behavior; to which argument other journalists pointed out that warfare, by and large, was the most competitive activity known to man, the stakes being so high.

Manfred Pelling had more or less come out and said that Nick was a world class liar, an immature egotist, that he was unfit to be an officer, a danger to his fellow servicemen, and a disgrace to Annapolis. Pelling claimed that it was only Mark Ferguson's pull with the navy which was keeping Nick from being summarily court-martialed, sentenced to hard labor, and thrown in the brig.

Rough stuff in anyone's book, Nick thought; but the kicker was that Manfred Pelling was tight as a tick with the president. Ed Billingsley didn't sneeze without Pelling knowing about it. It was said they talked two or three times a day, every day.

This was a set-up, orchestrated by Billingsley himself; he wanted Nick out of the navy, and he wanted him out with no further delay.

JENNIFER HAD thought it a good idea to spend the money Lily Zhang had given her during their meeting at the Jefferson Memorial. In fact, when she told Lily about the White House gala, Lily opened an account at Saks Fifth Avenue and told her protegee to spend whatever she wanted. She had high hopes for the evening, and wanted Jennifer to make the best possible impression on the largest number of people.

And so Jennifer had felt no compunction, guilt, or remorse about spending the funds of the People's Republic for a stunning silver evening dress, with matching shoes, purse, silver earrings and a diamond-studded necklace. If her objective were to draw attention to herself, she would spare no expense. A four hundred dollar bottle of perfume she found in Saks struck her as a quite justifiable expense.

The afternoon of the gala, she had her hair and nails done at the Four Seasons Hotel; someone she had once met at a Beverly Hills party had told her that movie stars visiting Washington often stayed at the Four Seasons, and they offered first class service for those seeking such amenities.

First class was what she wanted, and she was quite certain that the late great Chairman Mao would want no less for her.

When she was ready that evening, she came out into the living room and let the dazzling begin. "Oh, look, Gregory," Ellen exclaimed. "Doesn't Jennifer look beautiful?"

Greg wasn't admitting to *anything* but, if forced to, he would concede that he had never seen anything quite like her in his brief life.

"Now, what do you say to Jennifer?" Ellen said. "Do you remember what we talked about?"

He had promised that he would make his peace with Jennifer. "You look very nice, Jennifer."

She bent down, and gave him a little hug, suffusing him with perfume. "Oh, why thank you, Gregory," she said sweetly. "I only wish it were you going with me to the White House tonight."

This was too much for the lad. He fled to his mother, and hid behind her skirts. "Fighter pilots are not supposed to go on dates with girls," he said defiantly.

Ten minutes later Nick arrived. "Hey there, wingmate," he said as he walked through the door. Greg danced around him, ever careful of getting too near and wrinkling his uniform.

"Nick looks so handsome in his nice white uniform, doesn't he?" said Ellen. "Wait. Let me get a picture of the two of you," she said as she ran into the kitchen and returned a moment later with a camera.

Nick and Jennifer sidled up next to one another and posed. Nick started singing *Night of the Prom*. The flash went off. "There," said Ellen. "Now you can go."

"Now me and Nick," insisted Greg, pointing to the camera. His wish was quickly fulfilled. "Now you and Nick," he commanded his mother.

Ellen looked at Nick, and then at Jennifer, who happily reached for the camera. "Oh, what the heck," Ellen said. She stood next to Nick and had to admit that she still felt something from the old days. Still, time had moved on and so had she.

Nick and Jennifer said goodbye and walked down the steps to street level.

"Come on, Gregory," Ellen said. "Let's go watch them leave."

They rushed over to the veranda which opened out onto Q Street. They looked down and saw the waiting black governmental limousine, with men from the Secret Service stationed around it, forcing the dense, relentless Saturday night traffic to back up for several blocks.

They watched as Nick held the door for Jennifer. He looked up and saw them watching. He waved to them and they both waved back. "Good-bye," he called up.

Long after the limousine pulled off, they were still standing there waving.

THE MEDIA had been allowed to congregate in a designated zone tangent to the circular White House driveway which abutted Pennsylvania Avenue. Cars carrying guests stopped just past the cordoned-off media zone, and those arriving who wished to walk over and speak to the media could do so.

Nick chose to make no public statement, partly on the advice of his lawyer and partly due to Jennifer's request that they go straight in. Still, it was impossible to avoid being bombarded with questions as they made their way from the car to the front door.

"Nick! Over here!"

"What did you think of the article in the *Mirror*?"

"Are you going to resign your commission?"

"Are you being protected by the White House?"

"Why don't you just admit you got dizzy up there?"

"Don't pay any attention to them," Jennifer said quietly as they passed through the front door of the Nation's House and walked down the hallway. They were directed to the Green Room, where the family members of the candidates as well as top officials were gathering just prior to attending the main celebration in the East Room.

There were perhaps a dozen and a half people standing in the Green Room when Nick and Jennifer came in. No one noticed them, as all eyes were on a large man who was standing in the middle of the room. He towered over the man with whom he was apparently debating.

The vice president listened to the debate from a few feet away. Seated in a high-backed chair, and apparently enjoying the discussion, was the president of the United States.

"Well, Senator, I don't agree," said Uniqraft chairman Arnulf Kinder, the larger of the two debaters. "Every year you fellows have this huge battle over China, and you embarrass them over their human rights violations and then you finally rubberstamp their trade status and continue on your merry way. I say, what's the point of doing that year after year and causing all that heartburn between our two countries if the outcome is *entirely* predictable?"

"It sends an important message," replied Senator Lowe.

"Yes, yes, of course," said Kinder. "It's so easy to sit up there in your senatorial ivory tower and pontificate over issues that really don't affect your daily life; but guys like me, we're the ones who take the hits."

Kinder's audience was rapt; they knew exactly what was coming next.

"Do you think it was just a coincidence," he asked the senator, "that the Chinese took a multi-billion dollar passenger airplane order away from Uniqraft last year and gave it to Airbus – those damnable Belgians and French – and it all took place within a week of your big, superfluous senatorial debate?"

"Arnie," said Fred Lowe, "it's always easy to blame the politicians when the reality is that, by going with the Europeans, the

Chinese thought they were getting a better airplane at a better price."

"Senator, you really don't know what you're talking about," said Kinder with growing contempt. "Well, that's OK. You'll find out come election time that maybe your support isn't as strong as you think it is; some of you senators might take a hit or two yourselves."

At that moment, the president stood; immediately the debate came to a halt. All eyes turned to the direction that the chief executive was heading. The president approached and greeted the young officer. "Lieutenant Ferguson!"

"Why, good evening, Mister President."

"Good evening, Nick," he said, shaking hands. "And who is this lovely young lady you have with you tonight?"

"Mister President, I'd like to present to you Miss Jennifer Jiang. Jennifer, the president."

"How do you do, Jennifer," he said, taking her hand and enveloping it with both of his own. "It's certainly a pleasure to meet you."

"Thank you, sir." She lowered her eyes and found herself bowing forward ever so slightly. The reaction was instinctual; despite her years of Americanization, and despite the egalitarian socialist philosophy which had saturated her earlier education, the traditions of Old China still exerted a powerful pull on her psyche. Indeed, she was in the presence of a man so great that his power eclipsed that of any emperor or premier who had ever ruled her own country. And so she reacted the way that Chinese had reacted for millennia when in the presence of great authority: she felt deep humility.

The president seemed to be genuinely touched. "Miss Jiang, I must tell you honestly: I don't know what part of the country you're from, but I wish everyone I met were as reverential of the office of the presidency as you are. My goodness – you seem to be a bit overheated. Would someone get this young lady some punch?"

"I'm fine, Mister President," she said quietly, but the president insisted that she sit down in his own chair. "Really I am."

"Now, now, I'm not a deity or an emperor," he said as he took a glass of punch from a staffer and offered it to her. "Just a country boy from Alabama who did real well for himself. Here in America, we don't bow down before our betters." All eyes in the room were on her – and sympathetic eyes they were – as everyone laughed at the president's little joke.

She took a sip of the punch.

"Are you from the great state of California?" asked Billingsley. "Let me guess – San Francisco, from a very old and traditional Chinese family; am I right?"

"I'm from Beijing, actually, Mister President," she replied. "I've been studying here in the United States and I hope to find work as an interpreter."

She glanced up and her eyes met his dead on.

"Well, that's just wonderful, Miss Jiang," said he. "It's young people like you who do so much to promote good relations between our countries."

"I hope so, Mister President."

The president beamed. "Why, when I look at a young person such as yourself, it just fills me with hope."

Yeah, I know exactly what you're hoping for, Mister Prez, thought Nick to himself as he observed the scene. You're hoping to find a way to get Jennifer up to Camp David for a long weekend without the whole bloody world finding out about it.

Instinctively, Nick moved a half-step closer to her just to let his commander-in-chief know that Jennifer was – for the evening, at least – his date and that any encroachment thereupon would be regarded as a hostile act and would be met with rank insubordination.

The president read Nick's subtle come-about as clearly as it if had been signaled by a sixteen inch gun. He paid Nick his due. "I must say, I was sorry to see that column in the paper, Nick; I thought it was quite unfair in many respects."

"I totally agree, Mister President," said the lieutenant as he took a cup of punch being offered to him. Nick's flanking movement had created a conversational trio consisting of himself,

Jennifer, and the president, thus blocking off from conversation the others in the room. "Too bad Manfred Pelling forgot to run the column by you before he sent it to press."

The chief executive merely laughed. "Well, contrary to what people say, I don't discuss his work with him before it goes to publication, Nicholas. That's a silly thought; you should know better."

"What*ever* you say, sir." He took a sip of punch and the two men stared at one another hard. Nick could read undisguised fury in the eyes of his commander-in-chief, and the president saw the same in Nick's. "Good punch, sir."

"It is that, Nick. A strong punch, at that."

Nick escorted Jennifer away from the president's company, and then he was distracted for a moment by a member of the vice president's staff. Jennifer was left alone momentarily.

There was a distinguished looking man who seemed to be off in a corner by himself. His eye caught Jennifer's and he gave her a kindly smile. "Good evening, young lady. May I just say, you seem to be rather overwhelmed by it all."

She stepped over and spoke to him. "It *is* my first time here, sir."

"I see; and what brings you to Washington?"

"I was looking for work as an interpreter, and I just happened to meet Lieutenant Ferguson recently."

"Interpreter, eh? Are you a citizen or would you be a visitor to our country?"

"Visitor."

"Well, you understand that if you're not an American citizen then quite a bit of governmental translation work is going to be completely off limits to you," he explained. "Understandably, we just don't like the idea of foreign nationals having privileged access to our secrets."

"Of course."

"Still, if you're good, there are always opportunities to work for various agencies – as long as it doesn't involve national defense."

"Thank you, sir," she said with gratitude. "And may I ask what do you do, sir?"

"I'm the secretary of state."

Her hand covered her mouth. "Oh, I'm terribly sorry; I should have known."

"No, don't worry about it," he said with a laugh. "Half the American people wouldn't recognize me either; I'd hardly expect you to."

A few minutes later the official party moved to the much larger East Room, where they entered to the accompaniment of a long and sustained applause from top supporters, party officials, and White House staffers thronged about the room. The presidential party – including the elusive First Lady who had agreed to show up for a rare appearance – moved up a ramp *en masse* and ranged the length of a temporary stage.

The event was basically a pep rally in tuxedo and evening gown. Various members of the president's cabinet, the national party leadership, and members of the White House staff were introduced, allowed to say a word or two about what a great man Ed Billingsley was and how, if he were not reelected, the country would fail to thrive, crops would wither in the fields, our enemies would rejoice, the planets would deviate from their orbits, the ice age would return, and leisure suits would make a comeback.

When it was almost over, someone mentioned to the president that the vice president had not been introduced. The president handled that introduction himself. "And now it is my pleasure to welcome once again onto the team a great patriot, a distinguished American, a superb vice president, Mark Ferguson!"

When the vice president stepped forward, the loudest roar of the evening went up; the president naturally preferred to believe that it was the sight of both of them together that had so excited the crowd, and so he remained at center stage with Ferguson, basking in the communal glory.

"I was just telling your son that I don't review Manfred

Pelling's copy before his column gets published," said the president, forced to speak loudly in order to be heard as they waved at the crowd. "That's a myth and I don't know how it got started."

"Well, just once you might have, Mister President; it might have saved Nick quite a bit of aggravation."

"Now listen, Mark," Billingsley shouted over the continuing applause, "Despite what some people think, I do not have members of the press in my pocket."

By now the famous reserve had evaporated. "Who the hell do you think you're kidding, Ed?" the admiral snapped. "Do you think Washington doesn't know that all you have to do is pick up the phone and Manfred Pelling has the lead story of the day?"

"Why, Mark, I've never known you to be quite this vocal before." He waved at the crowd and beamed like a bride.

"Damn it, Ed," said Ferguson, "Why don't you just admit what you did? Why don't you just admit that you want Nick to plead no contest, admit fault and avoid a court-martial, or resign, or whatever it is you want him to do so it doesn't interfere with the campaign? You know that's exactly what you want. Why can't you just be man enough to admit it?"

"I don't know that I appreciate the tone of voice, Mark." Smile, wave. "It's very unbecoming a man of your great dignity." Smile, wave, feign delight.

"So is underhandedness, Mister President."

"Wave to the folks, Mark," said the president. "And smile; otherwise, people might start to get the impression you don't care too much for me."

## Chapter 24

Nick drove down to Norfolk to meet with his legal counsel. "I intend to resign my commission," he said just as soon as he sat down. The column in the *Mirror* had been the last straw.

"Excuse me?" said Neely. "I think we need to talk about this."

"Talking's over and done with," said the younger officer. "My mind's made up. Therefore I would like for you to approach the judge advocate and see if the charges can be dropped in exchange for my immediate resignation."

"Well, I assume that your resignation would be more than welcome in the halls of the Navy Yard," said Neely, "to say nothing of the White House, but let's not be so hasty about all this. I mean, I am your lawyer and as such I think we ought to look at the facts."

"Facts?" Nick laughed. "There are no facts – none that support me, that is. The only facts are medical facts, and they go entirely against me. As far as evidence that there were any problems with the avionics of this plane, there is none."

Neely raised an eyebrow. "How do you know that? We haven't even requested the flight records."

Nick wasn't sure if he should tell Jack about his road trip to South Carolina. "Can I tell you something off the record?"

"I'm not a journalist," replied Neely. "I don't go 'off the record.' However, anything you tell me is privileged. Have you done something you'd rather not have me know about, Nick?"

Nick paused and weighed his answer for a long while before he spoke. "I know for a fact that if you request the flight testing records you will find nothing of significance. Really, Jack, it's time to stop pretending."

"Nick, as your lawyer, I'll say it again: the best advice I can give you is to wait and see how this all plays out."

"Why? So you can get all this great publicity from a courtroom trial? So you can be on television every night making a statement to the press?"

For the first time in their brief association, Nick saw Jack Neely's lips purse in anger. "Don't question my motives, Lieutenant."

Nick had let his own anger get the best of him. "I'm sorry, Commander Neely; that was uncalled for."

"Look, Nick, I told you once before that I was a lawyer first. If you don't feel you can maintain your confidence in my judgment – which you obviously can't, since you won't take my advice – then get yourself another lawyer. OK?"

Nick sighed. "I think you're a fine lawyer, Jack. I just want out. I just want out, that's all."

TWO DAYS LATER, Nick was recalled to Norfolk.

Jack Neely had the paperwork spread out on a conference room table. "Here are the papers, expedited almost overnight – along with my advice for you to wait."

Nick approached the table. "Do you have a pen?"

It took all of five minutes. There were over two dozen signatures required. Four years at the naval academy and five minutes to resign. Nine months at flight school and five minutes to resign. Years aboard ships, wiped away in five minutes. Promotion, staff assignments, command, retirement. Five minutes – gone.

Five minutes to cut the lines and let his career drift away into the night, like a ghost ship without a captain – the good ship *What Might Have Been.*

Naturally, the Salivator was the only person that Nick wanted to share the rest of the afternoon with. They sat in a quiet, darkened bar off of Pacific Avenue in Virginia Beach and drank away the afternoon. "Damn, Nick," said his companion. "I can't believe it's done. How do you feel?"

"I'm all right, I guess. Hey, it's an honorable discharge; no shame in that."

The Salivator sighed. "Honorable discharge...I used to think that was nothing more than a Japanese medical term. Listen, Nick, Jeannine and I are going away for a long weekend; come with us."

"Nah, forget that, man."

"I mean it; it's no problem. Look, you can't be in D.C. when this thing hits. The damn reporters won't leave you alone; just get away with us for a good long weekend."

"I don't know..."

"You've been on a cruise for six months; you need a break. Hey, and you can bring Jennifer if you want."

"Well, now you're starting to talk some sense."

"See? I knew that would bring you around; think she'll go?"

"Who knows?"

"Well, she had a nice time at the White House, didn't she?"

"That was the *White House*, 'Vator. How could she not have a good time? Three days at the beach with a morose ex-pilot is a horse of a different color."

"All right, then, it's settled. You talk to Jennifer, I'll clear it with Jeannine. We sail at break of day."

"Well, I've got to run up to D.C. this evening and have a word with the Old Man."

THE VICE PRESIDENT received the news of Nick's resignation ex post facto, and in person. "You did *what?*"

"I did what was necessary."

"You threw your whole damn career away, that's what you did."

"I believe I did that the night I went up in my plane."

"Look, Nick, you had a fighting chance; *still* have," he said, reaching for the phone. "I'm reversing those papers."

"No, don't do that. Quite frankly, I don't need the hassle. And neither do you; all it's going to do is give your reelection opponents a lot of ammunition."

"To hell with them – the whole damn lot of them," said the vice president. "Look, I'm the one who should be resigning. Do you know how much I loathe sitting around this museum?"

"I appreciate that, but let's look at the long-term," said Nick, going through his paces. "Suppose I get cleared in the court-martial. That would be a miracle in itself and even if I can clear myself fair and square, people are always going to say that it was because of my connections. Don't you think I'm going to carry this around with me for the rest of my career? The publicity...everywhere I go in the navy..."

He shook his head. "Nope, sorry. No can do; without proof of a problem in the avionics, the best I can hope for is a severely curtailed career path."

Nick was right, but it was very hard for the admiral to admit it to himself. "What are you going to do now?"

"Go to the beach, I guess."

"I meant with the rest of your life; you're only twenty-seven..."

"You know, I haven't thought about it," he said quietly. "I never thought I would do anything else."

## CHAPTER 25

He had a hard time getting her off of his mind. The awe, the sense of wonder in her eyes when she was introduced into his presence, the trembling respect bordering on fear and yet, beneath it all, her gentle, elegant beauty – all combined to leave an indelible impression of loveliness in the mind of the president of the United States.

He wanted desperately to get to know Jennifer Jiang.

Ed Billingsley picked up his phone and asked Bill Robinson, the head of his Secret Service detail, to come to the Oval Office.

"Yes, sir. How can I help you, Mister President?"

"Bill, there was a young lady who attended the reelection kickoff on Saturday," he began. "A young lady by the name of Jennifer Jiang."

"Yes, sir. I recall that she was escorted here by Nick Ferguson."

"I believe that's the one I mean. Listen, I understand that she's a superb interpreter and, as you know, we have the Special Trade Conference with the delegation from Guangdong Province coming up soon. There's going to be an advance delegation which will be in Baltimore this weekend to discuss cultural exchanges, that type of thing. As you already know, I'll be going up there to give the keynote address on Saturday night.

"Now, as far as Miss Jiang's qualifications – I did speak to the young lady very briefly – she's quite polished and well-spoken and I think she would mix very well with that group. However…I understand that she's a Chinese national – which could be a problem."

"A very big problem – for you, sir." They both knew exactly what the chief executive had on his mind.

Robinson sighed. He would do everything he could to discourage this type of activity – not because he cared so much about the political fate of whoever held the highest office in the land; rather it was that, whether a presidential affair turned out well or badly, there was never an upside to it as far as the agency was concerned.

"Sir," Robinson began, "I'm going to give you the same advice I've always given you in these situations: patch up your relations with your wife, stop chasing skirt, concentrate on your job and keep your mind on your reelection."

Yes, folks, it was time once again to read the riot act to the president of the United States. The chief executive sat quietly and accepted the catechism.

"However, if you do choose to ignore my advice and are going to dally in the valley, I highly recommend you take up with some nice little Indiana farm girl, someone of whom the public might better approve if they happen to find out that you are not Family Man of the Year material. As for this Chinese girl, my official recommendation is that you stay the hell away from her, or any other foreign national for that matter."

The president nodded and checked his watch. "Sage counsel indeed; please continue."

"Never talk shop," Robinson admonished him further. "Furthermore, you may not introduce a foreign national into any kind of situation where United States policy is to be discussed and, if matters of national security, foreign policy, military, economic or trade issues are discussed in the presence of such a person, it is entirely possible that you will be in violation of federal statutes for which you may be impeached, tried, convicted and removed from office. Are we clear, sir?"

"Quite; an excellent recitation, Bill; as always." He stood and walked into the small kitchenette just off of the Oval Office. As he poured shots of whiskey for himself and Robinson, he continued to talk. "But, of course, you do know that your man Haraldsen gave her a clean bill of health; said that all of her references checked out fine. She was never a member of any political organization when she lived in Los Angeles. She appears to have had no real interests other than her studies." He walked back into the Oval Office and handed Robinson his drink. "And he *is* the best you've got, isn't he?"

"If he were the best we had, he'd be protecting you."

"So you don't give her a clean bill of health?"

"I don't give anyone a clean bill of health."

"That's pretty hardcore, Bill."

"Sir, as I always tell the new fellows, you don't have to be paranoid to be a good Secret Service agent, but it definitely helps."

The president sat down at his desk and held up his glass. "Bill Robinson, you are a wise and a sagacious counselor. Cheers!" He downed his drink and hammered his glass down on the desk. "So then! Now that we've got that little ritual out of the way, why don't you contact the young lady and see if she might be available to attend the Baltimore conference this weekend?"

Later, sitting in his office, Robinson weighed the pros and cons of this latest flirtation with disaster. On the credit side of the risk ledger, the president was certainly willing to go to great lengths to disguise his relationships with his women. He was actually quite good about that, and most cooperative with the agency. Experience had shown that, as long as the president were willing to stay within certain bounds, his various rendezvous could remain well below the relentless sweep of the national media radar.

And yet, speaking now on the debit side of the risk ledger, the president often failed to make a proper distinction between the lovely daughters of allies and those of hostile countries. His famously cautious nature had one blind spot: as a southerner, he believed no woman to be naturally capable of deception and manipulation.

The agency had had to intervene more than once to steer him away from unacceptable risks: the Iraqi graduate student studying at Georgetown who liked to jog down Pennsylvania Avenue; the Russian ballerina to whom he had been introduced backstage at the Kennedy Center; the Cuban concert pianist performing at the White House who had asked to see the Lincoln Bedroom and whom the president had been happy to oblige at three o'clock in the morning. And now – this lovely young thing, fresh from the People's Republic of China...

The relationship between China and the United States was hardly on a par with the hostile status existing between, for example, the United States and Iraq, but it was bad enough. The Sino-American detente had been fraught with tensions and hostilities for decades.

Clearly, both sides had something to gain from one another, and a peaceable relationship was in both of their best interests. Still, there were enough points of conflict between the two nations that the revelation of an affair between the president of the United States and a Chinese national would cause an unholy uproar. Forget reelection; just hope to get out of Washington without having to wear a disguise and take the Greyhound bus.

A short while later, Tony Phillips popped in to see the president. "Sir, it seems as though a young naval aviator by the name of Ferguson has just turned in his resignation."

"Really? Well, this is good news. That's one headache I won't have to worry about any longer. Me, oh, my! I can't imagine what could have caused this to happen so suddenly."

"I guess the lad just woke up, took a hard look at reality, and decided to throw in the towel, sir."

"Poor boy's going to lose his naval commission, his wings, and his little girlfriend all in one fell swoop. Well, this just isn't going to be his week, now is it?"

ELLEN AND GREG had gone out, and so Jennifer was alone when the knock came at the apartment door. She was almost finished packing for her trip to the beach with Nick and the DiSalvos. Nick had called earlier in the day and, as she had nothing planned for the weekend, she had accepted.

The knock was louder this time. She opened the door and saw two men in suits standing in front of her. "Jennifer Jiang?" said the older of the two.

"Yes? How can I help you?"

"Secret Service," said he, displaying a badge. "Agent Buel. May we come in?"

"Of course."

They stepped into the living area and Jennifer offered them seats, which they declined.

"Miss Jiang, we understand that you are a native of Beijing," said Buel. "And that you have been studying in the United States for the past four years. You arrived here recently from Los Angeles? Is that correct?"

"That's correct."

"And that you have stated your intention of working in this country as an interpreter?"

"Also correct; is there a problem?"

"No problem, ma'am. We're from the White House," said the second agent. "The president has requested that your name be added to the list of interpreters available to work at the Guangdong Province Advance Conference slated for this weekend in Baltimore. Would you be available to help out?"

"Why, yes, of course," she replied eagerly. "No problem whatsoever. Please tell the president that I would be happy to do so."

"Of course," added Buel, "we realize this is very short notice; if you can't make it the president will understand."

But there was no hesitation on Jennifer's part. She had not come to Washington to frolic with navy pilots on the beach. Granted, Taiwan would not be particularly interested in any information she might learn with regard to cultural matters; but this was a good opportunity to meet American officials and make contacts.

"I did have other plans for the weekend," she explained, "but I'll be happy to cancel them."

"Very well," said Buel. "We've been asked to escort you. The president didn't think you would be able to find the conference on your own. Do you need some time to get ready?"

"I'm practically ready now," she stated, knowing that she could repack in minutes. "I just need to leave a message for someone."

NICK ARRIVED at the DiSalvo homestead by mid-morning on Saturday. The DiSalvos lived in standard-issue junior officer quarters at the Norfolk Naval Base. Nick had traveled in his own car, with two agents following.

"Where's Jennifer?" asked Jeannine as soon as she saw Nick.

"Something came up," he said. "She got a translating job of some type; had to rush off."

"Well, daggone," said the Salivator, as Nick came into the house. "Must have been a good one to bail out like that. Tough luck, man. How did you find out?"

"She left a message for me at the BOQ." As a way of drawing attention away from the Old Man, Nick had chosen to live at the navy bachelor officer's quarters in Washington rather than at the vice presidential residence.

"So why didn't you bring Ellen and Greg?" asked Jeannine as she packed sandwiches for the trip.

"They're in Connecticut, visiting Tom."

"Sounds like it's getting pretty serious between those two," said Jeannine.

"Good," said Nick coolly. "Hope it works out. Look, guys, this is awfully nice of you to take me with you on your vacation, particularly since you two have been apart for six months. Jeannine, are you really OK with this?"

"I'm more than happy to have you along, Nick," she replied. "But if you want to know the truth, I think you're both nuts. I mean, haven't you seen enough of each other recently?"

"Nick's going through a pretty rough time, honey," said her husband. "Remember? We talked about that."

"Well, I understand all of that, Russell," she said. "But why the *beach*? The first thing you do when you get back from a six-month ocean cruise is you want to rent a house at Myrtle Beach with a view of the ocean? Not that *I* mind; believe me, I never get out of the house, but haven't you two seen enough of all that water?"

"We like the ocean," said her husband.

"The ocean is a special place," added Nick.

"Yes, well, the ocean is very nice," she admitted. "But what about the mountains? Wouldn't a nice cabin in the mountains have been nice?"

"I never thought of that; you, Nick?"

"Nope; mountains never crossed my mind."

"Don't either one of you have any sort of imagination?"

"Au contraire, ma cherie," replied her husband. "We have quite vivid imaginations."

"That's why we like the beach, Jeannine," Nick explained quietly, putting at last an end to Jeannine's puzzlement. "The girls get to wear their bikinis and we get to use our imaginations. It works out quite well."

"You're planning to go into the water, aren't you, babe?" asked the Salivator soon after they got under way.

"They make bathing suits for people in your…uh…condition?" Nick asked as diplomatically as he was able.

"Yes, Nick," she replied. "They *do*; they're called bikinis; but don't worry, fellows. I won't embarrass you; I'll go out after dark. You two just keep any comments about beached whales to a minimum and I'm sure we'll all get along just fine."

## 26

At the end of their first day at the beach, Jeannine advised Nick that he had received a call from Washington. He called the number she gave him.

"Lieutenant Ferguson?" said the voice at the other end of the line. "This is Chief Petty Officer Higgins at the BOQ here in Washington. We received a call at the desk from a young woman who says she needs to get in touch with you."

"Probably just a reporter," he said.

"No, sir. I don't think so. I asked her and she specifically said this was nothing like that. She said you'd be very glad she called."

"What's her name?"

"Sir, all she'd say is that it was urgent that she get in touch with you as soon as possible."

"Well, you can give her this number and she can call me here; one phone call can't hurt anything."

At eleven o'clock that evening the phone rang. Jeannine had already gone to bed and the Salivator was dozing away on the screened porch on the ocean side of the house. Nick grabbed the phone on the first ring and heard a soft-spoken female voice. "Lieutenant Ferguson?"

"Yes. Who is this?"

"I'd rather not give my name over the phone."

"Well, what is it you want?"

"I have some information on what might have happened to your plane."

"OK. Keep talking."

"Sorry; not over the phone."

"OK. How, then? You tell me."

"When will you be back in the D.C. area, Lieutenant?"

"What time is it now?" He checked his watch. "I could be there in eight hours."

"I don't think there's any need to rush, sir. I can wait."

"You don't understand," he replied. "Something like this, I need to know. Now tell me how we do this, and I'll be more than happy to meet you wherever you like."

"Meet me on the running path – the one that runs along the south side of the Potomac. Let's say one hundred yards north of the Alexandria city limits. Tomorrow at dusk."

"How will I know what you look like?"

"You won't, but I know what you look like. Sir, you need to come alone; I'm not looking for complications."

Nick was outside watching the black ocean waves break against the beach when the Salivator woke up and saw him standing there. "Hey, man, what's up? Did I hear the phone ring?"

"Yeah. Strange call; some chick wants to talk to me about my little aerial mishap. Says she knows something about it. I'll be leaving for D.C. first thing in the morning."

"Gee, your bodyguards aren't going to like that. They're having a real good time down here."

"They can stay here all they like, as far as I'm concerned. I'm going to have to lose them tomorrow anyway; whoever this girl is wants me to come alone."

Not long thereafter one of Nick's agents strolled up, flashlight in hand. "Good evening, gentlemen. Everything all right?"

"Everything's fine, Mike," said Nick. "Just couldn't sleep, that's all. How about yourself?"

"I'm on duty."

"Of course. Listen, Mike, I'm going to be heading back to D.C. in the a.m.; and I hereby exercise my right to waive my protection, so you guys can just stay here and enjoy the sun a little longer."

Eighteen hours later, Nick made his way along the pathway that ran beside the Potomac River. He was in his athletic clothes, and he wandered lazily along the riverbank. It had been a beautiful day, and so there were hundreds of people ranged up and down the river, doing the same.

He wore dark glasses, and had an old porkpie hat pulled down over his brow. His objective was to make himself conspicuous to the one person who happened to be looking for him, but unnoticed by everyone else.

At five minutes past five, he felt the presence of another walking along beside him. "Why don't we start jogging, Lieutenant?"

"I'm not a lieutenant anymore," he reminded his unknown companion. "I resigned."

"Premature decision," came the unsolicited opinion.

"That's easy for you to say," he said with a slightly irritated tone. "Why didn't you call me a week ago?" He glanced at her out of the corner of his eye. "And don't I recognize you? Don't you happen to be a sailor?"

"Yes, sir, that's right; stationed aboard the Jackson," she said. "Communications Specialist First Class Emma Walden; except this little jogging session never took place."

"Whatever you say, Communications Specialist First Class Emma Walden. So then, you say you know something about the night my plane fell out of the sky?"

"That's not what I'm here to talk to you about, sir."

"I'm confused already."

"Yes, well, I am here about your plane, but not the night you're thinking about," she explained. "It was something that happened about two weeks before that. I'd say late February – early March – somewhere right in there."

"I need the date; I need the exact date."

"Offhand, I can't remember the date," she stated. "I'd have to think about that."

"All right for now; just start at the beginning."

"Well, my cabinmate came in late that night – Rhonda Clement – and she was all giggly and laughing and happy."

"She came in late? And where had Miss Rhonda been?"

"With Corporal Benning."

"I know that name; he's one of the marine guards, isn't he?"

"That's correct, sir. He sometimes guards the Super Hornet squadron."

"And I'm guessing you're telling me that they were shipboard lovers; so what happened on the night in question?"

"Well, Corporal Benning was supposed to be on duty that evening but had been relieved temporarily and unexpectedly."

"Relieved by whom?"

"By one of the civilian techs."

"One of the Uniqraft techs?"

"One of the Super Hornet techs, to be precise."

"Which one?"

"I'm not exactly sure. Whoever it was, he told Grant to take twenty minutes – half hour, whatever – and spend some quality time with Rhonda – in the Uniqraft trailer."

All of the major defense contractors placed maintenance trailers in the vast hangar decks of the carriers. They were hoisted aboard the ship just prior to sailing; officially, they were used for storing engineering drawings and communications equipment. Unofficially, they usually housed impressive stashes of liquor and other contraband not considered regulation-issue.

"Very unusual, I would say," said Nick, "for a civilian tech to relieve a marine guard who's supposed to be standing guard."

"Yes, sir. Very unusual. Definitely non-reg."

"And so you think that this was done so that someone could tamper with my plane? Is that it?"

"I'm saying there was a window of opportunity," she stated. "For some reason your plane was vulnerable that evening; if one of the techs wanted to do something to your ride then he was certainly in a position to do so."

"All of that is very interesting," mused Nick. "Except that I didn't have any problem flying any other night of the operation."

"I can't explain the delay between the one night and the other, sir."

"Fair enough. Well, where can I find Corporal Benning?"

"Corporal Benning was end-of-tour at that time. Most likely he's out of the corps by now. My guess would be that Rhonda would know where he is."

"Then how do I get in touch with Rhonda?"

"Enlisted female quarters in Norfolk, sir. Building Two Seventy-six. Have a nice evening, sir." And then Emma Walden turned and ran the other way.

# CHAPTER 27

Lou Jian Ren heard from his Shanghainese contact with surprising speed. The message was clear: Jin Yi-bo was to be transferred from Harbin Prison to Shi Men Prison near the coast at the earliest possible moment.

The process of interprison transfers would be surprisingly easy. There were many perfectly acceptable reasons for transfer: to relieve overcrowding, to provide for work details, to distance prisoners from local contacts, to break up long term friendships and thus to prevent collusion. A certain percentage of transfers was done simply to keep prisoners off guard, to keep them guessing. There didn't have to be a reason.

The assumption at all times was that there was somebody, somewhere who thought it would be a good idea to send one hundred men to Guilin Province, or fifty to Shandong. The People's Republic was one of the most bureaucratic countries on earth. If the papers were in order, no one would question it.

## 28

Jennifer had arrived in Baltimore on Friday evening at the Guangdong Province Advance Conference for Cultural Exchange. Immediately she plunged into the work, meeting people from the American and Chinese arts communities.

She recognized nobody that she had ever met in Nanjing museum circles; but that was hardly surprising: the population of China was so vast that someone living and working in Guangdong Province might as well have been living on another continent.

She found the whirl of the conference thrilling. As an interpreter, she was constantly being pulled from place to place and her services were in constant demand.

Saturday was an even bigger day than Friday, with more meetings between American and Chinese officials. The president's arrival caused the customary stir, and Jennifer was assigned to interpret the speech that he would be giving at the conference banquet that evening.

The only jarring moment of the entire day was a dispute that developed mid-afternoon on Saturday. The topic was something she knew a little about: the Qing Dynasty vases which had been removed from China by Japanese soldiers during World War

Two and had been returned forty years later.

The Americans wanted to exhibit the vases in Washington; however, one of the members of the exhibition committee was Professor Leonard Kazmiersky of the University of Chicago. Kazmiersky had once declared that the Qing vases were of questionable authenticity. His words had caused an uproar years before in Chinese art circles, but he had never retracted his opinion. With his presence at the conference, the Chinese were now threatening to cancel the exhibit altogether.

Somehow, Jennifer knew what to do. In a quiet voice, she introduced herself, mentioned her own familiarity with the issue and suggested that the vases be submitted for evaluation using certain techniques that were being developed by a UCLA professor whom she knew. If the results could show that Kazmiersky were wrong, then he would retract his long-held view and the exhibit would proceed.

It was quite an unexpected move on the part of a mere interpreter, but when both parties realized that it was not only a good idea, but that she had found a fair way to end the impasse, all participants in the dispute broke out into applause for her actions.

She was instantly dubbed "The Peacemaker," and for the duration of the conference she became something of a minor celebrity.

She was assigned to work at the head table for the banquet that evening, and was seated between the president and the chief of the People's Delegation. She caught the president's glance on more than one occasion, but did her best to maintain the appropriate professional distance.

She did, however, feel a certain pride in seeing this most powerful man stand before her countrymen and speak knowledgeably about their concerns. He obviously had very good speechwriters working for him; still, she had the vague feeling that he could not have cared less about the topic on which he was speaking so eloquently.

The president chose to delay his departure back to Washington, and ended up staying in Baltimore for the evening.

It was very late when Jennifer finally returned to her room. She had been on the go for seventeen hours, focusing intently, talking much of that time, and she was exhausted. She decided to run a bath, and so she was wearing little more than a robe when there came a knock on the door. Standing before her were two gentlemen from the Secret Service.

"The boss would like to see you," said one.

"This late? Do you have any idea what time it is?"

"The president often works late into the night, ma'am."

"And he needs an interpreter at this hour?"

"We generally don't stand around and question the big guy, ma'am," the agent said drily.

Jennifer sighed. "Very well. Give me a few minutes and I'll get dressed."

"There's no time; the president needs to see you immediately."

She thought about it and, against her better judgment, left her room in the company of the agents, arriving at the president's room within a half-minute. "Good evening, sir," she said, standing in his doorway.

"Ah, Jennifer! Please come in," he said cheerfully, standing there in his trousers and a bathrobe. "I was just getting ready to retire for the evening. I hope you don't mind the informality. Come in, come in."

Jennifer took a step into the room and took a look around. The Secret Service seemed to have magically disappeared. "I thought there had been an emergency of some kind," she said quietly.

"No, no emergency. I just wanted to thank you for your great work today. I understand that you were quite a hit with everybody. And I was told about your handling of the situation with the vases –" He beamed. "Well, what can I say? I have a feeling you could teach the folks over at State Department a thing or two."

"Thank you, Mister President."

"Now then; I want you to consider yourself on call to the

White House," he announced grandly. "We could use someone like you – someone who can mix and move around easily – we need people who are a little less, shall we say, stodgy in certain social situations. We give the occasional state dinner, as you know; receptions, tours, luncheons, that sort of thing…"

"You're offering me a job?"

"Even better," he said with a wink. "I'm offering you a *role*. Oh, yes, of course – continue with your interpreting work, by all means. You're quite good; but I could see your doing much more than that." Quite a bit more, he thought to himself.

"Thank you, sir. Well, was there something you wanted, Mister President?"

That was the wrong question for her to ask. He approached her, placed his hand around the back of her neck, and pulled her gently towards him.

"Mister President!" she exclaimed, pulling away.

"Is there something wrong?"

She backed all the way to the door. "Sir, you're a married man!"

"Oh." He shrugged off that particular objection and sat down on a sofa. "Nothing to worry about there; my marriage has been over for a decade."

"Well, yes, but…"

"The Secret Service? No, don't worry about them. They'll never tell a soul; discretion is a big part of their job – "

"To make up for your lack of it?"

He laughed. "Well, yes; I suppose." He got back up. "I'm sorry. Where are my manners? What would you like to drink?"

She reached for the door handle. "I really must be going, sir, if you don't have any business to discuss."

He touched her lightly on the shoulder and edged her back into the room. "As one of my predecessors often said, 'Come, my friend. Let us reason together.'"

She faced him squarely and stood her ground. "Mister President, I should tell you that I happen to be in love with someone else."

That hardly slowed him down. "Well, it's not serious, is it?

Some young congressional aide you just met, or perhaps a reporter – something like that."

"No one you just described; but yes, I would say it's quite serious."

"I see." He seemed deep in thought. Wordlessly, he turned his back on her and strolled out onto the balcony, where he leaned on the railing and took in the stunning view of Baltimore Harbor.

She stood there, wondering whether he expected her to leave of her own accord.

She knew she had lost her cool in his presence. He had caught her off guard; she hadn't expected him to act so aggressively. Maybe he thought that because of who he was this sort of thing were simply to be taken for granted.

Despite the unlikelihood of someone of her background ending up in a hotel room with a man of his stature, she nevertheless faced a dilemma which was timeless and universal: she wanted to keep him interested enough in her for him to maintain a relationship with her, but she was afraid that if she gave in to his demands he would quickly lose interest. She had to figure out where the fine line was, and try to walk it as carefully as possible; this assumed that she hadn't already been dismissed out of hand.

After a minute, he turned and saw her standing there. He motioned for her to come out on the balcony with him, and she found herself doing as he asked. They stood side by side in the darkness; for security reasons, the balcony remained unlit. From their vantage point they could see armed Secret Service agents standing in nearby balconies of the hotel, watching them, as well as keeping an eye on the general area.

"Tell me, Jennifer," he said soberly. "How familiar are you with English history?"

"English...? Why, I know very little about it, I suppose."

"May I share with you a little of my own reading?" He didn't wait for an answer. "One of the things I find so interesting about studying other cultures," he began, speaking in his deep, mannered Alabama drawl, "is that we can learn so much from the way other people have lived their lives. Now you take, for example, the English. Throughout much of their long history, it was considered a great honor to have the sovereign take an interest in one of his subjects – one of his young, beautiful subjects."

She quickly saw where this line of thought was heading.

"Why, even a married couple did not view such an opportunity with opprobrium. In fact, many ambitious husbands welcomed the prospect of being cuckolded by the head of state.

"Why? Because the king had unlimited power and wealth, and he was in a position to reward handsomely the husband of a woman whose charms he particularly admired. Everybody benefited from this system – the king, the beautiful subject, and her practical husband.

"Indeed, the very word 'nobility' could be translated roughly as 'those who are our own.' And so – you see? – the sovereign viewed the wives of the uppermost classes almost as his far-flung national harem – his own! And – as with so many English traditions which may, with the passage of time, seem quaint and peculiar to us – it was in fact a very well thought out system." He took a sip of his drink and muttered under his breath. "God, how I miss the British Empire!"

"And is this the American system as well?"

"Well, that depends on the sovereign," he replied. "And, of course...on the subject."

She decided to deflect his suggestive response. "Mister President," she said quietly, "I can assure you that my country does not hold very fond memories of the British Empire. And – if I'm not mistaken – didn't one of your own predecessors fight a war to rid America of the British?"

He laughed. "Yes – Washington; what a schoolmarm he was. No sense of humor and bad teeth besides; the man could never get elected today." He turned and faced her. "Now then, who is the lucky man who has momentarily captured your attention? Perhaps there is something I could do for him to advance his career – put him in touch with someone who might prove to be of invaluable assistance to him."

She thought of Jin Yi-bo, a world away. "I don't believe there is anything you could possibly do for him at this time, Mister President," she said quietly. "He's beyond the reach of someone even as powerful as you are."

"Oh, I doubt that," he said with a laugh. "Tell you what: why don't you try me? I don't care what his situation is or what it is he wants to accomplish with his life. Whatever it is, I can help him. I have resources at my command that you just wouldn't believe."

Fine, she imagined herself saying. If you would be so kind as to drop an airborne division into Northern China, with the Seventh Fleet standing by on the coast, that would probably do the trick. "I'll think about it, Mister President; and now, if you don't mind, I think I'd like to return to my room."

"Are you sure I can't persuade you to stay here tonight? The view is so much nicer."

She had by now decided how she was going to respond to him. "Mister President, I don't do things like that. I don't just – what is the American expression? – 'hop in the sack' – with someone right off the bat – no matter how attractive I find him to be. It's not the way I was brought up. Where I come from, it's just not done."

He looked at her quizzically. "Where *you* come from? Well, you must be the rare exception; with one point two billion people in China, somebody over there is doing some serious hopping, I'd say."

She was still, and chose not to respond.

"I'm sorry," he said. "That was rather crude of me."

"I like to receive flowers," she offered.

"Flowers?"

"And walks together; perhaps a quiet dinner."

He laughed. "Oh, of course. Walks! As if I had time for walks..."

"And conversation...I do enjoy good conversation as well."

"Conversation? Conversation about what?"

"Why, conversation about anything...art, for example."

"I don't know anything about art."

"Well, it doesn't have to be about art; there are so many things we could talk about. Don't you have ever conversations with females just for the sake of it?"

He rubbed his chin. "Well, what would be the point of that? What I mean is…I suppose that is a weakness of mine…to a certain extent."

"There, then; you see? The change might do you good."

"You may not believe this," he said with just a touch of rebellion in his voice. "But people don't generally presume to put these kinds of demands on me."

She shrugged. "Fine; choose whom you like. Well, I've had a long day, so if you'll excuse me…"

"Oh! Well, let me get the door for you," he said, following her like an eager puppy as she left the balcony and crossed the room. "I suppose you do like to have doors opened for you – that sort of thing?" he said.

"I adore it, Mister President. Thank you so much, and goodnight."

He stood in his doorway and watched her walk down the hallway to her room.

THE PRESIDENTIAL motorcade was traveling back to Washington from Baltimore on Sunday morning. There were just the two of them in the president's car – Bill Robinson, leader of the presidential security detail, and the great man himself.

Of the two passengers, one was happy, and the other was not.

"And then it hit me," said the president. "She's fallen for that damned pilot, Nick Ferguson. Ex-pilot, I should say; he's not even a pilot anymore. He's a nobody."

"He is a rather handsome young man, sir," said Robinson. "Like his father. If I may say so, I could understand the attraction."

Billingsley looked at him as though he had just committed treason. "I'm the president of the United States, by Jenkins!" He returned to his brooding. "Now if I had met her twenty years ago..."

"You would have been dating a one year old..."

"Oh, you know what I mean: if she were twenty-one and I were twenty years younger." Robinson gave him a quizzical look. "All right – thirty-five years younger."

The president continued to ponder the situation. "In a way, I wish he hadn't resigned. That way I could just have the boy transferred to Timbuktu and be done with him."

"We don't have a naval base in Timbuktu."

"I'd put one there – just for him."

"But how can you be sure it's Ferguson? They've only known each other a short time."

"Listen, I offered to help the young man – the way anyone in my position would do, naturally. But she said – and I quote – that he was beyond the reach of even me. Now who else could that be but young Nicholas?"

"I see; so I guess you can write that one off."

"I don't know..." mused the chief executive. "She left a door open for something to happen."

"What do you mean?"

"Well, she dropped a few hints as to how she likes to be treated. I took it to mean that she was open to the possibility of something down the road."

"Wait a minute now. You're telling me that she's leading you on and setting conditions for some sort of relationship with you. What's going on here?"

"I didn't say she was setting conditions," said the president with some irritation. "People don't set conditions for someone in my position. She was just stating what it was she happens to need in order for something...a relationship...whatever...to have some possibility of success."

"Oh, I see. And what is it that she needs, Ed? Being involved with the president of the United States isn't enough for her? She has *needs* on top of that? Well, I'm sure you told her to her to take a hike."

The president was silent on that point.

"I said…I'm *sure* you told her to take a hike…"

"She does enjoy leisurely walks, yes; besides, the exercise could do me good."

"Oh, my god…you're serious; and what else does she like, Ed? Candlelit dinners?"

"There's nothing wrong with candlelit dinners; or even discussions about art."

"*Art?* Well, there's a subject you're an authority on."

"I know something about art. I happen to like that Norman Rockefeller fellow; I own an original print of one of his paintings."

"You mean Norman Rockwell? Oh, well, you are an expert then, aren't you? Do pardon me."

"And there's absolutely nothing wrong with giving a woman flowers."

"Flowers, is it now? You haven't sent flowers to a woman in twenty years."

"Well, maybe it's time I did."

"I've got to be honest with you, Ed: the girl has got you whipped."

"I don't need to listen to this from you."

Robinson made little whipping motions with his arm and wrist. "Whip. Whip."

The president was not amused. "You know, you can be replaced at any time."

By now Robinson was convulsing on the seat of the limo. "Whip. Whip. Whip."

The president stared at him. "I hear the Secret Service office in Montana needs a new detail leader. Just keep it up, Bill. You'd be perfect for Montana."

## Chapter 29

The soldiers of the People's Liberation Army came to attention, and stepped away from the doors. The massive doors were opened, and a great hall was revealed. He entered the hall, and walked the length of it upon a bright red carpet.

Against the back wall of the great room was a vast red flag, with five gold stars ranged in its corner. Under the flag was a long, curved table, around which were seated the men who ruled China.

He approached the table, stood quietly, and waited to be addressed.

"Song Bei!" said the premier, rising from his place of eminence. "We welcome you to the State Council of the People's Republic of China. We welcome you as its newest member."

"My humble thanks, Comrade Premier," said Song Bei.

The premier smiled. "Now that you have reached this level, Song Bei, you will have access to the highest secrets of government. There is one secret which we know that you are not yet aware of, but which you must be made aware of immediately, as you will play a role in this most momentous event in our nation's history."

Song Bei waited with great anticipation for the premier to

continue.

"It is the goal of this nation that the Province of Taiwan be fully reincorporated into the mainland within a year."

"Do I understand you correctly...?"

"An invasion, yes." The premier smiled. "Don't look so surprised. Surely you must have suspected that this would be a long-term goal of the government? The reincorporation of Taiwan into the People's Republic is not a matter which has been approached casually. It was Mao Zedong himself who first decreed it, in November of Nineteen Forty-nine, not long after he took over the government of China.

"Our strategy is really quite simple: we are going to take the island swiftly, and by force, and then dare the world to try to take it back; by that I mean, dare the United States to act."

"This is a most admirable goal," said Song Bei. "I am honored to be admitted to this council and to be allowed to take part in the planning."

"Oh, we have great plans for you, Song Bei," replied the premier. "After you have thoroughly absorbed all of the information having to do with our plans and strategy, you will travel to Taiwan and there you will assist General Bai. Upon the success of the invasion, General Bai will become the first governor-general of the Province of Taiwan, and in due time you will become its second."

"I am indeed most humbled."

"Indeed, you are most deserving. Your family has served the People's Republic with great distinction for many years. I am told that your niece, Jiang Ou, has surprised us all by making the favorable acquaintance of the American president himself. We hope that in short order her service will prove to be of great value to us.

"Now then, Song Bei, I have told you of our goal and I have told you our general strategy. For the rest of the afternoon, you will be briefed in much greater detail by a team of our most eminent strategists."

"First, Vice Premier Wang will review for you the history of the Taiwan Reincorporation Project." As the premier introduced the men, each stood in place.

"Deputy Minister of Intelligence Zhu will provide an in-depth analysis of the American leadership structure. And last, but certainly not least, Army Chief-of-Staff General Zeng will describe for you our military strategy."

Song Bei followed the senior officials to a lecture room, where the inculcation began. Vice Premier Wang began his highly learned lecture on the Reincorporation of Taiwan.

Its planning had gone on for decades. The most important element in the success of the plan, he explained, was the ability and willingness of the occupant of the American Oval Office to respond – or to not respond. The vice premier then discussed in great detail the long years of waiting for the perfect situation to present itself.

They were not about to try it while Truman was in office; anyone who had the nerve to fire General Douglas MacArthur was not going to be intimidated by the Chinese.

Nor would Eisenhower, who had gained lasting fame as the Liberator of Europe.

The Kennedy Administration presented them with their first real opportunity. The Bay of Pigs fiasco gave them hope, just as it gave the Soviets the courage to erect the Berlin Wall; but, just as suddenly, JFK's handling of the Cuban Missile Crisis changed their minds. The waiting continued.

Presidents Johnson and Nixon were looked at carefully. Neither would want to be associated with the loss of Taiwan on top of the tragedy of Vietnam and so, with a large American military presence fielded in such close proximity to China, the decision was tabled through the 1960s. Interestingly, the Chinese had learned valuable lessons in strategy from observing the war in Vietnam; but still they waited.

The Carter Administration presented them with their next opportunity. They were particularly intrigued by his willingness to give away the Panama Canal without a fight. And yet the more they thought about it, the idea of matching wits with someone *that* principled who had also spent his early career as a nuclear submarine officer unnerved them considerably.

When Ronald Reagan was elected, they put the program on indefinite hiatus.

Reagan's successors, however, offered some interesting possibilities. They considered launching the invasion while George Bush's forces were tied up in the Middle East in the Gulf War.

When Bill Clinton was elected they thought they had hit the *jackpot*. At one point they had the airplanes fueled and ready to go, but the premier stayed the hand of the generals. Where some saw weakness, the premier saw a pattern of surprise and recovery.

Clinton's willingness to send troops into Haiti was read in China as a sign that he might stand up for other smaller nations. Still, the premier permitted his navy to test the waters of American resolve. The 1996 standoff in the Taiwan Strait had shown to Beijing the futility of trying to approach Taiwan with a naval fleet – for the United States had only to send down the Seventh Fleet from Japan; hardliners in the American government would never allow an American naval blockade to be breached.

When the vice premier was finished, Deputy Minister Zhu stepped forward and delivered his political analysis of the American leadership structure.

"The presence of Edward Billingsley in the Oval Office presents us with a unique opportunity," he began. "We believe that his psychological makeup makes him the ideal presidential adversary for the sort of operation we have planned.

"First of all, he has never held military or been elected to office in his own right," said Zhu. "All of the positions he has held have been administrative. He is the consummate bureaucrat, and has always been able to thrive in that type of environment. He is a consensus builder; he never makes quick decisions, and the more murky and complex the problem, the longer it takes for him to work out the appropriate decision. He is capable of making decisions, of course, but always in his own time.

"His selection as vice president to the charismatic President

Lawrence Holdren was seen at the time as being a wise decision. As the consummate detail man, Billingsley seemed perfect as a counterpoint to Holdren, who was all personality and magnetism, but never spent much time on the inner workings of government. Unfortunately, no one ever anticipated that Holdren would die in office.

"Billingsley's psychological makeup, from what we can tell, is extremely rigid. He thrives by adhering to an amazingly complex set of rules. Think of him as being like a man who can't read, and who hides it from the world. He may have all sorts of strategies in order to deal with his disability – memorizing, avoidance mechanisms – but the day will eventually come when his success will depend on his ability to read, but he will not be able to do so, and he will fail.

"So it is with Billingsley; with the invasion of Taiwan, we are going to present him with a situation he has never had to face in his brief fourteen months in office: the requirement to make instantaneous life and death decisions. On top of that, we are going to present a scenario which will confuse him and make his decision-making much more difficult.

"We believe that he will react in his characteristic fashion: by refusing to make any consequential decisions until all the facts are clear. He will want to study, review and obtain a consensus. He will utilize decision-avoidance mechanisms wherever possible. He knows no other way.

"However, in this case, his decision timeframe will far exceed the time we need to establish a nearly unshakable beachhead on Taiwan. We need only two days.

"But we must also take into consideration the people around him, the people who influence him. Billingsley is like a large planet surrounded by influential moons. In fact, our code name for him is 'Jupiter.'

"The three biggest gravitational forces pulling on Jupiter are his chief political adviser, Tony Phillips, whose code name is 'Pan'; Admiral Mark Ferguson, whose code name, by the way, is 'Mars.'"

"The god of war…" said Song Bei under his breath.

"Correct," said Minister Zhu. "And finally, Uniqraft chairman Arnulf Kinder, whose code name is 'Judas'…

"The 'Betrayer?'"

"Yes, and I'll get back to him. Now, Tony Phillips is an opportunist; he has no compass. He pushes the president to make the most expedient decisions possible. Arnulf Kinder cares for nothing but money; he believes that the official American policy of standing by Taiwan is a detriment to the flow of business. He would love to see much more trade with China, and he will certainly push the president to abandon Taiwan, as more than one hundred sixty-one countries have done already.

"As far as Admiral Ferguson is concerned, he presents a real danger to our success; but we have a special plan to deal with him, which General Zeng will explain."

Song Bei nodded; he had had no idea that such a plan was in the works, much less that every aspect of the operation was being looked at so carefully.

"Now then," continued Zhu, "the first element in our plan is the creation of mistrust and division between the United States and Taiwan. In order to achieve this effect, we have tried to orchestrate the appearance that Billingsley has betrayed Taiwan by his taking certain actions which diminish the security of Taiwan.

"As I'm sure you know, the president's election this fall is not at all certain; we intend to capitalize on that fact. You will recall the passenger airplane deal, which we took away from the Americans at the last minute and gave to the Europeans?"

"Of course," said Song Bei. "The Americans were stunned by the loss of the deal; and it has hurt the president's standing in California. After all, as close as he is to Arnulf Kinder, Beijing had every reason to give the deal to the Americans so that we could thereby cultivate even more influence with the White House."

"Your analysis of the political ramifications of the deal are quite impressive, Song Bei. But you should know the real reason why we took the deal away from the Americans: we did it so that we could have even *more* influence with the president when we give it back to him …"

A smile lit up the face of the junior minister. "We'll be giving the deal back to the Americans?'

"Exactly. The president desperately needs that particular gift dropped in his lap; you can see how it would allow him to save face, to bolster his support in California, and thereby increase his chances of winning the election."

"I do see that, yes; and what do you intend to gain from this maneuver?"

"We will reoffer him the airplane deal at the same time we ask him to refrain from deploying certain military forces into the Pacific sphere; namely, an aircraft carrier and an advanced fighter attack wing which are scheduled to be deployed to Japan within a few months. If he will quietly deploy those forces to other parts of the world, we will give him back the airplane deal."

"That doesn't seem like too much to ask of him."

"It's not, Song Bei; however, the most important element in this planned discussion is that we will be making a very high quality tape recording of the conversation."

"You're going to record this conversation with the president! How?"

"Very simple: a friend of his will betray him."

"Judas?" That was Kinder's code name.

"Exactly. So then, at the appropriate time, when we release the recording to the world, it will cause a great deal of consternation in Taiwan as they realize that the president of the United States traded on their security in exchange for his own reelection.

"At that point, the president's credibility with the Taiwanese will be destroyed.

"However, just in case we have not done enough to damage the U.S. – Taiwanese relationship, we have one other little trick up our sleeve. This particular thread will connect the president to the secret manufacture of deadly weaponry intended to be used against Taiwan."

Song Bei nodded. "This is most interesting."

"There is a secret Pakistani factory, financed by us, in which a number of short-range, high-trajectory, deep-impact missiles are under construction. The missiles I have just described would seem to the world, if they were to be discovered, to be perfectly designed in order to attack the various underground electronic warfare defense systems to be found on the island of Taiwan.

"To complicate matters, we have hired a top international agent – Aji al-Houb – who has connections all over the world. Al-Houb was commissioned by us to obtain computer chips from the Qiryat Gat Manufacturing Facility located in southern Israel. This is a joint Israeli-American high tech lab and it is the site of a great deal of technology transfer between the United States and Israel. The computer chips are being installed in the missiles.

"And here is the clincher: Al-Houb worked briefly for Edward Billingsley when he was director of the Central Intelligence Agency ten years ago. Thus, the appearance will be given that the president used his connection to Al-Houb to obtain these parts. Once this apparent betrayal is revealed to the world – as it will be this coming winter – the Taiwanese will be faced with the realization that the president was somehow involved in this missile factory.

"When the Taiwanese see the airplane deal back in American hands, and the president reelected, and evidence of the president's involvement in the missile factory, how can they not then believe that they have been betrayed?

"At that precise moment we will issue a worldwide release of the recording of the president trading on the security in the Pacific region. The people of Taiwan will explode in anger and fear at the news of these acts of betrayal, and all of this emotion will be directed toward the United States.

"In order to ensure that these destabilizing actions are capitalized upon, we have put into place another element of our plan: a small but highly disciplined group of agitators and revolutionary elements. This group, called the TLA, or Taiwanese

Liberation Army, is working underground on the island at this time. They will assure that demonstrations and riots and various other civil disruptions take place in response to news of the president's betrayal.

"At the moment the invasion begins, the TLA will move into place and take over certain key government buildings. They will disrupt communications and will take actions which will discourage American intervention.

"The third and final element in our plan is the planned removal of Vice President Ferguson from the president's orbit. It is entirely predictable that, as these events unfold, the president will send Mark Ferguson to Taiwan. In fact, we know precisely where he will stay upon his arrival. His assassination will be prearranged, and a group identifying itself as a radical Taiwanese anti-American movement will take credit for the assassination, further inflaming Taiwanese-American discord. With Ferguson's death, our greatest military concern will be eliminated, and tensions between the United States and Taiwan will be at a breaking point. The Americans will deny that they tried to betray Taiwan, and the Taiwanese will deny that they were behind the assassination of Ferguson. Neither will immediately suspect that we were behind it all.

"And now at this time, I will call upon General Zeng to outline our military strategy."

General Zeng stepped forward, assisted by several aides who held maps and charts.

"It is clear," he began, "that China cannot match hardware with the United States. If it were to be tank corps versus tanks corps, or air wing versus air wing, or fleet versus fleet, the United States will always have the advantage. That lesson, along with those learned by observing the American failure in the war in Vietnam, has nevertheless yielded to us a coherent and workable invasion strategy.

"Thus has evolved the novel concept of conducting the invasion of Taiwan as a guerrilla operation. The idea is simple: thousands of troop transport planes will take off from all over

China." Here an aide produced a map of Eastern China. "They will leave from bases ranging down in Guangdong Province all the way up the coast to Korea. Lightly armed troops will be dropped by parachute at night, at very low altitude to decrease radar detection, and preferably through a cloud cover.

"The majority of the flights will be coordinated to enter Taiwanese airspace just over the tiny fishing village of Ming Hai, on the southwest coast of the island. The troops will rally on the inland plains, and will push north along the highway which runs along the west coast, driving straight for the heart of Taipei.

"There will be no armada for the United States to confront and stare down. All of the conditions of approach – nighttime, low altitude, cloud cover – will of course greatly increase the rate of jump casualties and air mishaps, but human beings are the most expendable commodity that we have. If ten thousand troops could be dropped every hour, even with an astonishing thirty percent casualty rate, perhaps fifty thousand highly mobile, lightly armed troops could safely land and regroup in a single night.

"Of course, the world community would know within hours what was happening, but how could they prevent its happening again the next night, and the next night and the night after that? Within a week there might be a half million Chinese troops on the island. Our troops will easily defeat the rather puny Taiwanese military forces and we will have entered Taipei.

"The strength of the plan lies in its simplicity. It will work, regardless of when it is implemented and regardless of any other factors in place. It will work because it will present the Americans with only two choices: they can provide a nuclear response, or they can mount a D-Day scale counterinvasion.

"The former, we believe, is almost completely out of the question. As far as the latter, how many American troops would it take to dislodge us from the island? Millions. And how many casualties would that entail? Hundreds of thousands.

"And how many casualties would the American public allow in an attempt to clear the Chinese from a small island in Asia? Few. Very, very few.

"And where would help come from? South Korea won't be able to spare any. Japan? Japan won't have any to offer. Australia? Yes, *Australia* could send a regiment or two.

"To summarize, the first strategic element in our victory is our preparation and planning. We have meticulously prepared; of course, we have had fifty years to do so. Other elements include overwhelming manpower; a critical difference between the American and Chinese abilities to tolerate casualties; and the certainty of a dilatory American response.

"And that, Song Bei, is how we intend to take back Taiwan; are there any questions?"

## 30

Nick drove onto the Norfolk Naval Base, ostensibly for a visit with the DiSalvos. After a brief visit with Jeannine, Nick and the Salivator left and together they made their way out of Officer Country and over to the bachelor female enlisted quarters.

Nick found Building Two Seventy-Six with ease and he walked up the stairs to her second-level door. He rapped on the glass of her door and waited for Rhonda Clement to respond. Eventually she did. She was an attractive woman – voluptuous, one might say – in her early twenties, with a come-hither look perceptible even through a screen door.

"Seaman First Class Rhonda Clement?" said Nick.

The door opened slightly. "Yeah?" She stepped out. "What can I do you for?"

"Good morning. My name is Nick Ferguson; and this is Lieutenant DiSalvo."

"Nick Ferguson...? Now where do I know that name?" Then her face lit up. "Oh, my God! From the *Andrew Jackson*. You're the lieutenant and your father is the – "

"Yes, *that* Nick Ferguson," he replied. "Former lieutenant, I might add."

"I was sorry to hear about your little aerial mishap. Would

you like to come in?"

"Thank you," he replied, as he stepped into her quarters, the Salivator directly behind.

Rhonda Clement had never before been visited in her quarters by officers. She attempted to do a quick straightening-up as she offered them a seat.

Nick declined her courtesy. "Thanks, but this won't take but a minute. The reason I'm here is that I need to get in touch with Grant Benning and I understand you happen to be a friend of his, and so I thought you might know where he lives."

She eyed the two of them warily. "He is an acquaintance, yes...Is he in trouble?"

"He won't be if he helps me out; all I need is to be able to talk to him."

She grew instantly defensive. "He's not in the service any more; we're no longer in contact with each other."

"I see; so then, the brief time which the two of you spent on the evening of February Twenty-sixth in the Uniqraft trailer was not enough to cement your undying love for one another, I take it?" He now knew the exact date because Emma Walden had called him again when she figured out the night in question. "I believe that was the night you induced Corporal Benning to desert his post so that you might entertain him in the hangar deck of the Jackson. Please understand, I certainly wouldn't want to see you charged under the Uniform Code of Military Justice for a moment of youthful exuberance."

Her face went decidedly pale. "How'd you find out about that?" In fact, she knew she had told a number of people; there could have been any number of ways he might have known.

"It doesn't matter," he replied. "Look, let me be clear. I'm not interested in getting you in trouble. I just need to talk to Benning."

She sighed, clearly relieved. "Well, he said he was going to Philadelphia to hook up with some high school buddies; they were thinking of maybe doing some traveling; but don't ask me where to. Look, I can give you his address but you gotta promise you'll leave me out of all this."

He nodded. "Deal."

JENNIFER FELT bad about canceling plans to go to the beach with Nick, and so on Sunday, when she arrived back in Georgetown, she called him and invited him to come over for dinner. Ellen and Greg were most likely going to be flying back from Connecticut later that evening.

Nick brought flowers. Jennifer had put together a fairly elaborate Chinese meal and she planned for dinner to be served on the veranda. "I'm very sorry about missing the trip to Myrtle Beach," she said soon after he arrived.

"No, I understand," he replied. "It's perfectly all right. So the president just had someone call you and boom! off you go, just like that."

"Well, he sent some men from the Secret Service to enlist my services. They had a limo on the street and before I knew it I was halfway to Baltimore."

He paused. "It's incredible to have that kind of power, isn't it?"

"I went because of the job," she said quietly. "Not because of the power."

He picked up a magazine and pretended to be interested in it. "And I guess you spent the night there…"

"Well, the conference lasted all weekend, and a room was provided."

He wandered about the living room, trying his best to appear nonchalant about the whole matter. "Spend a lot of time with the president, did you?"

"Oh, I hardly saw him." There was a long silence before she spoke again. "Nick, did you have time to get much fishing in while you were at the beach?"

"Fishing? No. Why do you ask?"

"Because you're doing an awful lot of fishing now."

He laughed. "Sorry, yes; I suppose I am." It was natural for him to wonder about what had really happened over the weekend. A sudden invitation…a government limousine…a luxury hotel room…the company of the president…

Still, Jennifer had invited him to be here with her tonight, knowing full well that Greg and Ellen wouldn't be there; she certainly hadn't been obligated to do something like that.

And so here they were – just the two of them. The calculations were simple enough: a beautiful evening, a beautiful girl, a fine dinner cooked for him. Yes, a quick reading of the Nick-o-Meter indicated that it was definitely time to make his move.

He lifted the lid covering a saucepan and at the same time managed to slip his arm around her waist. "Smells delicious."

She removed his hand. "I'm sorry, Nick, but I won't be on the menu tonight."

"Oh. Well, perhaps I misunderstood..."

"Tonight was just to thank you for your understanding, that's all."

"Well, there's thanks...and then there's *Thanks!*"

"Perhaps I should tell you...I happen to have feelings for someone else."

He took a step back. "I'm sorry; I didn't know. Is it serious?"

'Is it serious?' The president had asked the same question. That question was the standard opening gambit in the chess game that was the American mating ritual. She should have answered the president, 'Yes, and how about your marriage of thirty-seven years standing? Is it serious?'

But she did not resent Nick's asking; under far different circumstances, she could easily have succumbed to his considerable charms. "Let's just say," she answered him, "that the person I have feelings for happens to be someone that I can't be with right now. Perhaps some day that will change, but not now."

"SO HOW DID it go with Jennifer?"

"She's seems to have developed an interest in someone else."

"Really? Who?"

Nick looked him in the eye. "Take a wild guess, Salivator."

Lieutenant DiSalvo had a stunned look on his face. "My God! Doesn't she know I'm a married man? And a father-to-be at that. Granted, I'm youngish looking for my age, and many would associate a certain devil-may-care attitude in me with those of the bachelor set; but the reality is that in many ways I'm a settled man – a man much more mature than my years might suggest."

"Uh, 'Vator…"

"Now, if I had known her five years ago – or even three – that would be different." He sighed deeply and turned to Nick. "But now? No, it could never be. Nick, you must go to her immediately; entreat her of my deep regard…"

"Salivator…"

"Don't try to make me see the rightness of it all," he insisted, seizing his flightmate by the shoulders. "There can be no good to come of this! For the love of God, as you are my countryman, put an end to this madness!"

"Salivator!"

"What? What is it?"

"It's not you she's interested in."

"Right. I knew that. Of course; you didn't think I was serious, did you? OK, who, then?"

"You figure it out," said Nick. "First of all, she drops everything to go running off for this conference…"

"A good career move, the way I see it; there's nothing in that."

"She spends the night in the same hotel as the president," he noted.

"That's hardly unusual; it was an out-of-town assignment; the feds no doubt took over several floors and of course she needed a place to stay."

"And here's the clincher," said Nick. "She said that the man she cared for was someone she could hardly be with right now. Now I ask you – who else could she mean but a married president who's living in the fishbowl that is Washington?"

Salivator was stunned. "Billingsley? As in 'Leader-of-the-Free-World Billingsley?' You're kidding. I thought the girl had much more class than that. But still, I think you've got to ask yourself, do you really want someone who's that blinded by power? Especially when she could have you – with nothing going for you but Hollywood good looks and a complete lack of common sense."

"Thanks, Salivator; it's a real comfort confiding my innermost thoughts in you."

"Anytime, Nick. Any time at all."

## Chapter 31

Lily Zhang was dying to know how the Baltimore event had gone and so she arranged to meet with Jennifer on Monday. "It went quite well," Jennifer said. "The president offered me a role of some type."

"What do you mean – a role?"

"It wasn't that clearly defined. He said that there would be functions of various types at the White House where someone such as myself might fit in and act as a social butterfly – or words to that effect."

"Well, that's all well and good, but what about your personal relationship with the president? Did he not find you to be attractive?"

"Well, he invited me to his room at eleven o'clock at night..."

Lily's face lit up with delight. "So then...you are lovers! Well, why didn't you say so in the first place? I can't wait to inform Beijing; this is quite a coup for us."

"No, no, wait. I didn't say that. I think that's what he wanted but I'm not ready for all of that."

"You're not ready? Fool! Don't you understand what you have? The opportunity to have a close relationship with the most powerful man in the world! To learn so many things that will be of immense value to your country."

"Perhaps, but I feel as though I'm the one who must determine for myself the best approach to take."

"Oh, do you? And what approach are you taking?"

"If he wants me, he'll have to court me, the same as any other man."

"You child! Don't you understand anything? He won't do something like that. He gets what he wants or he moves on to someone else. It's that simple. We certainly know that much about him."

"He may move on," she replied philosophically. "But if that's the case, he would have moved on anyway, probably long before I would have gotten any information of value out of him. Do you think I can just give in to him for one night and then say, 'Tell me, Mister President – what are your true feelings toward the People's Republic? Oh, Mister President, how would you respond in thus and such a situation?' Do you really think that's the kind of information I can get from him after knowing him for such a very short period of time? If you want me to learn how his mind works, I need time."

Lily was steaming. "You think you know so much. Do you think you know more than I do?"

"Well...I don't know about that, but I suggest that if you think you can do better, why don't you try it yourself? The address is Sixteen Hundred Pennsylvania Avenue. He's home a lot; drop by anytime and give it a shot."

THE SALIVATOR was standing tall before the vice president of the United States. "Good morning, Admiral. You wanted to see me?"

"Thanks for coming by, Lieutenant. Stand at ease. Now, I want your honest opinion. How do you think Nick is doing?"

"You mean with the new babe? Oh, he struck out bad, sir. It was not a pretty sight."

There was a slight pause and a repressed smile. "I meant...with the resignation."

"Oh, that. Well, basically he's fine, sir. Feeling a little lost at the moment, but that's understandable."

"Yes, I suppose it is," said Ferguson, as he stood and strode the floor of his office and looked out the window. "Salivator, I had some turnover on my staff recently, and I was thinking that I could use a good, seasoned junior officer on board; someone who's loyal, hard-working, intelligent. Know anyone who might fit the bill?"

"I could put the word out, sir."

"I was talking about you, son," said Ferguson. "That way you'd be in the same geographical area as Nick; the two of you could see each other more often and he'd feel a little less lost; not to mention, serving on my staff might be useful to your career."

"Oh. Oh, I see. Indeed, it might."

"Of course, it might mean having to give up deployments for a while," said the senior officer. "Then again, maybe your wife would prefer living on the Norfolk base rather than here in Washington…"

"I think we can make our adjustments, sir," said the Salivator, extremely pleased with the offer. "I'll be more than happy to sign on."

## CHAPTER 32

She came to him as in a dream.
In the dusky room she glided across the floor, her form light and ethereal, draped in a cloudy mist. She was as lovely as he had ever remembered seeing her, with her black hair wafting about her face and shoulders, her eyes bright and piercing, her face sweet and angelic.

He rose up from his bed, propping himself on one arm as best he was able. With the other arm he reached out as far as he could, desperately wanting to hold her again, to draw her to him, as he had done many years before.

"It's you!" he called out in a hoarse whisper. "You've come at last!"

She came forward to his bed and kneeled down, so that her face was close to his own. In the darkness, in the mist, he could barely see her face, but he could sense her soft, calming presence. "Little Ou!" he exclaimed, addressing her in the traditional Chinese style of familiarity. "You've come at last! You've come for me! I can go home now!"

As through a tunnel, he heard his name being sounded. "Jin Yi-bo? Is that you, Jin Yi-bo?"

"Yes, Jiang Ou? Don't you recognize me? Don't you know

me?"

The woman spoke quietly. "Jin Yi-bo, my name is Doctor Yang. Please listen to me. I'm with the International Red Cross. I'm here with other medical personnel and we want to try to help you."

He seemed lost, fearful. "You are not my love?"

The doctor looked over at one of Jin Yi-bo's cellmates.

"He's been hallucinating quite a bit in the last few days," said Bao Luan, the young man who had done the most to help to care for Jin Yi-bo after his surgery. Bao Luan stepped across the tiny cell, looked through the small window of the cell door and saw a guard standing only a few feet away. He stepped back over to Jin Yi-bo's bed, squatted down and wiped a wet rag across Jin Yi-bo's fevered brow. He spoke quietly to the doctor. "His injury has never healed properly. Doctor, Jin Yi-bo is very important to many people. Can you save him?"

She opened Jin Yi-bo's shirt, carefully removed the crude bandages, and examined the wound, as well as his torso. "He has a very serious infection, I'm afraid," she said after a moment. "It's systemic; he's in grave danger."

Doctor Yang sighed as she reached into her medical bag. The British-led contingent, composed of six doctors and ten nurses, as well as ancillary medical personnel, had spent the entire day trying to work their way through just one section of the lao gai at Harbin. The scope of the task was overwhelming: although many prisoners could be helped by the prompt administration of basic medicines and minor surgical operations, there were all too many prisoners who could not be helped at all – their care would exhaust the limited resources that the Red Cross had brought with them.

But Jin Yi-bo had to be helped; those were the orders which came directly from International Headquarters in Geneva. Doctor Yang did not know why this young man was of particular importance, or why his care was to be given special consideration. As a doctor, that wasn't important to her; she wanted to help them all.

She couldn't, of course, but she had agreed to do everything she could for him and she had agreed to pass a certain message to him. Of course, she could see quite clearly that he was in no condition to understand or remember what she would say to him. She spoke quietly to Bao Luan as she prepared an injection for the desperate patient. "Jin Yi-bo is going to be leaving this prison. He will be transferred to Shi Men, near the coast. There is going to be an attempt made to get him out of China."

They heard the guard step over to the door and look through the window. Feeling the guard's stare, the doctor worked silently, administering the injection. After that procedure was completed, she began to examine the wound closely, looking for the best place to insert a drain. Bao Luan drew very close and assisted her as best he could.

As the wound began to drain, the doctor asked Bao Luan to step away from the bed. When he did so, the sight of the draining wound was directly within the view of the guard. He found the sight to be so repugnant that he turned away from the cell and walked to the end of the corridor.

As the doctor checked the wound and began to apply a salve to it, she continued to speak quietly to Bao Luan. "Here is what must happen. In Shi Men, they are using quite a few prisoners on various work details. He will be assigned to one of these. He will be outside from morning until dusk. The Taiwanese will find him and he will be taken from the fields to the coast, and from there to Taiwan. You are going to have to tell him all of this when he comes out of his fever. I'm leaving salves and other drugs for him, which you must help him with until he is better."

Bao Luan nodded his understanding of everything she had said. He also understood that he could be losing his friend and leader. "He will need me to look after him," the young man said quietly.

Doctor Yang instantly understood his meaning. "Your name?"

He told her and she wrote his name on a prescription pad which she carried in her pocket. "I will try to see that your name is added to the transfer list. I'm sure you will take good care of him."

As she packed her medical kit, she looked around the tiny cell. She spotted a small photograph set in a recess in the stone wall. It was a picture of a girl of about sixteen; she was fresh-faced, smiling and quite beautiful. "This is Jiang Ou, I take it?" asked the doctor.

"Yes."

"Well, then you must take very good care of him. He has a great deal to live for."

## CHAPTER 33

The campaign was by now in full swing. The president and his running mate were traveling constantly. Nick had been hired by the vice presidential reelection committee – a harmless bit of nepotism which nevertheless gave him the opportunity to stay busy and not have to think too much about his future.

The Ferguson campaign had discovered one unexpected dividend of Nick's presence on the campaign trail: he drew girls and young women to the rallies. Thousands of them.

Nick had expected to stay completely in the background, but the sympathy that had welled up over his resignation and ruined career had somehow redounded to his advantage. The circumstances of his resignation were by now quite well known; whereas many people believed that he had been quite lucky to be allowed to resign his commission, many others felt that his willingness to sacrifice his career without a fight demonstrated a noble quality within him.

The crowds gathering to greet the vice president were in many cases larger than those for the president, the difference largely due to all the younger women who came to see Nick. Learning of this, the president jealously demanded that Nick be removed from the campaign trail.

The vice president was aware of the problem, and felt that it was wrong to upstage the president. He asked Nick to stay in the background during the Kentucky-Tennessee leg of the campaign trip. Nick complied, but the crowds grew smaller and seemed less lively without all the girls in attendance. Everyone noticed it, but Tony Phillips knew that he, as the president's chief political adviser, was the right person to speak up.

He knew the president wouldn't want to hear it, and he was right. "I don't like that little ex-flyboy," said Billingsley with some bitterness. "First of all, he embarrasses his father and the campaign by losing his plane; then he refuses to cooperate with his commanding officer. And now he tries to upstage me on the campaign trail."

"Mister President," said Phillips, "a vote for Nick Ferguson – Mark Ferguson, I meant to say – is a vote for Ed Billingsley. Now, as the head of the ticket – and the party – you need to be more concerned about the real possibility of losing the election than being too choosy about where your help is coming from."

The president didn't like it, but he listened; within hours, Nick was back in business.

The president had not forgotten Jennifer, although he was trying. After their late-night Baltimore meeting, he had gone back and forth about her. At first he was so taken with her that he was willing to change and do the kinds of things that she had suggested.

But then he had opened his mouth about the matter to Bill Robinson, who had mocked him for his folly. He should never have told Bill Robinson in the first place; and yet the more he thought about it, the more he thought that Robinson was right; even to entertain her silly ideas, he would be making a fool of himself.

He had decided to forget all about her. He didn't need that level of involvement with someone like that. There were plenty of others; he met them every day. No one else put conditions on him like that. It was outrageous of her! He resented the very idea!

He resented her as well; and so, as of right now, he would put her completely out of his thoughts. He checked his watch: three twenty-seven and seventeen seconds. From this moment on, his entire being would be cleansed of every thought, every memory, every inclination and every impulse having to do with Jennifer Jiang. Gone forever, as of right…now!

He sat on the dais of the Dayton Arena and resumed listening to Ohio Congressman Tom Fenster's fascinating discourse on the relationship between water use rights and agricultural tax rates. It was truly an intellectual tour de force.

He wondered what she was doing. She certainly wasn't with Nick, because Nick was here in Dayton with the vice presidential campaign. So who was she with, and what was she doing with him?

Did she have his flowers on her dresser at home? Was she sitting in a Georgetown restaurant, engaged in witty conversation with him? Were they walking hand-in-hand along the Potomac, laughing over some little bon mot, joking about the foolishness of aging politicians?

Was the boy some rich kid who loved to take her to parties? Or perhaps some goateed Georgetown University intellectual, majoring in Maoist political philosophy with plans to become an investment banker? He hated intellectuals; he wasn't going to get their votes anyway, so why pretend to like them?

It was driving him to distraction. He had to see her. He had to know where she was. He wanted her to be with him. He wanted her to be with him right then, that day. He wished Congressman Blowhard would keel over from heat exhaustion, so he could get the hell out of there. The man had so much hot air in him he could heat the Chrysler Building.

When would this infernal day be over?

He reached into his pocket for a notepad and pen. He wrote a note to Bill Robinson, instructing him to have an agent drop by Jennifer Jiang's Georgetown residence and induce her to come and join the campaign. He would have no trouble finding a low-visibility job for her. He handed the note over his shoulder to

Robinson. He could hear Robinson opening the note and reading it. He could feel the man's sarcastic smile, but he didn't care.

He would be happier on the campaign trail, knowing that she were always in the vicinity. He could have one of the boys keep an eye on her, and fend off any young campaign staffers who might mistakenly think she was fair game. And late in the evening, when the day's campaigning was done, he would court her, as she desired.

Oh, yes, he would court her all right. He would show her that he was still young enough, and virile enough, and suave enough and debonair enough and all those other qualities enough that he had thought were long since extinct within him, but which were not, because *she* had seen those qualities in him, and therefore they must be there.

JENNIFER RECEIVED a message from Major Chen and she met him in Washington's Chinatown district. They sat in a restaurant and talked quietly.

"It was a Doctor Yang, and she examined him thoroughly and found him to be in very bad shape..."

Jennifer put her hands to her face. "Oh, no..."

"But she saved his life, that's the important thing," he assured her. "And he seems to have a very reliable cellmate who is helping to keep him alive. Now he has the right medicines, and he'll be all right...in time. He should have been told by now that he'll be transferred to the coast. So now it's up to you: give us something we can use, and we'll send in the commandos."

She nodded knowingly; her contribution remained to be delivered.

"Now then, as far as the president," Major Chen continued, "I understood from your message that you did spend some time with him in Baltimore. How did that go?"

"Oh, he's quite the charmer; I think he'd like to have a harem, truth be told, and me in it."

"Are you...?"

"I'm taking my time; and whereas your Chinese counterpart

seems to differ with me on the finer points of presidential-level espionage, it is my contention that if I am going to gain his confidence, then I need to take the time to develop a relationship."

"In other words, you don't really want to be his lover…"

"That would be a great sacrifice for me; I'm sure that Jin Yi-bo would understand, but I'm sure he would expect it to be a measure of last resort. At any rate, I will soon be in a position to test out my theory. The president's men came around this morning and asked me to join the presidential campaign."

"Doing what?"

"Mainly staying in the background, doing a few odd jobs here and there, and being available for whenever His Majesty deigns to call upon me. All in all, it will be a good opportunity to keep my ear to the ground. In a campaign, they have to formulate policy as they go from city to city, responding to the needs of the people. My feeling is that the farther west the campaign trail goes, the higher the likelihood of hearing some talk of policy vis-a-vis China. Do you agree?"

"Absolutely. With the loss of the airplane deal to Europe, an awful lot of people are going to want to know what the president has in mind for future trade relations with the East. I'm sure you'll hear quite a bit. Very good, then. Well, I'll be following you out West; I'll be available at all times if you need anything. Let's try to talk every day if possible."

## Chapter 34

Chen Wei Dong had assembled the three hundred members of Section Six of the People's Reeducation Camp Number 216. He had in his hand a list of twenty men who were to be transferred to Camp Number 743 in Shi Men, near the coast.

Jin Yi-bo's name was called, as well as that of his two closest friends, including Bao Luan.

There were two trucks waiting in the prison courtyard. The transferees crowded on, along with their very meager possessions, and they began the long trip to Shi Men. It would take three days of travel over bad roads to get there.

Jin Yi-bo was now feeling much better, thanks to the drugs he had been given by the Red Cross. Still, a heavy jolt of the truck going over a pothole in the road sent a searing pain up and down his side.

He had no idea how he would make it through three days of this torture.

# Chapter 35

Jennifer had been on the trail with the Campaign to Reelect the President for four days. The campaign had moved from Dayton to Chicago to Kansas City.

She fit in well, from all the reports the president had received. She had done whatever was asked of her – making sandwiches, putting up banners, handling information requests from the media. They were all so busy that not once had anyone raised the question of who she was or why she was there.

And tonight, she would be coming to dinner.

The president was booked in the presidential suite in the Kansas City Sheraton and now he was prancing about the room, checking the fold of the napkins, inspecting the verticality of the candles, noting the cut and color of the flowers, adjusting the bass and treble of the stereo system. He had called and asked the concierge to select appropriately romantic musical selections for the evening, and he had been provided with Rachmaninoff's *Rhapsody on a Theme by Paganini*, and Chopin's *Piano Concerto Number One*. The menu was being specially prepared by the hotel chef according to his order: chateaubriand, and candied vegetables, and a very fine selection of wines.

She wanted a romantic evening; and in this, he would not

fail to please.

Bill Robinson had just then come into the suite and was watching him carefully. "What's all this, Ed?"

"What's all what, Bill?" He checked the mood lighting one final time.

"All this: the flowers, the nice table setting, the classy long-hair music. What is this?"

"It's dinner for two, Bill, and you're not invited, OK? Any more questions?"

Robinson picked up a piece of the fine china and inspected it. "Well, it's just that you don't normally go to all this trouble for a single dinner guest, especially out on the campaign trail. I would say it must be very special dinner guest. Well, who is she? Do I know her?"

"Questions, questions; so full of questions."

"Oh, wait a minute. Could her name be Jennifer Jiang? Could she be a young, beautiful Chinese national who happens to set conditions for her relationships with various heads of state?"

"No, Bill, you're wrong; perceptive as you can sometimes be, you happen to be mistaken on that point. The fact is that she just happens to be a young lady of excellent taste and refinement and, for my part, I just happen to be a gentleman who knows how to please such a person. It's never wise to read so much into these kinds of things."

"Fair enough. Well, then, shall I call the local fine arts museum – have them send up their Van Gogh collection? You'll want to have something to talk about over the chateaubriand, won't you?"

"Oh, we'll have something to talk about, Bill. I think we'll talk about how there needs to be a number of personnel changes within the Secret Service, especially at the highest levels."

NOT LONG thereafter, political adviser Tony Phillips hurried into the room. "Mister President, there's a matter we're going to have to deal with right now."

It turned out to be a bombshell: Billingsley's opponent had come out that day with a plan to overhaul certain aspects of the federal tax system. The timing of the announcement couldn't have been more unhelpful: with the president's speech that evening before the Kansas Business Alliance, the White House would be shown to be woefully unprepared to come up with anything nearly as innovative.

The president's mood was radically altered by the news. "Well, Tony, shouldn't we have seen this coming? Why didn't we come up with our own plan first? How could you let me get blindsided like this? How am I supposed to respond to this in just a few hours?"

"Mark? What do you think?"

The vice president had been asked to sit in on the meeting. Ferguson had been studying a copy of the press release. "Mister President, this is nothing more than smoke and mirrors."

"I respectfully disagree with the vice president." They all turned to Arnulf Kinder who happened to be in town, as he maintained his usual close contact with the president even on the campaign trail. "This proposal on the part of your opponent is quite serious. The business community will embrace a concept like this. You have a serious problem on your hands, Mister President."

The president could scarcely contain his irritation. "Well, you have influence with the business community, Arnulf. You can torpedo this idea."

"Not very easily. The basic idea has merit. The business of America is business, and this proposal happens to address a number of important issues."

"What do you say, Tony?"

"Mister President, I say let's do whatever it takes to get us out of this crisis and then we'll worry about the consequences down the road."

"Mark?"

"I disagree; no need to respond so quickly. Your opponent knows you're making a speech tonight. He's playing you for all you're worth; he's hoping you'll respond quickly and that you'll blunder."

"You know what the problem with you is, Ferguson?" said Kinder. "You've never had to scrape for money the way most people do. You're completely insensitive to the economic aspects of life."

"I've given the president my opinion on the matter," said Ferguson tersely.

Arnulf Kinder did not enjoy being dismissed by anybody, particularly by someone whose net worth was minuscule compared to his own great fortune. "Oh, I see. Your opinion is above reproach; no one can question your infallible judgment. Is that how it is?"

The vice president refused to respond to the attack.

The president sank into his chair; he was clearly shaken by the succession of events. He looked at his watch. "Why do you people put me in this kind of position?"

The president's speech had turned out to be a disaster. Ever suspicious of his own vice president's motives, he had ignored Mark Ferguson's cautionary advice and had instead allowed Arnulf Kinder and Tony Phillips to craft a poorly constructed alternative to his opponent's plan.

And now, the president was furious and Tony Phillips was the one who was forced to endure his wrath. They were sitting in the presidential limousine in the garage of the Kansas City Marriott, where the president had given his speech earlier in the evening. "I was told by you and Kinder that your idea would work!" said Billingsley, almost at a shout. "And yet, to my amazement, my speech before the Kansas Business Alliance was not well received, now was it?"

Phillips was silent and hunkered down in the facing seat of the president's limo.

The president continued. "And on top of that, now we find out that my distinguished opponent had never authorized the statement which you came running in to tell me about this afternoon! It was all a hoax, but no one bothered to check it out. Oldest campaign trick in the book and we fell for it – hook, line and sinker.

"So not only am I a sucker for falling for the hoax – and of course that makes me look like a complete idiot – but now the media is blasting the hell out of my speech – my poorly prepared speech which you and Kinder threw together at the last minute – all full of wonderfully unworkable ideas.

"Now do you see why I never rush into making decisions, Phillips? Now do you see why I check and double check and triple check everything that I do? Now do you see?"

Phillips saw, and he realized that he had blundered badly. As they sat in silence, Bill Robinson opened the president's door and spoke to him. "Mister President, Arnie Kinder asks whether you could step into his limo for a few minutes."

The president could see Kinder's limo not fifty feet from his own. "What the hell does he want at this hour?"

"All he said was that you would be very, very interested in what he had to say."

The president reluctantly agreed; Kinder's limousine was waved forward, and it came to a stop only a few feet from the presidential limo. Doors on both vehicles opened and the president emerged from his vehicle.

"By the way, sir," added Robinson, "there's a Chinese governmental official named Qian in Kinder's limo. We've already checked him out; he's clear."

The chief executive walked three paces and stepped into Kinder's luxuriously appointed vehicle. He settled in the facing seat, opposite from Kinder and a man whom the president did not recognize. "Well, what is it?"

"Mister President, would it come as a very big surprise to you if I told you that California is in worse shape than you thought?"

"You think I need more bad news?" Billingsley said grimly, and then he thought about what Kinder had just told him. "I thought things were holding steady out there."

"Up until recently they were," said Kinder. "However, with the loss of the plane deal there's been more deterioration of your support. It's a big political issue and your opponent is using it more and more against you; they're saying it reflects on your ability to get things done. A poll they're going to release tomorrow shows you trailing in California. And if you lose The Big One, you may lose it all. However, I think we can help."

"I think I've had all the brilliant ideas I can take from you for one day; and who is *we*?" he added, staring at the other passenger in the limo.

With regard to the president's poorly received speech earlier that evening, Kinder was completely unapologetic; he had moved on to other matters. "Mister President, may I introduce to you Deputy Minister Qian from the People's Republic?"

"I don't understand...why would I be meeting an official of the People's Republic in an unscheduled meeting at eleven o'clock at night?"

"Trust me on this, Ed," said Kinder. "I'm confident that it will be in your best interests to listen to what the gentleman has to say."

Deputy Minister Qian leaned forward and spoke quietly to the chief executive. "Mister President, the Chinese people feel a certain sense of dismay at the continued American military presence in the Pacific sphere."

The president shrugged. "We've had a military presence there for decades."

"How well we know that," said the soft-spoken official. "But we believe that China does not pose a threat to the region. And yet, each time a new carrier or fighter aircraft is assigned to bases in the Philippines or Japan, it creates a loss of face for us. Certainly you can understand that?"

The president was unmoved. "We all have our crosses to bear," he said with some irritation. "So what is it you want?"

"If the new aircraft carrier – the *Franklin D. Roosevelt* – which is scheduled to be deployed to Japan early next year, could be stationed in another part of the world, this would be seen by many in my country as a gesture of good will between the peoples of our two nations."

"You want me to redeploy an aircraft carrier?"

"And the advanced fighter attack Raptor squadron," added the minister, "which we understand is to be deployed into the region. We feel that we pose no threat which justifies these military elements in our region of the world."

The president was totally baffled. He turned to Kinder. "I think you know what kind of day I've had. And now you bring this man here, someone I've never met in my life, and he's trying to tell me how to deploy our strategic forces...? I hope there's something more to this conversation because, so far at least, I'm not shouting halleluya." He turned back to the Chinese official. "Minister Qian, what exactly do I get for these little gestures of good will?"

"Perhaps as a quid pro quo," the man replied calmly, "there could be a reversal of the passenger airplane deal. I know the American people would certainly sit up and take notice."

The president was sitting up and taking notice already.

"Mister President," Kinder added, "what Minister Qian is so generously offering would go a long way towards turning California back around."

The president was well aware of the ramifications of the offer. "That's all you want? You just want me to send a carrier and some planes to another part of the world, and the United States gets the airplane deal back?"

"The continued addition of new ships and planes is a source of discomfort to the Chinese people," explained Qian with careful patience. "It makes us feel as though we cannot be trusted to act as good citizens of the world community. Surely you can understand our viewpoint, Mister President? It is a matter of national pride."

The president was silent for a good while. "How much of the airplane deal can you give us, and how soon can we get it?"

"I believe I can speak for the highest levels of my government when I say that we are in a position to be as flexible as possible. The cooperation of the American government will determine everything."

The president shook his head. "I don't even know if that carrier deployment has been announced. I don't always keep track of those things."

"I believe I can answer that question, Mister President," offered Kinder. "It was announced only as a possibility. The Joint Chiefs are supposed to discuss the issue in full next week."

"I see you're on top of things, Arnie."

"I'm just looking out for your best interests, Mister President."

Ed Billingsley, the candidate, wanted to shout Yes! to the idea. Ed Billingsley, the politician, knew better. He would not give his answer now. He would pretend to mull it over – for days, perhaps even for weeks; but in the end, he knew exactly what he would do. He would consult with the chairman of the Joint Chiefs of Staff, and he would suggest that the East was secure enough for the time being, and that the carrier should go to some other part of the world. "I'll need some time to think it over."

"Think it over?" exclaimed Kinder with obvious impatience. "Hell, Ed, it's a gift! With one fell swoop, you can secure California, win the election, and improve relations between China and the United States. You can't lose on this."

"I don't like to make instant decisions, Arnie," said Billingsley coolly. "After tonight, I'm sure you can understand *why*." He turned to the Chinese official. "Minister Qian, you pin down for us the exact terms of the deal and we'll give it very careful consideration."

The man bowed slightly. "We hope you will be able to arrive at a decision quickly, Mister President. The need to go forward with the contracts is becoming urgent. We certainly don't want your country to lose out on a very lucrative arrangement."

"Well, if you were so concerned about us, you would have given us the deal in the first place, right?" the president said with a sense of skepticism which was simply for show. "Like I said, I like to consider these kinds of decisions with great care."

Kinder was right, though. It was a gift, and it was just this sort of gift placed in his lap that could ultimately be his salvation. The only question was whether he could keep his decision low-key enough that no one would raise any issues. The American presence in the Far East was as strong as it had ever been. If the Chinese felt threatened by additions to those forces, well, he could hardly blame them.

It wasn't like they were asking him to take standing forces out of the area; that would be much harder to explain; but to divert a carrier here – an air wing there – for the president to do that, it was simply a judgment call.

After all, he was the commander-in-chief. No one else could possibly know as much as he did about the security needs of the country. The country, did you say? The world!

If he felt those forces could be put to better use in another part of the globe, who, in the final analysis, could say that he was wrong? If he could get those plans reversed, and no issue made of it, he would be home clear for the election.

Best of all, the campaign was headed toward California. If he announced the reversal of the airplane deal in his big speech in Los Angeles, things could start to turn around for him. California would turn around, and perhaps the country as well.

Yes, Los Angeles would be the place where he would make his stand.

He bid adieu to the gentlemen and stepped back over to his limo. As it whisked him back to his hotel, he reached into a secret compartment of the limousine and took out a flask of brandy. He took the top off the flask and began to sip from it.

He hated the stress generated by the types of situation he had been presented with today – the quick reaction required to deal with an opponent's unexpected announcement, and decisions to redeploy forces – decisions which could be questioned by various people.

No, he definitely didn't need any more days like today.

NOT LONG after the president's limo left the scene, Kinder's limo had also taken to the highway. After they had been riding for a few minutes, Kinder reached into a console and pushed a button. "Let's play it back."

He and Qian listened with rapt attention as the president's words as well as their own were heard coming from six speakers ranged throughout the passenger compartment.

Qian's soft voice was heard first. "'Perhaps as a quid pro quo, there could be a reversal of the passenger airplane deal. I know the American people would certainly sit up and take notice.'"

Then Kinder. "'Mister President, what Minister Qian is so

generously offering would go a long way towards turning California back around.'"

There was a pause before the president spoke. "'That's all you want? You just want me to send a carrier and some planes to another part of the world?'"

Qian again. "'The continued addition of new ships and plane is a source of discomfort to the Chinese people. It makes us feel as though we cannot be trusted to act as good citizens of the world community. Surely you can understand our viewpoint, Mister President? It is a matter of national pride.'"

"'How much of the airplane deal can you give us, and how soon can we get it?'"

Kinder turned off the equipment. "That's enough of that, I think."

"Very nice recording equipment," said Qian. "Japanese?"

"American," replied Kinder. "When only the very best will do." He laughed. "Yes, indeed, when all this comes down, the vice president takes a dive, the president takes the rap, and Arnie Kinder reaps the rewards."

"You've been a big help," said Minister Qian.

"I want to help," replied Kinder. "We have the same goals, don't we? I'm tired of that puny little country standing in the way of trade between our two great nations. Just about the whole world recognizes your sovereignty over Taiwan. Once your little police action becomes a fait accompli, I think the United States will secretly breathe a sigh of relief. Sure, there may be some editorial protest – all the human rights purists and so forth – but I think the general sentiment will be, 'Finally, we can get down to business with China.'"

"There will be a great deal in it for you once the dust settles," said Qian. "Although, I must say…"

"What's wrong?"

"The president did not seem as eager as we might have hoped."

"That's just his way," said the American. "Believe me, I've known the man for a long time. He has to mull things over; but don't you worry, somewhere inside that slow-moving ox is a tiny little beacon that sends a constant message to his brain, minute by minute, day in and day out."

"And what does that message say, Mister Kinder?"

"That message says, 'Survive! Survive at all costs, but survive!'"

JENNIFER ARRIVED at the Sheraton at ten-thirty in the evening. The president had not yet returned from his last campaign appearance following his speech, and so she asked to be allowed to wait for him in the presidential suite. She had been advised by a member of the president's staff that she should not expect him to be in the best of moods when he returned from the post-speech reception.

The president finally arrived at the hotel just after eleven. Instantly, Jennifer could see that his mood was dark. He was quiet and subdued.

Jennifer did her best to take his mind off the day. "Everything looks lovely - " she said. "The table, the décor, the place settings..."

He lurched toward her and planted an awkward kiss on her cheek. "Evening, m'dear." She could smell the alcohol on his breath. He plopped down in a chair. There was a knock on the door. "Who the hell is it?" he called out.

"Dinner is served, Mister President," came the reply.

Jennifer opened the door and a crew of hotel personnel brought in the dishes and set them out on the side table. "Oh, it smells wonderful," she exclaimed. "What is it?"

"Chateaubriand, ma'am, and a wonderful pinot noir," said the chef, as he directed his crew in setting out the elaborate dinner. "Will there be anything else, ma'am?"

"No, I believe that will do quite nicely. Thank you."

The president addressed the steward. "Gimme a glass of that wine before you go."

"Yes, Mister President."

"A big glass; yessir, fill 'er right up. Don't be stingy. Oh, hell, just gimme the whole bottle." He took it from the steward. "Now I don't want to be disturbed. Do you understand? Capiche?

Comprendez-vous?"

"Yes, Mister President."

When they were alone, Jennifer tried valiantly to pretend that everything was normal. "Well, it all looks so wonderful," she said. "Shouldn't we sit over here and try some of it? Surely you must be hungry, Mister President."

"At the moment, my needs are thirst-related. My needs, one might say, are spiritual. So bring on the spirits – the wine, the nectar of grape, ambrosia of the gods." He took a gulping swig and set his glass down. "Damn them. Damn them all. The Three Stooges. Damn the Three Stooges. I'm supposed to have a political adviser who actually understands politics; but does he? Does he know anything about politics?"

"That would be Mister Phillips?"

"Phony Tony, that's what I call him." He had already downed one glass of the wine and he sloppily poured himself another, half of which he downed almost as fast. "You can't believe a word he says. And Arnulf Kinder. Such a lousy, money-grubbing, self-centered fatcat; just out for himself."

He finished the glass, stood up, picked up the bottle, and strutted about the room. "And then there's our lordly vice president. Oh, how great he is in his own mind! So self-righteous, so sure of himself. The great He Who Walks On Water. The Great Disdainer of the ordinary ways of all us mortals. Who put him in the position he's in? I put him there! So who in truth is the great one?"

She felt terribly uncomfortable; this was not turning out at all the way she had expected. "Would you like to sit down and have something to -"

"They're all leeches, leeching off my reputation, my position," he said, lifting the bottle to his lips and guzzling it straight. He lowered the bottle and wiped his mouth with his coat sleeve. "They all use me for their own purposes. Do you see it? Do you see it? I ask you now, do you see it?"

"Well, I..."

"Oh, don't try to defend those weasels," he countered just before taking another big slurping gulp of the wine and then setting the bottle down. "Please, give me a little credit that I know what I'm talking about. You think Ferguson doesn't want my job? He would kill for my job. Sure, he comes across as some modern day Saint Mark – all noble and restrained and loyal-seeming...seeming, I said – but he's plotting. I know he's plotting. He'll find a way if he can, you watch him. It will be President Ferguson, and Vacuum Cleaner Salesman Ed Billingsley. You watch. You mark my word. You 'Mark' my word. You 'Mark Ferguson' my word. Fark Merguson, your Kiwanis-stamp-of-approval president, your board-certified waterwalker. Oh, President Merguson, may I call you Fark? May I fall on your carcass, Fark? I'll have one carcassfark of your starkest fodder, Mrs. Farquhar, and make that 'to go.'" And with that, he flopped face down on the couch.

Jennifer got up immediately and went to check on him. "Mister President, are you OK?"

He rolled over and tried to kick off his shoes; she ended up helping him do that. "Don't get me started; I'm just getting started. And take Arnulf Kinder – please! Everything for the Almighty Dollar. Let us bow down and worship thee, O thou great and holy Dollar! To Thee alone we sing our hymn of praise, glorifying in Thee, reveling in Thee, making Thee to be manifest and ever-present in our wallet and in our bank account.

"No compunction about morality, or the needs of the people of this country. None. It's all, 'What's in it for me?' Do you think I don't see that? Well, do you?"

"Yes, Mister President. Whatever you say." She was trying to loosen his tie; it had gotten twisted around his neck.

"Oh, don't patronize me with your patronizing... patronization. If I wanted your opinion I would have asked for it. Phony Tony...why on earth did I ever hire him? Mister Opportunism! Mister Anything to Make Tony Phillips Look Good.'"

She helped him off with his coat.

"I like you, Jezebel."

"It's Jennifer."

"I like you anyway. I trust you. You're straight up with me. No games. It's all, 'This is what I like, Mister Prez, this is what I want.' Straightforward. It's a great quality. Don't ever change. You are the embodiment of perfection. And may I just say, what a fine little embodiment you have there."

"Thank you, Mister President. Here, why don't we have a glass of water?"

"I trr-usht you," he continued. "You're different from all the others. And I not jusht saying that. You're different from all the kowtowing, sycophantic power-mad hustlers I meet every day."

"Well, one of the ways to get all of that off your mind is to – "

"You want to know about my marriage, don't you? That's what you secretly want to know about, isn't it? All of my girlfriends want to know the secret of what happened there. Not to mention the whole country. Well, do you want to know or not?"

"No, it's not really my concern."

"I'll be happy to tell you." He sat up and took another frothy swill from his drink; he refilled his glass to the brim and beyond; the overflow went directly to the carpet. "She says – and this is a direct quote – she says I'm a mean drunk. I don't think I'm a mean drunk. Do you think I'm a mean drunk?"

"Not so far. Not mean, exactly; a little bitter, perhaps."

"Who wouldn't be bitter? With the right people around me, I could have been a great president. Some people think I'm through, did you know that? Have you heard that on the street? Some people think I'm going to lose the election. Why? Because of California. I'm going to lose California."

"I didn't think it was definite one way or the other."

"Oh, in some people's minds it's quite definite. Lemme explain the facts of life to you, Jezebel. Not those facts of life, the political facts of life. You see, when a major state such as California loses a major piece of industrial business, they have to have a politician to blame. It's a law; I'm sure it's actually on the books. I think it reads: if you lose a profitable enterprise in your state, find the most prominent politico you can reasonably lay the blame on, and blame away. Do not vote for that person again. So you see, Kinder lost the Chinese passenger aircraft business. Kinder is closely associated – in the public mind – with me. Ergo – and thusly therefore – to wit, ipso facto and videlicet – California will vote against me, and I will lose the general election. Clear as a drum?"

"I'm sorry, I didn't realize things were that bad."

"They think I'm defeated, but they may be in for a *lit-tle* surprise." He stood up and walked over to the couch located underneath the window. "In the not too distant future, we will be in California, we will. And in Los Angeles, things will turn around. There I'll take my stand." He managed to step up on the couch and he balanced himself on the cushions.

"Mister President, please come down from there!"

"Remember Kennedy's speech at the Berlin Wall? No, you're far too young for that."

He began speaking in a remarkably accurate Kennedy accent. "There are some who say that Ed Billingsley is washed up. Let them come to Los Angeles! There are some who say that Ed Billingsley cannot win the general election in his own right. *Lasst sie nach Los Angeles kommen.* Let them come to Los Angeles! There are some who say, Ed Billingsley has let things slip away from him. And I say, let them come to Los Angeles."

"Mister President, please! You're swaying back and forth. Oh dear!"

The kennedyesque speech continued. "Two thousand years ago, the proudest boast was '*civis Romanus sum.*' Today, in the world of partisan politics, the proudest boast is '*Ich bin ein Losangeliener!*'"

"Mister President, I think you've had a little too much too drink," she pleaded. "Please get down from there. If you don't, I'll have to get help."

He took her hand and stepped down to the floor. "'Ee-ask not what yoah country can dew fo' yew, ee-ask what yew can do fo' yoah country!' That's from the inauguration speech. Do you remember that one?"

"Yes, I do know that one, but – "

He staggered over to the desk which had been provided for him. He sat behind it and picked up the phone. "Attorney General's Office, please. Yee-uss. Say Bobby, I understand that

Ethel and Jackie will be at the spa-hr for the weekend. What say you and I round up a few chicks and we go skinny-dipping in the White House swimming pool. And see if Martin King can send over a few girls; I wouldn't mind integrating with some of that brown suga-hr, if you gather my drift."

He stood and pointed directly at her, his arms wobbly. "Now there was a president! Staring down the Soviet Union, staring down Big Steel, staring down the Southern governors and all the while he had the most alluring women in the country traipsing through the White House, just like on a treadmill. And the secret? He had good people around him. People who knew how to look out for his interests.

"Not like my people – self-serving, back-stabbing, uncoordinated, narcissistic, infantile, greedy, self-righteous…not like Tony Phillips. Not like Fark Merguson."

He picked up the empty bottle and threw it against the window. The bottle shattered, sending glass everywhere. "Not like Arnulf Kinder."

At the sound of the breaking glass, the doors to the suite flew open and the Secret Service intervened. There were half a dozen of them. Four of them grabbed the president and helped him to his room. Bill Robinson and one other agent took Jennifer gently by the arm. "Miss Jiang, why don't we call it an evening?"

JENNIFER AWOKE early, deeply bothered by the president's bizarre behavior of the evening before. She hardly knew how she would face him, or what she expected him to say about the whole episode. She half expected him to dismiss her from the campaign, just so that he might avoid being reminded of the incident. But then again, maybe not; it was entirely possible, she supposed, that he had little recollection of it all.

She had to laugh about it; if only she had had a means to record the evening on film, she could have sold it to a television station for a fortune.

Her first visitors of the day were neither – as she had half-expected – the Secret Service nor were they members of the president's campaign staff. Instead, she found herself on the receiving end of a phone call summoning her to a suite of rooms six floors above her own floor.

The caller spoke with a perfect Beijing accent, and he identified himself as Deputy Minister Qian. She dressed hurriedly, and arrived at the designated suite a half-hour after receiving the call.

"We are very, very pleased to meet you," said Qian, grinning broadly as he introduced himself and his fellow officials. "All of the senior leadership of the party are quite pleased that you have done so well. To have gained the confidence and trust of the president, and in so short a period of time – this is quite remarkable."

"Thank you."

"But then, members of your family seem to find their way to the top with great regularity," added the minister. "Your uncle Song Bei, as you know, has recently been appointed to the State Council."

She had only recently been made aware of that development, through the good offices of the consul general. "Yes, the family always believed that my uncle would succeed to a very high position." He never had any compunction about clawing his way to the top, she thought to herself.

"Many people believe that he will one day become the premier," added a second official, who stood next to Qian. "Undoubtedly, your ability to influence events here in the United States will reflect very favorably on your uncle."

"I hope I may be a credit to him," she said through nearly-clenched teeth. She waited for them to continue, but they merely stood there, beaming at her. "What can I do for you gentlemen?" she said at last.

"Ah, yes!" exclaimed Qian. "Yes, the reason for our visit: we would like for you to use your influence with the president…"

"My influence?"

"Last evening, I approached the president with a very important offer. Has he mentioned it, by chance?"

"He came back to his room very late last night," she explained, "and very tired. He just wanted to relax." She left out the part about the drunken rant.

The officials smiled knowingly at one another, and then

Qian turned back to Jennifer. "Perhaps his fatigue would explain why he was not anxious to make a decision when I spoke to him. Well, then, perhaps we should give you the basic terms of our offer – just in case he may not remember them."

Now here was something worth hearing! What terms, what deal had these high-ranking Chinese officials given to the president of the United States the evening before? She remained placid in her demeanor. "If you like...I'd be most happy to learn of these terms, in the event that the president wishes to discuss the matter."

They were more than happy to tutor her, and mentioned the reversal of the airplane deal, and the redirection of the aircraft carrier and the fighter wing. They did not go into the reasons behind this offer.

"It seems like a reasonable proposition," she said when they were done. "And you want me to use my influence with the president in order to get him to accept these terms?"

"You would have the undying gratitude of your country," said Qian.

"Very well," she said. "I'll do my best."

An hour later, Jennifer was summoned to the president's suite. "You wished to see me, sir?"

The great man was half-sitting up on his bed, wearing a robe. He had a large ice-pack on his head, and was drinking something intended to settle his stomach. "I feel as though I owe you an apology for my behavior."

"It was not exactly as billed," she said, "but it was definitely interesting."

"I'm sorry," he said. "It was a rough evening for me. Well, I can make it up to you, can't I? As soon as we wrap things up in Los Angeles, you'll come to the White House and I'll show you a first class evening."

"If you like, Mister President."

"Call me Ed."

"Fine. Mister Ed – I mean Ed."

He picked up the front section of the *New York Times* and

waved it around. "All this trouble in the Middle East…It worries me, you know…"

"Trouble?" she inquired. "Something happened in the Middle East? I hadn't heard."

"Oh, yes. There was a killing there recently…and a bus was vandalized."

"A bus?"

"The Middle East," he sighed. "It's always been a very volatile part of the world. I don't think we worry enough about the flow of oil through the Arabian Sea. I sometimes think we've pulled back from that area a little too radically. I sometimes think, well, what if something happened, would we have the forces in place to deal with any problem?"

"I don't know; would we?"

"I think we need another carrier in the Mediterranean," he said. "You just never know when that oil situation is going to get out of hand again."

He threw the paper down on the floor and tried to stand. "Well, my speech in Los Angeles is only a week away. When we get to Phoenix, I guess I'll be making a few changes to it."

## Chapter 36

Shi Men, China. Jin Yi-bo awoke in his new cell. It had been a rough journey from Harbin, but he had made it, and he would live, thanks to the Red Cross.

But now he had another problem to deal with. Almost as soon as he had arrived, he had been sent to the prison administrator's offices. There he had been asked to read a few pages out of a book. They saw that he could read extremely well and so they made him a clerk in the office of the prison administrator.

He was to report at seven in the morning and was to work until five. He was not going to be working in the fields, after all.

But if he could not work in the fields, he could not be rescued.

# CHAPTER 37

And lo! it came to pass that the president of the United States did travel unto the fabled city of Los Angeles, as had been foretold. Yea, verily, before the assembled multitudes of ye party faithful, did the Embattled One prophesy that the Great Airplane Passenger Deal, long since believed forsaken, had been raised from the dead and was made whole once again.

And it was good; it was very good, in fact, for said multitudes of ye party faithful were right joyous and, filled with the spirit of hosannas, did raise a great cry of jubilation, saying unto all who came unto them, "Praise be unto our president, for he hath shown unto the nation a unique and uncanny ability to pull yon rabbit out of yon hat when the need doth arise."

And it was cool.

JENNIFER WAS on the phone to Major Chen almost as soon as the president's speech was over. "I suppose you heard the president's announcement," she said.

"Every word of it. Obviously, he's agreed to redirect the carrier and the planes out of the Pacific sphere. The Chinese save face, and the president saves his – hold on; I've got another call."

He came back to her a few minutes later. "There's been a

development."

"What do you mean?" she said.

"There's a sub which is getting ready to deploy from Taiwan. They have room to take the commandos, but the authorization hasn't been given."

That statement created enormous anxiety in her. "I'm doing the best I can," she said. "I can't put a gun to their heads and make them spill all their secrets."

"I'm not complaining," said the major. "You've found out some interesting things, and you're getting to know all the right people. I've passed along everything you've given me; everything goes to the Presidential Palace in Taipei. Just continue to follow up, talk to people. What's it all about? Let's try to piece all this together. Get us something we can use, and I might be able to get those commandos on that sub."

"I'll try," she said wearily. "By the way, have we confirmed that Jin Yi-bo has arrived safely in Shi Men?"

"I'll confirm that for you," he replied. "I'll get back to you as soon as I can."

When she got to her hotel room that evening, Jennifer was surprised to receive a message from Ji Wan Li, the consul general. He had asked that she come to his offices the next morning.

She woke up early, dressed conservatively, and made her way to the Los Angeles Industrial Trade Building, where her voyage of espionage had begun not too many weeks before.

This time, she was ushered into his office and she found that his demeanor was entirely different. He was beaming at her. "Little Jiang!"

"Honorable Consul General," she replied. She noted the presence of Arnulf Kinder in the room as well. She was quite surprised to see him.

"Jiang Ou," said the consul, "I want to congratulate you."

"Congratulate me? For what?"

"Don't be coy with me, Little Jiang. You know perfectly well that you had a hand in getting the president to go along with our offer. He took a much shorter time to make his decision than we were expecting. Obviously you helped him understand the benefits of reelection."

She could not honestly claim credit for the president's decision, but she would not correct the consul general. "The president is a very pragmatic man."

"But why should any of us be surprised?" said Ji Wan Li. "Did I not choose you for this very role? Was it not I who saw your potential – your ability to vault into any social circle, meet with people at any level?"

"I am quite grateful for the confidence you have placed in me, Honorable Consul General."

Arnulf Kinder approached her and offered his congratulations as well. "When do you go back to Washington?" he asked.

"The president asked me to visit him in the White House as soon as the campaign returns to the East Coast."

"Listen, why don't you come out to my estate this weekend?" he suggested quietly. "You can relax, enjoy yourself. You've been traveling around the country for a couple of weeks now, living in hotel rooms; that must be getting a little tiresome."

He didn't have to ask twice; of course she would go. If Arnulf Kinder were this closely allied with the Chinese, he must know everything that was going on. And if the president had been manipulated into something, then Arnulf Kinder must be fully aware of what was happening. Just as importantly, they all seemed to believe that *she* knew what was going on. She didn't, but they thought that she did, and that was all that mattered.

She would go, of course, hoping against hope that she could keep up the charade without getting caught. And if she could find out more of what Arnulf Kinder knew, perhaps those commandos could be aboard the submarine when it sailed.

ARNIE KINDER lived like an emperor. He owned a stunning estate which was located on a cliff overlooking the ocean about fifty miles north of Los Angeles. The limousine which brought Jennifer up from Los Angeles passed through the guarded gates of the estate, and the vehicle made its way to the mansion by way of a beautifully landscaped mile-long paved driveway.

She was met at the front of the mansion by a butler, who escorted her into the palatial house. As she walked through the cavernous foyer, she glanced from side to side and scanned the rooms which she passed.

She was astounded by the extravagance of the place. Money dripped from the walls in the form of priceless artwork. Money oozed from the floors in the form of vast Indian rugs. Money sprawled about the rooms in the form of hideously expensive furnishings and sculpture. Money, money everywhere.

Finally, after walking the equivalent of a city demiblock, she was shown into a room which appeared to be a study. Books lined the walls, and maps and globes were placed throughout the room.

Kinder was waiting for her, dressed in tennis clothes. He was still excited about the role she was playing – or the role he *thought* she was playing – a role which he believed to be serving his ambitions. "Super job," he said. "Really, I mean that. Super job with the president. We're all quite impressed with you."

"Thank you."

"No, I'm serious," he insisted. "I was told you had a gift, the ability to go to any level – and it's true. I'll be completely honest with you. I didn't think the president was going to redeploy that carrier and those planes. He's so cautious about everything – scared of his own shadow; but you pulled it off, there's no question about that."

"It wasn't as difficult as you might think."

"False modesty doesn't impress me, young lady; I think you should tout your accomplishments."

"Fine. In the future, I will."

"Now, I was told that you were filled in on everything in Kansas City," he said, fixing a drink for himself and one for her. "Personally, I think they kept you in the dark for far too long – against my advice, I might add. I was in favor of telling you everything from Day One. I mean, if you're going to play in the game, you need to know what the score is, am I right?"

"Oh, definitely. I think it's so important that one know the score."

He handed her drink to her. "But others saw it differently. I think they would agree with me now that you could have handled all the information we could have given you."

"If they had handed me the playbook, I definitely would have read it."

"Yes, you do your homework, I can see that," he said. "You and I – we think exactly alike. I like that. I like to talk to people who are on my wavelength; intuitive; sure-footed. What do you think of the idea with the missiles?"

She had no idea what he was talking about. "Oh! The missiles – well, I think that will prove to be a formidable idea...the missiles...yes."

"Very, very intuitive of you. See – same wavelength. The missiles were my idea. Put that factory right there in Pakistan. Get the best technology. The connection to the president – all of it. My idea, too. And Mister Al-Houb. I've known the president a long time; so I know most of the people he knows. And then Pakistan, of course. And why not? Perfect place, right?"

"I couldn't agree more." She had no idea what he was talking about; she just hoped she could remember all the allusions he was making.

"We won't use them of course – that would be counterproductive. No, they'll just keep tinkering with them, adding some parts here, some parts there, and then one day we'll find a way to leak the information to the world, and somehow it all gets connected to the president and well, all hell will break loose. It'll be great, won't it?"

"I can't wait."

"Not soon enough if you ask me. Well, then, what do you plan to do when all of this is over?"

When all *what* was over? "I hadn't thought that far in advance."

"Next spring is not that far away; may I make a suggestion?"

"Please."

"I could use someone like you on my team. With your connections to China – everyone keeps saying your uncle will be premier one day – and with all the business opportunities opening up, I think you and I could make a pretty good team."

"I appreciate the offer."

"You don't have something going with the president, now do you?"

"Uh...no, not exactly; friendly, of course."

"Of course," he said with a wink. "Well, you don't have to tell me. You want my advice?"

"Of course."

"Never back a loser."

"OK, LET'S SEE if we've got this straight," said a rather amazed Major Chen. "Next spring something is going to happen and it will involve some missiles which aren't going to be fired. They're in Pakistan, but they belong to the Chinese.

"However," the major continued, "when the information about the non-firable missiles is leaked, it's going to ruin the president and all hell will break loose. Also, there's going to be one fewer carrier in the Far East and one fewer air wing, but the Americans will be building passenger aircraft for the Chinese. Any idea what all this means?"

"None whatsoever," she said. "What do you make of it?"

"I'm wondering what the Chinese are really up to."

"What do you mean?"

"Well, normally, when China and Pakistan get together, you can pretty much assume they're up to no good," he explained. "In the diplomatic community, China is regarded as the four hundred pound ex-convict that nobody wants to tangle with and Pakistan is like the weird little guy who sits down in his basement all day and reads books on how to blow stuff up. You really don't want those two spending much time together."

"I didn't realize that. Well, what should be done?"

"I need to notify Taipei immediately. I'm sure they'll want to check out this factory. You might have done yourself some good, Little Jiang. If we can piece together what all this means, it might amount to something. And I suppose that if it amounts to something, then the commandos can be given the green light to go."

## 38

Otsiru Kawagaki had been in training for nearly a year. After being denied tenure in the Department of Art History at UCLA, he had decided to return to Japan in order to become a Buddhist monk. The training had been arduous, bone-wearying, and all-consuming. He had left his former life behind, and had had no contact with it for many months.

Finally, he had been accepted into the novitiate ranks of the monastery located outside of Nagano. He was then allowed a short break in order to return to his hometown of Tokyo in order to settle his affairs before beginning his new life.

His mail had been piling up in his parent's home for many months. He went through it, discarding most of it without a care.

Finally, he came to one which caught his interest. It was from the Student Records Office at UCLA. He opened it and read. It was a simple request. They merely wanted to know whether he had ever taught a student by the name of Jiang Ou.

If he had information on the matter, he could send it to them or he could directly contact the Secret Service in Washington.

The Secret Service! That was most intriguing. He had to think. From the ascetic regimen imposed upon him over the many months just past, his mind was remarkably clear, and yet he could not recall a student by the name of Jiang Ou. Still, it had been a long time since he had been in the classroom. It was possible he was simply overlooking someone whom he would recall quite well if his memory could only be jogged. He would need to check his class records.

Unfortunately, they were in storage. For UCLA, he would perhaps not go to so much trouble as to search for the records; but for the American Secret Service…well, that was different.

JIN YI-BO had been working in the prison administrator's office for three mornings now. He had grown increasingly desperate to find a way to join the field worker details, but it was made quite clear to him that his personal interests were of no concern to those who ran the prison.

And therefore it came as a surprise to him, on his third morning at work in the office, to find himself being addressed by a supervisory official whom he had seen coming in and out of the administrative offices from time to time.

"What are you doing here, my friend?" said the tall, quiet man.

Jin Yi-bo looked up. "I beg your pardon?"

"Shouldn't you be out in the fields, working with the others?"

"I was assigned to the office," the prisoner replied.

"I see that you were," said the man in a friendly tone as he repeated the question, this time more slowly. "But shouldn't you be out in the fields, working with the others?"

"Perhaps I would have preferred the open air and the exercise," said Jin Yi-bo, beginning only now to understand his questioner, "but this is where I was assigned."

"I'm sure you do quite good work," said the official. "However, I'm even more sure there would be many advantages to being in the fields. Why, you never know when some great whale may land on the nearby shore, and take you away to far and distant places…"

Jin Yi-bo managed a slight smile. This man, whoever he was, knew of his plight and his predicament. There was a network of people working carefully, quietly, and in subtle ways, to see that he got out of China.

Jin Yi-bo could only reply truthfully. "Given the opportunity, I would be happy to work in the fields."

The man paused and then spoke with quiet confidence. "Don't worry; I will see to it."

## Chapter 39

When the campaign finally returned to the East Coast, Nick had some unfinished business to take care of; it had taken him weeks to find out when ex-marine Grant Benning would be back in Philadelphia. When he did finally come back, Nick paid a visit, with the Salivator in tow.

Nick found Benning's parents' row house in South Philadelphia with little trouble, and the young man himself answered the door.

"Grant Benning?"

The young man was clearly surprised to see the young officers, both present and former. "Say, you're Lieutenant Ferguson! Sorry about your career, sir."

"Thanks, Benning. Look, you got a minute? We need to talk."

Benning looked around and then stepped out onto the stoop. "OK. What's up?"

"Mind if I ask what you were doing in the Uniqraft trailer on the night of February Twenty-sixth?" said Nick. "As I understand it, you were lured away from your post by Rhonda Clement."

The young man was taken aback. "'Tenant, I ain't in the service no more; and neither are you, for that matter."

"I see; well, then, apparently you haven't read your discharge papers."

He tensed slightly. "What are you talking about, Lieutenant?"

"It always pays to read the fine print. I'm referring to Article Seven, Section Twenty-nine of the Uniform Code of Military Justice which provides that any member of the armed services who is suspected of having been involved with a crime while on active duty may be recalled to active duty for the specific purpose of giving evidence or being himself subject to prosecution. Didn't your gunny sergeant go over all of that with you at the time of your discharge?"

"Gunny didn't explain nothin' to me like that."

"Well, he should have."

The young man shrugged. "OK, fine. I'll talk." He sat down on the stoop in front of the row house and lit a cigarette. "It was Mike Taylor with Uniqraft. He set the whole thing up. Told me if I wanted to use his trailer, he would be working on one of the planes and he would keep an eye on things. I figured that was all right since the only reason to have a marine guard on duty is if nobody's around; but if somebody's around working on the planes, that's different, the way I saw it."

"And did you see him working on any of the planes?"

"Well, when me and Rhonda left the trailer, we walked over to my post together."

"And he was working on a plane. Whose plane?"

"Yours."

Nick and the Salivator were heading back to Washington a short time later. "Is that true about his discharge status?" asked DiSalvo. "About being subject to recall to active duty?"

"Not that I know of."

"He seemed to believe it readily enough."

"So he did, Salivator; so he did."

It took Nick an entire afternoon to find Uniqraft senior technician Mike Taylor. He was living in – what else? – a trailer, which was located in a lonely, desolate area in rural Eastern Maryland.

Nick drove to the location by himself and wandered around the property for a while, calling Taylor's name. He checked his watch. The Salivator was supposed to have met him in the little one-horse town of Dawson about two miles back, but his wingmate had never shown up and so Nick had come on his own.

After a few minutes of calling, a wiry, fiftyish man came around the end of the trailer and stopped.

"Mike Taylor?"

"Yes? Who is that?" The man was squinting.

"It's Nick Ferguson."

He finally recognized the ex-pilot and sauntered forward. "Well, well. Imagine you coming all the way out here. I'm honored indeed. What can I do for you, Lieutenant?"

"You can tell me what you were doing to my plane on the night of February Twenty-sixth."

He laughed. "Lieutenant, we used to work on those planes around the clock. How would I remember what I was doing on a particular night?"

"Let me see if I can aid your memory. It was the same night you allowed Corporal Grant Benning – who was on guard duty at the time – to meet his girlfriend Rhonda Clement in your trailer for about a half-hour. I have three witnesses – Grant and Rhonda and one other. Care to corroborate their stories?"

Taylor was very quiet. "Oh, I don't know what I could possibly add to all of that."

"You could tell me what you were up to, for starters."

"I ain't gotta tell you nothing, Lieutenant." He turned and walked to his door.

But Nick Ferguson wasn't leaving empty handed. He had lost too much, been through too much, to give up now. He grabbed Taylor by the arm. "Look, my friend, I want to know what you did to my plane."

"Hey, take it easy!" He tried to pull away, but Nick yanked him from the steps and shoved him roughly against the side of the trailer, with his forearm on his neck. "Talk!"

"I can't breathe!"

"Talk!"

Taylor swung around and hit Nick in the stomach. Nick grabbed him by the collar and slammed his head into the trailer wall. Taylor dropped down, picked up a loose board, and swung it at Nick, hitting him on the side of the head. Nick felt dizzy and nearly blacked out. He looked up and saw the board coming around again. He ducked and body-slammed Taylor, who fell. Nick jumped on top of him and shoved his head into the dirt. "Talk!"

"Lieutenant, you're crazy!"

"Oh, truer words were never spoken," Nick said in a hoarse whisper. "So crazy, in fact, that I might just say to hell with it and break every bone in your body. That's what I *might* do; what I'd prefer to do is just get the pure unadulterated truth out of you and let you live."

Taylor knew he couldn't break the younger man's hold. "I was told to stand by for special instructions that might or might not be coming in," he said. "I was told to get the guard away from his post."

"What do you mean 'special instructions'?"

"I was told to photograph the wiring in the avionics of your plane."

"Now why would someone want you to do that?"

"No idea."

"What's so special about the wiring in my plane?"

"Every plane is slightly different, depending on the repairs and modifications that we've done."

"Did anyone ever say what they wanted these photos for?"

"Lieutenant, I've worked for Uniqraft for over thirty years. They've always treated me well and I've learned over the years not to sit around questioning every decision."

Nick elbowed him in the jaw. "Not good enough!"

"It might have been a test they wanted to run," said Taylor, breathing hard. "It might have been a repair of some kind."

"It might have been for placing an explosive device or damaging a part in some way?"

"It might have been; but the point is the instructions never came. In fact, I got a code that said, 'Stand down. Nothing's going to happen. Test cancelled.'"

"Who sent the message to have you stand down that night?"

"Lieutenant, I've told you all I know."

"Who sent the message?" He slammed Taylor's head into the dirt.

"Jesus!" Taylor moaned.

"I don't think so; try again."

"All right, it was Kinder."

"Arnulf Kinder?"

"Yes-s-s."

Nick reached into his jacket and took out a portable recording device. "I want to tape your confession. Let's start from the beginning."

But just before he pressed the play button, he saw that Mike Taylor was looking at the edge of the tree line. Nick followed Taylor's gaze, and saw two large men lumbering across the dusty yard towards them. Slowly, he got up off the ground, and Mike Taylor did the same.

The men approached within ten feet, and one of them spoke. "Something the matter, Pops?"

"Nick," said Taylor, as he stood and dusted himself off, "I'd like you to meet my sons, Junior and Tiny. Boys, this is ex-Lieutenant Nick Ferguson. Don't hurt him too bad, boys; his old man is vice president and we don't need us any congressional investigation."

Junior was every bit of three hundred pounds; and he was the baby of the family. Tiny was the one with all the heft. Junior lumbered toward Nick, who tried to make a run for his car. At his car door, he was grabbed by the collar and thrown to the ground. Tiny reached down and picked him back up. Nick took a swing, connected to Tiny's jaw, and sprained his hand in the process.

Tiny dropped him and kicked him on the way to the ground. Nick tried to crawl away, but Junior kneed him in the face, and the blood started flowing. Tiny kicked him several times in the ribs.

Just as the bell rang for the second round, the Salivator came tearing up in his car. He saw the condition Nick was in, and he reached for his service revolver which he carried on the front seat of his car. He stepped out of his car and fired into the air. Everyone froze and stared at him.

"The next round goes into your gut, Tubby," said the Salivator, approaching the fight scene. "And you'd be awful hard to miss."

The Taylors, pere et fils, backed away from the Salivator as he assumed a shooter's stance and aimed his revolver at chest height and pointed it at each man in turn. Slowly, Nick got up, picked the tape recorder up off the ground, and made his way to his car. When Nick was safely away from the area, the Salivator backed up his own car, turned around, and followed Nick back to town.

By the time they got back to the Washington area, Nick was starting to reel from the pain and swelling. The Salivator wanted to get the Secret Service involved, but Nick protested loudly. He wasn't about to have another media frenzy.

Nick transferred into the Salivator's car, and they rolled slowly through the back alleys of Georgetown, arriving just after dark behind Ellen Conley's apartment. The Salivator helped Nick up the back stairs, and they knocked on the door just as Ellen and Greg were having dinner. Tom Yancey was their guest for the evening.

Ellen was appalled at the sight of Nick's black eyes and swollen mouth. She immediately came to his aid, providing a couch, ice packs, ointments, bandages, pillows, aspirin and whatever else came to mind.

Greg was proud of Nick for showing up unannounced with genuine war injuries. "It's Nicko Ferguson!" he exclaimed. "Shot down six German planes, wounded in sixteen places, but he's gonna pull through!"

"Seventeen places," said Nick.

Tom Yancey volunteered to do nothing; rather, he grew

increasingly annoyed with the attention given to his ex-rival. "Well, this is absurd," he exclaimed. "Let's just call the Secret Service, and have them come and take care of him."

"Don't touch that phone, Tom," said Ellen tersely, as Greg hovered nearby.

"Well, I think you have my feelings to consider, Ellen. Bringing another man in here, taking care of him like this…"

"Right now, Tom, your feelings are not my highest priority."

"And what is? Your feelings for Nick?"

"No, I didn't say that. Right now I'm most interested in avoiding a scandal that would cause a problem for the admiral. He always treated me decently; and so I intend to keep this little problem away from the media and under wraps, even if Nick has to stay here for a week."

"Well, I appreciate your very fine motive, but the fact remains that you are placing your concerns for another man ahead of my wishes; and so I say, either he goes or I do."

"Well, in that case, Tom, I believe you know where the door is."

## CHAPTER 40

Buddhist-monk-in-training Otsiru Kawagaki had traveled several miles from his parents' apartment in downtown Tokyo to a storage facility where many of his personal belongings were kept.

He spent the morning going through a number of boxes, until he finally came to the one which contained his academic papers from the days when he taught art history.

He found all of his class rollbooks, stacked and bound in the bottom of the box. He sat down on a trunk and went through every page of every rollbook, looking for the name of Jiang Ou. He amazed himself that he was able to recall the face of every student who was listed in his rolls, and he could even picture exactly where that student had sat in the classroom.

It took him twenty minutes to go through all of the rollbooks, and then another twenty minutes to double check himself. After that time, he was forced to admit that there was no question about it: he had never taught anyone by the name of Jiang Ou.

# CHAPTER 41

As Pakistan was known to be an occasional philosophical ally of China, the Taiwanese government had always maintained a staff of operatives working in Islamabad, along with an extensive list of sympathetic contacts who despised the autocratic power of their country's government.

The discovery of a factory outfitting American-made missiles became at once the only priority of that secret and clandestine force.

Despite the agrarian base of the country's economy, the fact was that there were hundreds of buildings across the land which were large enough to be used for such a purpose. And so it was that, throughout the next few nights and days, men and women and, in some cases, children, found their way into these buildings and tried their best to determine the activity being conducted there.

In some cases, access to these buildings was easy; in other cases, ingenuity was required. Sometimes an activity as simple as the mistaken delivery of goods would be sufficient to allow the agent to determine the nature of the business.

After a period of six days and nights of continuous work, all but three buildings in the entire country of Pakistan had been eliminated as suspects by the Taiwanese agents and their Pakistani accomplices. Those three buildings were subject to round-the-clock surveillance. Those who left the building were trailed, their identities ascertained, and the nature of their employment determined.

In time, the first of the three unknown buildings revealed itself to be a site used for the piracy of American musical recordings. Interesting enough, but not a pressing matter at the moment. The second building proved out to be a governmental laboratory used for testing military protective equipment. No planes in sight.

The third building proved to be the charm. A truck approaching the building had broken down in the gathering heat of Pakistan's June weather. The driver had been assisted by a helpful young man who proved to be an adept mechanic. While the engine was being worked on, a second operative got into the truck and hid with the cargo. He managed to get photos of the interior of the plant and within hours they were on their way to Taipei.

## Chapter 42

Lieutenant and Mrs. Russell "The Salivator" DiSalvo were sleeping soundly in their Northern Virginia home which they had recently moved into. It was past midnight when the missus rocked her husband's shoulder. "Russell…! Wake up. I need you."

"I'm too tired right now, Jeannine," muttered the Salivator. "Let's wait 'til in the morning."

"Not that, you idiot!" she said, kicking him awake. "I think it's time for the baby."

He bolted upright in bed. "Oh, my god!"

He had her in the car and roaring towards Bethesda Naval Hospital within minutes. By the time they arrived, Jeannine's labor had subsided, but she was so far overdue that they knew it was a matter of hours at the most.

The Salivator had put a call in to Nick, and he showed up, with Jennifer, Ellen, and Gregory in tow, just as Jeannine was being wheeled into the delivery room. The father-to-be had donned a hospital gown, and he followed the delivery team close behind.

He was a Big Help during the delivery itself. "Look lively there, mates!" he called out to the doctor and senior nurse who were running the show. They rewarded him with dirty looks and told him to stand a few feet away.

Which he didn't. As Jeannine went into a major contraction, the Salivator was right by her side. "Just give it some forward throttle, baby!"

Then he moved around to where all the action was so he could be there for the big event. He stuck his head in between the doctor and the nurse. "Come about starboard, ten degrees!"

"Russell, will you shut up!" yelped Jeannine just after a major contraction.

"Yeah, Russell, shut up," said everyone else, pretty much at once.

He was so excited he couldn't control himself. "OK, now, full speed ahead! Bring it out of port, baby!"

The baby came a-flying, and the Salivator rejoiced with a rebel yell. "Let's check the stern!" he commanded the doctor. "Yep, she's a boy! And that makes me a dad!" He turned to the nurse. "Do you understand me? This has never, ever happened before!"

"We've seen it a few times, Lieutenant," the nurse replied blandly.

"Not to me, it hasn't? Cigar?" he offered.

"Don't even think about lighting that up in here," she threatened.

He strutted around the delivery room, unwrapped his cigar, stuck it in his mouth, and then glanced down and saw all the blood which he had somehow not noticed up until that precise moment. He started to turn white, and the nurse observed that he was a little shaky. "Are you OK, Lieutenant?" she asked. "You look a little pale."

"Steady as she goes," he replied just before he fainted dead away.

Twenty minutes later the nurse came into the waiting area, where the proud father was resting comfortably, surrounded by his friends. "Lieutenant," she said. "Your wife has a slightly irregular heartbeat, which we understand is a part of her medical history. So we want to keep her here for forty-eight hours, just for observation, and then she can go home. Now, if you would like to join your wife and son in her room, please follow me."

The Salivator invited the others, and they all walked in to see the newborn.

"Lieutenant, your son," said the nurse, placing the infant in his arms. "What do you wish to name him?"

"How about Torpedo?" he replied. "Did you see the way he shot out of there?"

"Put down Russell as the first name," said Jeannine groggily. The nurse did so. "And middle name?"

"The middle name will be Nicholas," declared the Salivator, shaking hands with his best friend.

The nurse turned to Jeannine. "Is Nicholas OK, Mrs. DiSalvo?"

"Nicholas is OK."

Everyone decided to hang out at the hospital as long as possible. Ellen and Jennifer took turns walking the hallways, carrying Torpedo in their arms.

Late in the afternoon of that day, Jennifer received a message on her pager. It was Major Chen. "Your lead turned out to be a pretty good one," he said when they spoke a few minutes later.

"What did they find?"

"A missile factory in Pakistan," he replied, "just as you said. We got a pretty good look at it. It's a special kind of missile, from what they can tell, designed to go high and bury deep into the ground before it explodes. They'll take out underground defense systems, which we have on the island; and because they have such a high arc, they go only a relatively short distance."

"Meaning they're perfect for lobbing over from the mainland towards Taiwan," she supposed.

"Right. The good news is that there didn't seem to be any completed or stockpiled missiles; they seem to be in the early stages of construction, which means it was great that we found out about this when we did – thanks to you. Now, let me ask you, did Kinder ever mention the name of someone named Aji Al-Houb?"

"Al-whom?"

"Al-Houb."

"Well, yes, now that you mention it, he did. When I was at his house, he was making reference to a number of things which I couldn't connect or halfway remember, but I do recall that he referred to someone named 'Mister Al-Houb' and he seemed to be implying that this guy was someone the president knew, and so that's how Kinder knew him. Why? Who is he?"

"A rather notorious international agent-for-hire," replied the major. "And I'll read you what they have on him: native Moroccan, more or less stateless, and has been so for a decade. Architect of several important political assassinations that they know of, and probably quite a few that they don't. Has at least three major felony warrants outstanding against him."

"How did they find out all of this, and where is he now?"

"Our agents had a long-range telephoto camera, and they photographed him coming out of the plant, sent the photos over the internet to Interpol, and Interpol identified him. Right now they're following him halfway around the world."

"Where is he going?"

"We'll know when he gets there. He does have an interesting itinerary: he left Islamabad Airport yesterday morning at ten sixteen a.m. Greenwich Mean Time on Flight Six Ten bound for Singapore. We had agents in place and waiting for him there. Met with a group of Chinese businessmen in the Singapore Marriott and he then took off once again for the airport. Changed into a disguise at this point.

"He was spotted leaving Singapore at three thirty-three GMT and he headed non-stop to Nairobi, Kenya. Once again, more meetings, another change of disguise.

"He arrived in Tel Aviv late yesterday and took a taxi out of town to a point thirty miles south of Tel Aviv. This is where the Qiryat Gat Manufacturing Facility is located. It's a joint Israeli-American high tech lab; they make computer chips for military applications. Here he met a contact about a mile outside the plant, in some little village café. As we speak he's on a flight from Tel Aviv to Paris; the flight lands in an hour. Interpol is prepared to pick him up for questioning under any of the murder charges, if President Liao gives the green light. And you say Kinder confirmed that President Billingsley knew him?"

"He seemed to be saying that. Why?"

"Al-Houb once worked for the CIA at a time when the director was Edward Billingsley."

"So has anyone figured out what this means yet?"

"It's hard to say, but whatever it is, it's starting to look like Billingsley had a hand in it. If they have Al-Houb picked up in Paris, they may be able to find out the answer to that question."

NICK ALSO received a phone call while he waited with the others in the hospital. It was from a Lieutenant Commander Teddy Rayburn, who flew the Super Hornet out of San Diego. Rayburn had been aware of the problems Nick had claimed to have with his flight control on the fateful night, and Rayburn had experienced much the same problems on a recent flight. As he had explained to Nick, he had been luckier and had managed to keep his plane out of the drink, but he felt that there was something wrong with the avionics systems which had nothing to do with pilot performance. Rayburn was more than willing to provide testimony in support of Nick, and offered to come to Washington in order to testify if necessary.

Nick asked Rayburn to write down everything, and told him that he would get in touch as soon as possible.

He could sense that the tables were at last turning. He decided that this would be an opportune time to pay a call on Arnulf Kinder, who had a suite of offices in Virginia. He drove south from Bethesda and headed west to Tyson's Corner. He found the twelve story glass-walled building where the East Coast offices of Uniqraft were housed. He entered the building and made his way to the penthouse floor. Arriving on the executive floor, he approached Kinder's secretary. "I'd like to see Arnie

Kinder, please."

"Your name?" she said, without looking up. "Oh, you're...Lieutenant Ferguson."

"The same," he replied, breezing right past her. "Is Arnie in his office?"

"He's in a meeting," she replied, standing up and following him. "Lieutenant Ferguson, you cannot just barge in like this...!"

But Nick Ferguson was a man on a mission; he pushed open the door to Kinder's office. It was the size of a small airplane hangar.

"I'm sorry, Mister Kinder," exclaimed his secretary. "I tried to stop him."

"What's the meaning of this, Ferguson?" demanded Kinder.

"Gosh, I don't know, Arnie," said Nick, sauntering into the room. He tossed the tape onto Kinder's desk. "What's the meaning of this?"

Kinder stared at the tape. "What is that?"

"It's a tape recording of a little chat I had with Mike Taylor, one of your employees. You just won't believe some of the things Mike told me; but don't take my word for it; listen to Mike explain it all."

Kinder grabbed it. "Let me have that." He broke the tape cassette and began pulling out the ribbon.

"Actually this is just a copy," said Nick. "There are numerous others which I've already made for the *New York Times* and the *Washington Post.* They could be in the mail this very evening. In fact, they will be. So you don't have to explain anything to me, Arnie. But consider this fair warning – along with my recommendation that you call in your entire public relations department; and I strongly recommend you get yourself a lawyer. You're definitely going to need one. "

# CHAPTER 43

Aji al-Houb was exhausted from his tricontinental trip just now ending. He was bleary-eyed and slightly disoriented. And so when members of the Metropolitan Police of Paris approached him in the airport lobby, they found him to be initially confused and offering no resistance. "Pardonnez-moi, monsieur," said one of the plainclothed gendarmes who took one of his arms. "Est-ce que vous avez un moment?"

They took Aji al-Houb to Interpol Headquarters on the outskirts of Paris, where they relieved him of the contents of his briefcase. Interpol's Chief Inspector du Martin was called in, and the analysts displayed for him their findings.

"Six microchips, of highest grade, appearing to originate in the Qiryat Gat Facility near Tel Aviv. Microchips designed for installation in missiles.

"Next, electronic files, showing electronically how the microchips would increase the accuracy of the missiles they were used in. All of the electronic projections show major Taiwanese cities as targets."

Chief Inspector du Martin was duly impressed. "I think we know what we have. It will be my duty to inform the president of France and obtain his approval for the release of this information."

The president of France was astounded by the report from Interpol. "Release it," he ordered, as soon as he had fully digested the meaning of it all.

His minister of state was more cautious. "But Monsieur le President, perhaps we should discuss this with the Americans before taking such a step."

The president of France was adamantly opposed to the idea. "I ask you, where was Edward Billingsley when we needed his help six months ago with respect to the import crisis? Completely unwilling and unable to make a decision. With no risk to himself, he could have helped me enormously, but did nothing. Now it is my turn; the facts which we shall release are clearly indisputable. Let him try to refute them; he gets no favors from France. Call our friend Monsieur Hebert."

Jacques Hebert was the most respected reporter working for *Le Monde,* which would be the first newspaper to break the story. When he arrived at Interpol, Hebert was shown all of the relevant information; he recognized the situation instantly for what it was: the scoop of a lifetime.

Missiles designed to attack with amazing precision any Taiwanese defense system.

The capability of reducing to rubble all of Taiwan's underground defense capabilities in a matter of days. The most stunning news of all was the connection of al-Houb to Edward Billingsley through his days at the CIA.

And so Jacques Hebert – as any so-informed reporter would – could easily piece together the notion that the president of the United States was the architect of a deal to put the military defense of Taiwan in jeopardy in return for a reversal of a major trade deal with China and his own reelection. If that were indeed the case, it was a travesty of the first magnitude.

The news of the apparent treachery flashed around the world. Every wire service picked up the story, and within hours the details were being dissected in London, Moscow, Tokyo and every other major world capital.

The arrest of al-Houb in Paris was given top story and headline coverage in Taiwan. President Liao of Taiwan made sure that all media on that island had complete access to the information. The president of that republic condemned the situation in the harshest possible terms, terming it a deep betrayal.

With the fear of a closer-than-previously-thought relationship between the United States and the People's Republic, Taiwan now knew that they had little else to rely on but themselves and world opinion.

China's State Council was as surprised as anyone to see these unexpected developments. The revelation of the factory in Pakistan and the role of Aji al-Houb had come about six months prematurely. Nevertheless, China had been planning for this eventuality for over fifty years. They were not as prepared as they would have been had they stuck to their timetable, but the basic simplicity of the invasion plan allowed for plenty of room for error.

The White House issued an immediate denial of the allegations, but it was hard to refute the objective facts in the matter.

The Chinese immediately countered the American denial by releasing the taped conversation between the president and Minister Qian. Copies of the tape were sent to all of the major broadcasting companies in the United States, Europe, and Asia. In the United States, there was an immediate attempt by the White House to suppress the release, but as soon as the tapes were released in the rest of the world, the effort to suppress American broadcasters ceased.

Selectively edited, the conversation on the tape was devastating to the White House. The president's credibility was destroyed, even though his claim of innocence with respect to the missile factory was valid.

The reaction of the people of Taiwan, aided and encouraged by elements of the TLA, was thunderous. Oblivious to the storm of armed paratroopers about to be unleashed on them, they directed their anger at the Americans. Within hours of hearing of the betrayal, protests formed in the streets of Taipei. As there was no American embassy to complain to, the offices of numerous American corporations were inundated with phone calls.

The protests turned into anti-American demonstrations such as had never before been seen in Asia.

In Taipei, General Bai was notified by Beijing that the Liberation of Taiwan was on, and that he and his people were to do everything they had planned on doing in order to magnify disorder and instigate disruption. With the demonstrations going on in the streets, the general could see that his job was half-done already.

Newly appointed minister Song Bei left for Taipei immediately, via Hong Kong, posing as a businessman and traveling under a false passport.

Within the borders of China itself, thousands of planes were moved into position in staging areas adjacent to the military airfields. The planes would remain camouflaged or hangared until shortly before takeoff. Paratrooper regiments had been recalled to base and were gearing up for their brief flight from the mainland to the island.

## Chapter 44

Jennifer was sitting in one of the hospital waiting rooms, holding Torpedo and watching the events unfold on television. When she received a call on her pager, she carried Torpedo over to the phone and called Major Chen. "I'm afraid I have some bad news for you," he said.

"Not Jin Yi-bo!"

"No, we don't know anything about his situation at the moment. The problem is that...well, I'm sorry to say this but they can't send in the commandos right now. The Taiwanese submarine fleet has been put on full alert. There's a lot going on."

"It's going on because I gave you the information you wanted," she said bitterly.

"Look, nobody knows better than I do that this whole crisis has come about because you found out about the missiles," the major said, "but now they're afraid to deploy their military forces for anything but essential action. I'm sure you don't like it but I know you can understand that they just can't tie up an entire sub right just to get one man out."

"Of course I understand; it's just that the irony is rather stinging."

"Look, I have some connections fairly high up. I'll see what I can do."

Jennifer put the phone down and sat down in a state of dismay.

"Is there anything I can do to help?" asked Ellen, who had taken Torpedo from her while she spoke on the phone.

"No, thanks."

"Want to talk about it?"

"I'm fine."

"Look," said Ellen, "this is none of my business, but you've been watching all the events on television very closely, and you seem to be on the phone a lot. Are you – by any chance – connected to all of this in some way?"

Jennifer breathed a sigh of relief. She had desperately needed someone to talk with. And Ellen was completely trustworthy, there was no question of that.

She paused for a moment before she answered. "I may have had a little to do with it."

# 45

Former professor Kawagaki sat down and began to compose his letter to the Secret Service. "Honorable Conrad Haraldsen," he began. "Agent, The United States Secret Service. Washington, D.C. 10011.

"Honorable Mister Agent,

"This is in response to your request for information regarding Miss Jiang Ou.

"As you have correctly understood, I was for some time an assistant professor of art history at UCLA, although I no longer work in that capacity. Indeed – as you have been informed – I did teach a class in Eighteenth Century Japanese Art.

"Allow me to make a most humble apology for the lateness of this response. After returning to Japan, I have spent many months in seclusion and isolation in my effort to become a Buddhist monk.

"I am sending, by following mail, copies of all of my class rolls for each year in which I taught the subject. As you will see for yourself, no such individual is listed in my class rolls.

"Respectfully, Otsiru Kawagaki"

He would take his letter to the local telegraph office and have it sent immediately.

## CHAPTER 46

They gathered in the Oval Office, the president and the Big Three: political adviser Tony Phillips, Uniqraft Chairman Arnulf Kinder, and the vice president.

The tension in the room was electric, the president apoplectic. He raged at Arnulf Kinder. "How could you let this man get into your limo with a recording device? How could you do that to me?"

Kinder was cool as a cucumber as he lied to the man he had betrayed. "Ed, I had no idea the man had a tape recorder on him."

Of late, it seemed as though tape recorders were playing an increasingly ominous role in Kinder's life.

The president stared coldly at Kinder, and the others sat or stood in uncomfortable silence for nearly a minute. There was nothing anybody could say; the damage to the president's credibility was catastrophic.

Finally, Tony Phillips spoke. "Mister President, I think it would be a good strategy to perhaps detail your exact relationship to Aji al-Houb, just so people will know the…uh…truth."

"I don't have a connection to Mister al-Houb," the president said icily.

"Isn't it true that you've met with him in the past?"

"As director of the CIA, I did meet with him, yes, but that was ten years ago."

"Still, you can't say you don't know him…"

"I've admitted that, Tony," he replied with barely checked fury. "Look, you're not a prosecutor and I'm not on the witness stand. OK?"

Phillips smiled grimly as he paced back and forth in the Oval Office. "Well, not yet anyway; they do have impeachment hearings for this kind of thing. The president of the United States has been implicated as an agent of Taiwan's destruction; gentlemen, we have met the enemy and he is us!"

Phillips was so stressed out by the intense pressure of the past twenty-four hours that he was starting to unwind. He sat down and put his head in his hands. "The Taiwanese have been rioting for sixteen hours straight. Every world capital is calling here and wanting to know if the White House has gone mad. I can't wait to see the polls coming out next week. This is a public relations nightmare of the highest order. Just what we don't need: incontrovertible evidence of our colossal stupidity in the handling of foreign affairs. Start brushing up on your golf game, Ed; and I suggest you check out your retirement plan."

"Tony, shut up!"

Every face snapped to the back of the room. Every pair of eyes turned and stared.

It was the vice president. He had stood and he was glaring at the president's political adviser. His eyes were piercing and black.

Mark Ferguson was rumored to have a temper, but few people had ever seen evidence of it. Here was evidence manifest.

He walked to the center of the Oval Office. "Phillips, I am sick and I am tired of the way you talk to the president," he said through clenched teeth. "I won't stand here and listen to this a minute longer."

Tony Phillips smirked insolently. "I don't know that you have a choice in the matter, Mark. You're just the vice president, after all."

"Just the vice president" approached Phillips slowly and leaned down close, his hard, chiseled face only three inches from the fat, blubbery face of the political adviser. "I beg your pardon? What did you say, son?"

He was on his own now; Billingsley was far too debilitated to intervene. Phillips thought better of saying anything else. "Nothing."

With his presence, Ferguson had instantly transformed the room from a squabbling bag of cats into a military situation room. When he began to speak, no one dared interrupt.

"I think we're looking at this whole problem incorrectly," he declared. "In the first place, there are several points that don't add up.

"Number One: why would the Chinese allow a factory to be built outside their own borders in order to produce such a highly sensitive weapon as short-range missiles?"

"Second question: if the Chinese could gain access to microchip technology through the Qiryat Gat plant," he continued, "why not just add it to their existing line of missiles? No one has answered the question as to *why* the Chinese would do something so irrational. Isn't that the real question we should be trying to answer right now?" He glared at Phillips, who cut his eyes to avoid the stare.

"On the surface level, the obvious answer that comes to mind," continued Ferguson, "is that, by connecting these two threads – the al-Houb Thread and the Forces Pull-back Thread – somebody wants to ruin the president four months before the election. The fact that he can be connected in this way is being interpreted worldwide as evidence that he wished to betray Taiwan. It's not true, of course, and eventually we can prove our case, perhaps, but right now we happen to have a political earthquake of the first magnitude on our hands. But that's the surface level; my question is, what's below the surface? Has anyone tried to dig into that?"

Tony Phillips was silent; he hadn't bothered to look below

the surface.

"I believe that we have a Trojan Horse in our midst," declared Ferguson. "What we are looking at is not what it seems; but whatever it is, we need to figure it out and we need to do it fast."

There was nothing but silence in the room. Ferguson had a rapt audience. "We turn now to the next important question, how did al-Houb manage to get himself arrested at this most opportune moment? After all, he's an experienced international agent. He does have felony charges hanging over him, but somehow he's managed to elude the authorities for six years. And yet now, after all this time, he's been picked up in Paris – wearing a disguise, no less – and at the exact moment he's picked up, he just so happens to have some very important computer files and microchips on him. I ask you, what would be the odds of that?"

This was a new line of thinking; no one had considered that Ferguson had been analyzing the situation to this extent.

"Maybe these same folks who have been orchestrating all of this decided that it was time to set al-Houb up to be arrested," Ferguson suggested. "After all, they knew what he would be carrying on him, and they knew that the president would be implicated by this evidence.

"This begs the following questions: why wasn't he picked up in Nairobi or Singapore? Could it be that the news coverage wouldn't be as good as it is in Paris? Or could it be that Interpol is located in Paris and so it would be easy to figure out very quickly what it was he had in that briefcase of his? And it begs this question, more than any other: who is it who wants to cause this huge stir, and why? Ed, any idea?"

"Well, of course I have enemies," said the president, "but I can't imagine why someone would want to make it look like I'm out to betray Taiwan; but, now that you mention it, how exactly did this arrest of al-Houb come about? Was it a routine check or did someone alert the French authorities?"

"They were alerted by Interpol," replied Bill Robinson of the Secret Service, who had stepped into the room.

"And who alerted Interpol?" asked Ferguson. "Tony, you seem to have all the answers."

"No idea," he said curtly.

"Well, it shouldn't be that hard to find out; look into it for us," ordered the vice president.

Phillips nodded respectfully and left the room in a hurry.

The fact was that the vice president had started to ask the right questions. Of course, he was wrong in thinking that the people who were behind all of this had themselves betrayed al-Houb. He could not have known that it was Jennifer Jiang's report to Major Chen here in Washington that had led to the quick arrest of al-Houb in Paris. He could not have known that Jennifer Jiang had gotten her information from Arnie Kinder; but that was his only error.

There was indeed a Trojan Horse. The picture would soon crystallize and the Americans would in time come to understand what the truth was, but by then it would be too late. The biggest tragedy of all was that Mark Ferguson, the first person to identify the existence of the Trojan Horse, would himself be its first victim.

The hour was late and, with Phillips gone, it was now just three of them in the Oval Office: Billingsley, Ferguson and Bill Robinson.

Politically, the president was in deep trouble. He had had no idea about the missiles, of course, but that fact was of no relevance whatsoever. The spotlight shone on one place and one place only.

The president sat brooding. "I did it with the best of intentions, Mark. I saved a major aeronautical contract for us – for my *country*! – and you can't tell me that's not important."

"Taiwan feels betrayed."

"I don't give a damn how they feel." He paused. "Well, of course, that's not true..."

Ferguson did not offer much in the way of consolation. He and Billingsley had never been on the same wavelength; now they were as far apart as they had ever been.

The president seemed fearful; he saw the election slipping away. "Well, I suppose you already figured out that you are going to be the one to go over there. They'll listen to you."

"I know many of the players there. I hope they will listen."

"You can make them understand what was behind it, can't you? For our part, it was just a trade deal, that's all."

"I can make them understand it, Ed," said Ferguson as he stood to leave. "Unfortunately, I can't make them like it."

AIR FORCE TWO had been checked out, was fueled up, and was warming up on the runway at Andrews AFB. It was six p.m. The flight to Taipei would take the better part of a day.

The vice president would be arriving within a few minutes. Nick was already there, and the Salivator had just then arrived, with Jeannine and Torpedo along to see him off.

Nick stood on the flightline, near the ramp, waiting for the Old Man, when a familiar car was waved up to the gate and two individuals, also quite familiar, got out and approached him. It was Ellen and Gregory.

Gregory was thrilled to see Air Force Two, and begged to be allowed to go aboard. Ellen had to restrain him. "Another time, Gregory."

Nick greeted her, surprised to see her at this time of the morning, but she had a ready explanation. "You left your sweater at my apartment. You may need it."

"You came all the way out here to bring me a sweater?" he asked.

"Of course not," she replied with a slight nervousness. "Actually, I thought you might like some cookies. I was doing some baking last night, and I happened to remember how much you like chocolate chip cookies."

"Won't Tom be jealous?" said Nick, accepting the box of cookies. "Listen, I'm really sorry if I caused a rift between you two…"

"You didn't cause a rift, Nick. You merely exposed one. Tom will be much better off with some New York City socialite."

There was an uncomfortable pause. "Well, I hope you have a nice flight, and perhaps…well, that is, when you get back I think that Gregory would very much like to see you."

## 47

General Bai was pleased with the enthusiasm of the riot agitators. There was pandemonium throughout the land, and chaos and confusion ruled the day. Anti-American sentiment was at an exquisite level of intensity, and the bomb which would kill Vice President Ferguson would soon be in place.

All that remained was for the final signal to be given, and his men would move into their assigned places in order to paralyze the government of Taiwan. Then it was just a matter of waiting for the paratroopers to regroup and battle their way up from the south end of the island until they liberated Taipei from its democratic form of government.

And then General Bai would become Governor-general Bai.

CAPTAIN LI BIAO of the Taiwanese Marine Special Assault Force was worried. He and his team of six enlisted men, armed with submachine guns, knives, binoculars, and the bare minimum of supplies they would need in order to operate in-country for a day, had just left the submarine *Tiger Claw* and were paddling in their rubber boats toward the Chinese coast, less than a mile away.

It was four a.m. They had until midnight to retrieve Jin Yi-bo from Shi Men Prison – a distance of six miles to be traveled over mostly desolate, brushy and hilly country – and get him back to the sub.

They would spend the morning looking for him. With their high-powered binoculars, the commandos would be able to pick him out from the thousand or so men who would be engaged in hard, backbreaking labor, working the fields from morning until dusk.

Jin Yi-bo had been told to carry a red bandana and to wrap it around his forehead while he worked. If he were questioned about it, he was to tell the guard that his wearing of the color red was representative of his newly-acquired reverence for the glories of communism. They would doubtless believe it.

Then it would be just a matter of getting him away from there. The plan was to approach the edge of the fields, wait until dusk, and then find some way to distract the guards and move in. Once they had Jin Yi-bo and his companion Bao Luan, they would lead them back to the shore.

And then all they had to worry about was whether the *Tiger Claw* would still be there. The sub commander was not highly experienced, and had seemed nervous the evening before. The political situation in Taiwan was worrisome, and the sub commander would not give an absolute guarantee that he could wait the entire twenty hours before pulling away from the coast.

JENNIFER WAS having a late dinner with Ellen, and they were sitting quietly. Gregory had already gone to bed.

During dinner, Jennifer had received a message to call Major Chen and she intended to do so at the first opportunity. In the past, she would have found an excuse to leave the apartment – offering to go to the corner drugstore to get some milk for Ellen, for example, in order to use the payphone there.

But this time was different. Ellen knew the whole story – or certainly a great deal of it.

Jennifer dialed Major Chi and he answered immediately. "It's me," she said.

He was expecting her call. "Well, I've got some semi-good news for you…"

"Semi-good?"

"The Taiwanese did manage to come up with another submarine."

"Really? That's wonderful."

"No, it's semi-good. This sub is very old, and basically they've been cannibalizing electronics out of it in order to rebuild other vessels. It can travel, but it can't fight very well. So they have to have a very clean mission, and get out of there with no problem. The sub commander will wait twenty hours, and then he will have to come back to Taiwan, with or without the commandos. Those are the best terms I could get you."

She could hardly contain her excitement. "When will we hear something?" she asked.

"Understand, now, they're going to be completely incommunicado until they get back to the submarine; we won't know a thing until then. And let me tell you also, these guys they sent in are the best – absolutely handpicked – but anything could happen. They not only have to get him away from the prison alive, but they have to get him back to the coast; being hunted down and recaptured is always a possibility; and I don't have to tell you what that means."

"I understand," she said, almost in a whisper.

"I'm telling you this because it's absolutely essential you understand how dangerous it is for him right now. You *must* not get your hopes up. Now, if everything goes OK, they should be picked up by the sub. Naturally, with all that's going on over there – the political turmoil, I mean – he'll have to stay on the sub until it's allowed to dock in port. Could be a while, but he should be OK. You with me?"

"I'm with you."

"I've arranged a ticket to get you out of the United States," he added. "I suggest you go to Japan, maybe wait a few days, and from there you can get to Taiwan."

"I think…I think I'll wait a while before using that ticket," she said quietly. "In case something happens...I want to be with friends; but thank you, Major Chen."

"No, it's you who deserves the thanks, Jiang Ou."

## CHAPTER 48

At seven o'clock in the morning, the agricultural details began trudging out of Shi Men Prison. Included in the regiment of workers, for his first day on the job, was Cabbage Field Specialist Jin Yi-bo.

All he knew was that he had come to work that morning, had been dismissed from the prison administrator's office, and had been told to join the agricultural workers. What he did not know was that his beneficiary had secretly contacted Lou Jian Ren in Beijing and together they had concocted the idea that Jin Yi-bo had been exposed to tuberculosis during his time at Harbin. When Lo Jian Ren informed the head of Shi Men Prison of that undocumented fact, Jin Yi-bo instantly became a field worker.

And so Jin Yi-bo marched along with hundreds of other raggedy, weary men who were soon to populate the vast fields, fields which were bounded and interspersed with densely wooded tracts.

Captain Li Biao had spread his men out along the edge of the woods, and they took up positions and began looking for Jin Yi-bo. They were able to communicate by means of radios, and they spent a good part of their morning in their search.

Late in the morning his red bandana was spotted. He had been assigned to work in a cabbage field located in a low-lying area. The field was so large that it was assumed that he would be in that area for the entire day.

They had been given a picture of him, which Jennifer had given to Major Chen. With their binoculars, they were almost certain that it was the same man. He was now even thinner than his picture indicated and that had been taken when he was still a teenager. They watched him carefully as he worked a row of cabbages. They had been told that he still walked somewhat stiffly, not having fully recovered from his injury.

From the way he walked, they were now certain it was Jin Yi-bo.

His location on the workfield wasn't bad; even in a live fire-fight, they would be able to get to him fairly quickly and pull him back into the woods. His friend was assumed to be working close by, and he was expected to help Jin Yi-bo when the time came.

The commandos studied the guards carefully. They were a sorry lot – undisciplined, oblivious to their surroundings, careless, unmilitary. There were only two guards in the cabbage patch, and they were both overweight and slovenly.

One worrisome note was the presence of dogs. The animals were spotted in the distance, under trees about a half-mile away, at the place where the guard tower and the supervisor's station were located.

Captain Li Biao took note of all of these factors and in the early afternoon, he communicated his plan to his men.

DESPITE WHAT they asked of him, Ma Chang Lin had no intention whatsoever of dying for anyone's cause. He had risked plenty just in driving an explosives-filled truck through the streets of downtown Taipei the day before. He had driven it into the basement garage of the Emperor Hotel and through the length of the garage. Carefully, oh so carefully, he had managed to get it through the doors of an underground storage room.

He had been told exactly where inside the room to place the

truck in order to destroy the hotel.

The vice president of the United States would be coming to the Emperor Hotel within a day and he would be staying in Room 301, just as he had done every time he came to Taiwan. For that was where, as a young naval officer, Mark Ferguson had spent part of his honeymoon. Subsequently, throughout his naval career, he had always stayed in the Emperor Hotel – in the very same room – when visiting Taiwan and, especially after his wife died, he would have never consented to staying anywhere else.

Underneath the gruff exterior, Ferguson was something of the romantic type. Ah, but the admiral would pay for his silly sentimentality.

He would pay with his life.

Ma Chang Lin snorted at how easy this all would be. He had done all that could reasonably be expected of him: the truck was sitting there, undisturbed. The door to the storage room had been quickly plastered over and painted during the night. When the Secret Service came to do their check, they would have no reason to suspect that there was anything behind the wall.

At just the right time, Ma Chang Lin would push a button on a remotely controlled ignition device, and the truck would explode, sending its tremendous force directly up into the building.

Moments after the blast, an individual claiming to be a member of a Taiwanese anti-American extremist organization called Strike Dragon would contact the Department of State in Washington and take credit for the bombing of the hotel.

AIR FORCE TWO landed at Chiang Kai Shek Airport, west of Taipei, at four in the afternoon. The vice president and his staff – including Nick and the Salivator – deplaned rapidly and were met by the Taiwanese army chief-of-staff, General Shen, whom Ferguson had met on several occasions in the past. Formalities were handled quickly and then Ferguson and his key staffers headed for waiting limousines. The vice presidential limousine left the airport and headed east towards Taipei; General Shen rode with Ferguson.

"Was my arrival announced in the Taiwanese media?" asked Ferguson.

"Absolutely. Your presence here is most urgently desired, Admiral."

"And what have the Chinese said about my visit?"

"There have been no comments."

"Don't you think that's strange?" asked Ferguson after a period of contemplation. "The Chinese usually go ballistic anytime there's contact between an American government official and Taiwan. They would normally consider this to be blatant interference in the internal affairs of their country. Why aren't they saying anything?"

"Good question, sir; I hadn't thought about it."

When the vice president arrived at the Emperor Hotel, there was a vast, angry crowd lining Nanjing Road. The crowds were chanting furiously. "Sold out! Sold out! Sold out!"

There were thousands of police in riot gear – as well as elements of the Taiwanese army – lining the streets, trying to hold back the crowds.

Mark Ferguson was used to friendly crowds wherever he went outside the United States. He had never faced anything like this, certainly not in Asia; but now his car was pelted with every kind of object coming from the crowd.

The limousines were driven into the basement garage of the hotel, and security was extremely tight as the Americans were hustled out of the cars and into the hotel.

As they rode the elevators to the third floor, they could still hear the chants of the protestors. "Yankee go home! Yankee go home!"

The president of Taiwan would keep Mark Ferguson waiting, merely as a way to show his displeasure with the government of the United States. The vice president had arrived at his hotel at five in the afternoon, and he had been asked to wait until Liao was ready to see him. He didn't like it – he and Liao had once been good friends – but he understood why Liao felt he had to do this.

Across the street from the Emperor Hotel, in the General Trade Building, Ma Chang Lin waited, his remote control in his hand. He was under strict instructions not to set off the explosion until he had been told that the vice president was in his suite of rooms. His accomplice, Su Yu Juan, was working on the housekeeping staff, and would let him know.

But what was taking Su Yu Juan so long?

## Chapter 49

Administrative Assistant Eugenia Waters was always glad to see Secret Service Deputy Detail Leader Conrad Haraldsen leave for an overseas trip with the vice president. It gave her an opportunity to reorganize the office and make a few changes which she thought were needed.

Haraldsen had left for Taipei the day before; he should have been arriving there just about the time she started her workday.

She had not been at work more than an hour when she received the telegram.

The sender was located in Tokyo, Japan. She opened it and read; in so doing, she remembered the need to research Japanese art for a lead her boss was once tracking down. She didn't know if this matter were still pending in any way, and so she decided to send a message to him via electronic mail.

THEY USED a mirror to get Jin Yi-bo's attention. The late afternoon sunlight hit him in the eyes and he looked up and saw the mirror and instantly knew who it was. Quietly, he communicated the news to Bao Luan; they knew now that the rescuers were on the scene.

At dusk, the diversion began. There came the sound of a

duck call emanating from the woods. The cabbage field guards heard it and they looked at one another and smiled. They both had the same idea: a fat duck would be an excellent addition to their bland diet of rice and cabbage.

One of the guards led the way towards the tree line and stepped into the woods, which were now grown dusky with the fading light. "Here, ducky, ducky, ducky."

The guard saw no immediate sign of the feathered creature, and yet the quacking calls continued, giving hope of a sumptuous feast. The second guard moved to the edge of the wood, checked on the prisoners, and then stepped into the wood and joined the hunt. The guards searched the bushes, looking low, looking carefully. The light was fading fast, but the duck, they were quite sure, was close.

The hunters, as it turned out, quickly became the hunted. The first guard took another step, and he looked up just in time to see the butt of a rifle coming directly for his nose. The second guard was grabbed from behind, and his throat was slit.

A few minutes later, a siren sounded from the prison wall, signaling the end of the workday. The cabbage patch prisoners began to line up, facing the guard tower, as they always did, in order be marched back to the prison.

Jin Yi-bo and Bao Luan moved to the rear of the formation, close to the woods and away from the guard tower. Jin Yi-bo turned and saw the Taiwanese marine captain signaling for them, and so he and Bao Luan turned and slipped into the woods, their escape being shielded from view of the guards by the emaciated bodies of their fellow prisoners.

MA CHANG LIN finally got through to Su Yu Juan. "What the devil is going on?"

"He didn't go to his room right away," she replied. "He met some people he knew and he went into the bar and talked to them."

"Where is he now?"

"I think he went up the back way to his room just a few minutes ago."

"You *think?* After all this, you missed him?"

"The Secret Service is here. They've taken over the place; it's very hard to move around and go where you want."

"Su Yu Juan, where is the vice president right now?"

"He's in his room," she said. "I heard someone say he was coming down soon."

"Why didn't you call me as soon as you knew that?"

"They secured the exit I was going out of; I had to find a different way out."

"What does that matter?"

"I don't want to die in here!"

"You idiot! You're sure he's still up there?"

"Yes, I'm sure."

"All right, then. I'm blowing the building."

From the outside, the explosion didn't look like much. A few windows puffed open and some dark smoke began billowing out. The building sagged slightly on one side, and debris started falling off and landing in the streets.

The shock and noise from the blast silenced and then frightened many of the protestors who were standing on the sidewalks surrounding the hotel.

Within moments, fires were blazing, and firetrucks could be heard coming in the streets.

The explosion in downtown Taipei was the signal long awaited. It was now nearly dark. And across the Taiwan Strait, it was growing dusky as Chinese paratroopers boarded the planes and the planes began to leave the airfields.

The Chinese invasion of Taiwan had begun.

## 50

Captain Li Biao held up his arm, and his men halted in place. They all strained to hear the long and mournful wails of the prison sirens.

The bodies of the guards had been discovered. Two prisoners were missing.

Undoubtedly, the dogs were tracking them.

The rendezvous with the submarine was still two hours away.

They couldn't expect to merely hide and wait it out. They would have to deal with whoever was coming after them.

They would have to stand and fight.

JENNIFER DECIDED to go ahead and leave for Japan. If the final outcome of the rescue attempt were to be unhappy, she had decided that she didn't want to learn the news in Washington.

The timing of her flight meant that the final resolution would be played out while she was in the air, and she would find out when she landed in Tokyo whether she would ever see Jin Yi-bo again.

Ellen and Gregory drove her to Dulles International Airport. She checked her baggage at the counter, but was given some surprising news. "There's been a delay," said the clerk. "Due to the problems in the Far East."

"I see," said Jennifer. "How long of a delay?"

"Perhaps three hours."

"We'll wait with you," said Ellen when Jennifer explained a moment later.

"No, that's not necessary," insisted Jennifer. "I think it's best if we say our goodbyes now."

And so they did. Young Gregory, who had once been concerned that Jennifer would steal away his idol, had now become instead her great admirer, and was truly saddened to see her go. Ellen, who believed that she had finally come to know this elegant, mysterious woman from a distant world, was just as sorry to lose her newfound friend.

And so they hugged, and they waved, and they wished each other well, promising it would not be the last time they met, although they knew beyond a doubt that it was.

THE PLANES came in low, barely one hundred feet above sea level. It was now past sunset, but the moon was nearly full.

The first wave of planes was composed of radar jammers. These planes contained the world's finest and most sophisticated jamming equipment, the technology having been stolen from some of the most advanced military research institutions in the United States.

All of the Taiwanese army radar located along the western coast of the island was rendered ineffective. Even the radar installations operated on the island by America's National Security Agency were flummoxed.

Cloud cover was moderate over much of China, the Taiwan Straits, and Taiwan. The airplanes, as they left the various fields, were directed under cloud cover as much as possible, in order to reduce the possibility of large waves of planes being picked up by satellite surveillance.

The Chinese knew that they could hardly keep the secret of the invasion for much more than a few hours at best, but they wanted to conceal the size of the invasion force for as long as possible.

Agents of the Taiwanese Liberation Army had built bonfires along a three-mile section of the coast, near the tiny fishing village of Ming Hai, so that the planes could see their way to the drop zones. The name Ming Hai means "brilliant sea," and the sea was indeed brilliant with the light coming from the bonfires as well as the intermittent light from the moon, when it broke through the clouds.

Just as the Chinese planes arrived over land, they increased their altitude to barely one thousand feet, to give the paratroopers room to open their chutes.

Silently, the white parachutes billowed open and wafted their way to the earth.

Reforming on the ground, the platoons formed into companies, the companies into battalions, and the battalions into regiments. The units formed up in fields and along country roads and waited for orders to move up the coast.

Meanwhile, in Taipei, members of the Taiwanese cabinet were detained in their homes. Key military officials were arrested; those resisting were shot on sight. Key governmental buildings were quickly occupied and communications were disrupted in accordance with prearranged plans.

CAPTAIN LI BIAO, along with his marines and his two charges, had managed to cover more than a mile of the wooded landscape before the prison sirens had begun to go off. There was little doubt that the dogs would find them before they could get their boat into the sea. They continued at a half run, and the captain was on a steady lookout for a place to make his stand.

At last, the officer chose his spot. There was a place where the road leading to the beach narrowed considerably, and it cut through numerous small hills.

The marines formed an ambuscade on the beach side of the road. They took cover behind the slopes of a small hill, and they readied their rifles and set out their grenades. Jin Yi-bo and Bao Luan were handed pistols, which they readily took up against their former captors.

Within ten minutes, the pursuers came into view in the distance.

Now the marines could see what they were up against. Leading the way were several dogs, eagerly straining at their long leashes. The dogs had the trail cold, and were relentless in their pursuit.

Following the dogs were a half-dozen armed men, stalking the trail.

And following the men were two Chinese army halftracks, with tops removed; each vehicle carried a dozen armed soldiers.

The marines were outmanned and outgunned, and the captain had less than two minutes to decide what to do.

## Chapter 51

The White House. "Mister President, the Emperor Hotel has just blown up."

"And the vice president?"

"He was inside at the time."

"Oh, my God!"

The atmosphere in the Oval Office was bordering on pandemonium.

"Mister President!"

"Mister President!"

Roy Kelly, the president's chief-of-staff, intervened to calm things down. "Not everybody at once." He acknowledged the assistant secretary of state for the Far East.

"Mister President, we just now received a communiqué from the Chinese," said the official. "They categorically deny any involvement in the civil unrest in Taiwan. They say that it's part of the coup being attempted by anti-American extremists."

The chairman of the Joint Chiefs offered contradictory evidence. "The Taiwanese air force has spotted planes on the northwest coast of the island."

"What do the Chinese say to that?" asked the chief-of-staff.

"Beijing has reported that they have sent a number of observational planes over Taiwanese airspace," replied the military officer. "They consider Taiwan to be their territory and they want to know what's going on there. They say they will be happy to provide us with any information they come up with."

"Observational planes?" said the chief of staff. "Well, tell them we don't need their interference right now. We're trying to figure out what's going on."

"We also have some reports of Chinese aircraft activity near the Korean border," said the general. "The Taiwanese army reports massive jamming in the middle coastal areas of the island."

The official from the state department was handed a message. He read it silently and then announced its contents. "Beijing has said they are considering sending in troops in order to help the Taiwanese army quell any civil disturbances."

"Get back to them immediately," ordered the chief-of-staff. "Tell them to back off."

The head of the Central Intelligence Agency had just been shown into the Oval Office. All eyes turned to him. "Mister President, there are unconfirmed reports coming in that Chinese troops have been spotted in the Taiwanese countryside."

"What does Taipei say?" asked Billingsley. He had taken a seat and seemed to be highly stressed by these darkening reports.

"We're getting conflicting information," said the CIA man. "Officially, the Taiwanese government has made no announcement along those lines; others we have talked to are not so sure."

"What about ships in the area?" asked the chief-of-staff. "If this is an invasion of some type, there have to be supply ships at the very least, don't there?"

"No reports of ships, sir," said the general.

"Well, that's encouraging. What about our own observational planes?"

"The navy sent up EWACS just a very short while ago," replied the senior officer, referring to the navy's 'flying radars'

– airplanes which had the ability to take in the scene for hundreds of miles around. "They're looking at everything from twenty-five thousand feet on down. So far all they have is the observational planes, same as the NSA. We've sent them to look farther south."

The chief-of-staff turned to the commander-in-chief. "Mister President, what do you want to do?"

There were too many people standing in front of him, demanding answers. How could anyone expect decisions at this point? "Don't ask me what I want to do," Billingsley said with great irritation. "Don't bring me all this disjointed information. I think maybe you folks need to start confirming a few things. I can't deal with this. I need it all laid out for me, all the facts, clearly – everything.

"I can't start World War Three because of a few hunches. I want to have all the information I can get in order to make a rational decision. Does anyone understand what I'm talking about? I want options, damn it! Prioritized options! I want people to make recommendations and sign off on them. Come on, we have to have a system. Do you understand?"

All in the room were silent. The president glared at them all, as though these problems were collectively their fault. "Then clear out of here. Find out what's going on and give me my options."

After most of them had left the Oval Office, the president turned to Bill Robinson. "Go find Jennifer Jiang and bring her right here. If I have to talk to the premier of China, I want her to act as my interpreter."

"I don't like that idea one bit, Mister President."

The president bristled. "I don't give a damn what you like, Bill. Maybe it's time someone explained to you that you take orders from me and not the other way around."

Robinson was stunned; he had never heard Billingsley talk that way before.

"Well, go on. I want her here in half an hour."

THE TAIWANESE marines lay motionless along the edge of the ridge. Their pursuers were fifty yards away and were lumbering relentlessly towards them.

The plan was to wait as long as possible and, on signal from the captain, to attack.

The captain had nerves of steel, for he allowed the pursuers to move closer and closer, until the separation of forces was less than twenty yards. Jin Yi-bo and Bao Luan held their pistols firmly, and lined up their own targets of choice. Jin Yi-bo silently vowed to die before he would be retaken prisoner.

The captain was watching the dogs closely. They would be the ones to detect the ambush. They would be the ones who would effectively signal the attack.

And so it happened. The lead dog stopped suddenly, and began to growl. He looked over at the ridge, and began to pull in that direction.

The captain rose to his knees and hurled a grenade at the first truck. It landed in the truck bed, exploding violently and killing or wounding several of the soldiers.

The other marines, along with Jin Yi-bo and Bao Luan, began firing at the men who were trailing the dogs. The men were cut down, and the dogs ran loose, howling frantically.

Two other grenades were hurled at the second truck. One missed altogether, and the second failed to go off. The soldiers in the second truck had time to escape the fate of those in the first, but there was gunfire to back up the grenades, and several were shot before they could react.

A few soldiers managed to escape the withering barrage of Taiwanese gunfire, and they took up positions behind the damaged trucks. Still, the marines had gained the advantage by surprise, and they continued to lob grenades and fire deadly rounds at the soldiers and prison guards.

Eventually, the Chinese were forced into retreat. They scampered back down the road and raced up and over the ridge which ran along the other side of the road.

The marines left it at that and moved at a double time in the direction of the beach.

It was now past eight in the evening. They had less than an hour to get to the beach and only another hour after that to get out to the rendezvous point, assuming that the sub were still waiting.

**THE VICE PRESIDENT** of the United States and the Salivator had just stepped from the third floor into the elevator when the bomb went off. They had absorbed much of the stunning force of the explosion but had been protected from the worst of it by the thick doors of the elevator.

The elevator cabin had drifted down to the basement, and they both now lay at the bottom of the elevator shaft, their presence and condition unknown to the rest of the world.

The Salivator awakened slowly; he felt groggy and disoriented. In the darkness, he reached over and rocked the shoulder of the vice president, who was not moving. "Sir, are you OK?" He heard no answer. "Admiral?"

The lieutenant heard breathing, and then coughing. "I'll let you know in a minute." Ferguson pulled himself to his feet. "Little dusted up, that's all. Where's Nick?"

"No idea. He had gone on ahead of us, sir."

They managed to pry the doors of the elevator open and they stepped out into the basement, which was choked with tremendous amounts of dust. Slowly they made their way through the basement, until they came to a door which led up and out onto Nanjing Road.

The vice president of the United States emerged from the dust and the rubble with the cuffs of his suit trousers tattered and his coat ripped in several places. He was bleeding from his forehead, and he walked with a slight limp.

He and the Salivator were met by two Secret Service agents, both of whom were shocked to see the vice president walking around under his own steam. "Admiral, are you OK?"

"I've had better days." He turned to the Salivator. "Get the president on the horn."

"Right, sir; as soon as I can find one, I will."

THE SECRET SERVICE, in the person of Agent Buel, arrived at Ellen Conley's apartment within a few minutes of the president's directive. "We need to see Jennifer Jiang."

"I'm afraid she's left," Ellen replied.

"I see," said Buel. "And what time will she be back?"

"Well, what I mean is..." explained Ellen. "...she won't be back. She's gone to Japan, in fact."

"When did she leave?"

"This morning; is something wrong?"

"Sorry, Ellen," said the agent. "It's nothing I can discuss with you right now."

"I see. Well, I dropped her off at Dulles. I just got back, as a matter of fact."

"Do you know the flight number?"

She told him what she knew. The agent shrugged and punched a button on his cellular phone. "This is Agent Buel. Flight Nine Sixty to Japan, leaving Dulles. If it's still on the ground, hold it there. If it's taken off, turn it around and land at Reagan National. I'll have the runways cleared."

"This must be awfully important," said Ellen.

Agent Buel shrugged and smiled. "If the president says he wants to see Miss Jiang, he sees Miss Jiang."

## CHAPTER 52

Within minutes, the surviving members of his Secret Service detail had surrounded the vice president. They had managed to get to their weapons van and they were armed with rifles and submachine guns. They were locked and loaded.

Members of the Taiwanese Seventh Infantry Regiment had raced to the Emperor Hotel, joining their compatriots who had been guarding the streets during the demonstrations. They were now rallying around the vice president as well, under orders from their commander, who approached the American official a short while later and saluted him. "Mister Vice President, I'm Colonel Dow, Taiwan Seventh Infantry. Is there anything you need?"

"I should have my communications restored momentarily, Colonel," said Ferguson. "Then maybe I'll know what the hell is going on. What can you tell me?"

"Sir, I just received a call from General Cheung, military commander of the Capital District. Unconfirmed reports are coming in from the countryside that Chinese paratroops have landed in the south."

A moment later a Secret Service agent approached the vice president. "Sir, communication is restored."

Ferguson did not hesitate. "Get me the commander of U.S. forces in Korea," he ordered. "They watch everything that moves in this region. We'll see if they have anything on this." He turned back to the Taiwanese officer. "What are your HQ people telling you?"

Colonel Dow shook his head. "We're having a lot of problems with internal communications right now."

The vice president was interrupted once again. "Sir, Air Force Two has been sabotaged. It got hit by a bazooka shell. I don't think you'll be able to fly out of here."

"We'll worry about that later. Have you got me a line to the White House yet?"

"We expect to have the president on line momentarily," came the reply. "Meantime, this is a call from the carrier. Admiral Townes."

Ferguson took the call from the carrier group commander. "Go ahead, Chuck."

"Mark, I think we need to come get you."

"I've got a lovely suite at the Emperor Hotel; good luck finding it."

"We've got choppers inbound at this time with overhead fighter escort. We'll set down at Chung Hsia Road and you can board there. Please advise personnel status, sir."

"We've got Secret Service dead and wounded, and several unaccounted for. Medical supplies in dire need here."

"Roger that, sir."

"Chuck, what the hell is going on?"

"I've sent E-Two's up," the officer replied. "They've started picking up Chinese observational aircraft coming in right over the island."

"Observational aircraft? What exactly do they think they're looking for?"

"The Chinese made an announcement less than ten minutes ago that Taiwanese anti-government factions are fighting in the street and in the countryside, and they want to monitor it."

"Amazing how they know all that," said Ferguson. "Think they had anything to do with it? Or, for that matter, with my hotel going up?"

"Anything's possible," replied Townes. "The state department got a message less than twenty minutes ago that Strike Dragon, some Taiwanese radical group, is taking credit for the explosion at your hotel."

"At least we know who to send a thank-you note to."

"We've also gotten preliminary reports of Chinese troop sightings in the interior," added Townes. "Completely unconfirmed, but we're going to be checking it out. My E-2s are heading south."

"Well, you certainly know more than I do, Chuck; keep me informed."

"Will do, sir. Choppers should be on scene in less than ten minutes, Mark."

Conrad Haraldsen sat in the communications van which was parked on the street near the damaged hotel. With communications restored, there had been a flurry of messages back and forth between the vice president's staffers and the White House, the Pentagon, and the commander-in-chief of the Pacific Fleet.

When the message traffic died down momentarily, Haraldsen checked his own electronic mail. He read the message from his secretary, Mrs. Walters. In his typically meticulous way, he responded without hesitation. "Contact Jennifer Jiang. Hold for questioning. Conduct complete background investigation. Urgent."

He hit the send button.

THE 747 RACED down the runway, lifted its wings, and began its steep climb into the air. After a few minutes of steady climbing, the plane leveled out and turned in a westerly direction. Before long, the pilot allowed movement in the cabin, and the passengers began to relax.

But that period came to a sudden end. The captain came onto the loudspeaker and made an unexpected announcement. "We're sorry to inconvenience you folks, but there's been a slight change in plans. We will be turning back and landing at

Ronald Reagan National Airport in Washington for just a few minutes.

There was a slight air of concern among the passengers, but the captain anticipated as much. "Please be advised there is no emergency; the plane is doing great. We simply have to drop off one of our passengers, and then we'll get right back in the air and be on our way."

As he spoke, the plane began a slow drifting turn to the north, and then to the east.

In less than ten minutes the plane was hurtling toward the runway at Reagan National. When it came to a stop, Jennifer glanced out the window and saw several government vehicles idling on the runway curtain.

A ramp was flung up against the exit door, and several men in dark suits entered the plane. They knew exactly where her seat was. "Miss Jiang?" said the lead agent.

She looked up, and could feel the stares of dozens of her fellow passengers, more curious than angry about the delay. "Yes?"

"Agent Redding, United States Secret Service, ma'am. I'm afraid I'm going to have to ask you to deplane at this time."

"Is there a problem?"

"Perhaps we can talk about it in the car."

THE E-2 RADAR surveillance aircraft from the USS *Ronald Reagan* had been ordered to head southwest from its current position and to increase altitude in order to obtain a better view of the island.

The pilot leveled out at thirty-thousand feet and headed along the coast toward Tainan. The radar operators carefully watched their radar scopes.

After twenty-five minutes in the air, the crew of the E-2 realized that they could see something which all the coastal ground radar had been prevented from seeing.

There were long lines of white markings on their scopes. The lines moved slowly, inching along from west to east.

Each marking represented a single plane.

## Chapter 53

When the marines arrived at the beach, they were confronted with another problem: the rubber boat had a hole in it the size of a fist. They lost precious time repairing their boat; but when it was once again seaworthy, they carried it over the beach, pushed it into the sea, and boarded it.

There were six lightweight paddles, and the highly conditioned men made light work of moving the boat rapidly out to sea. They reached their rendezvous position at ten p.m. As planned, they shone their light – three short bursts followed by a longer burst, repeated every thirty seconds.

This activity continued for seven minutes, but there was no response. There was no submarine waiting for them.

And then their worst nightmare came into view, in the form of a Chinese naval gunboat. It had seen their signal light, and was bearing down on them.

It would be armed with machine guns, no doubt.

And the marines were nearly out of ammunition.

"MISTER PRESIDENT, it's the vice president."

"My god, he's alive!" Billingsley grabbed the phone. "Mark! How are you?"

"Still kicking. Ed, listen to me. If you don't act immediately, Taiwan is going to be overrun. It's going to take an expeditionary force to scrape the Chinese off this island."

"Admiral, I have the word of the Chinese ambassador that his countrymen are not anywhere near Taiwan. The only thing that naval surveillance has picked up is a bunch of observer planes."

The vice president was handed a message as he spoke to the president. "Your information is outdated, Mister President. I was just advised by the navy that they picked up a caravan of planes to the south, just north of Tainan. This caravan extends west from central Taiwan all the way to China. We have visual confirmation coming from all over Taiwan that they're fighting in the countryside. Reports of casualties, including deaths. If they're landing troops, they have to be stopped now."

The president did not process new information very quickly. "We had an official communiqué from the Taiwanese government saying that it's some anti-government forces in the south. We have reports of a popular uprising."

"The Taiwanese government? Ed, have you talked to President Liao?"

"Well, not directly. We're having some trouble establishing communication, but all of that is being worked on."

"Ed, I've heard that the Taiwanese generals are getting their orders from a brand new defense minister. They don't even know who this guy is. I seriously doubt the government would make such a change if an invasion were going on. Does that make any sense at all?"

"All I can tell you is that the Taiwanese government is giving us conflicting information," said Billingsley, unnerved by the relentless onslaught of ominous news.

"You're getting conflicting information because they've infiltrated the government," said Ferguson. "My guess is that there's been a takeover of certain key communications. They must have had some units in place. Ed, we have elements of the Seventh Fleet standing off the coast. I say let's act."

"Admiral, we're not in a position to act until I have firm

information. I intend to go about this in a deliberate way. This thing started less than two hours ago. I want to convene my national security staff and the entire Cabinet. I want a complete briefing. I want every bit of information I can get."

"You'll lose Taiwan if you delay."

"My methods have always served me well, Admiral; and I'd say that right now I'm in a better position than you are to see the big picture."

Had the Chinese been in a position to monitor the phone conversation between Billingsley and Ferguson, they would have been pleased at just how well the president was conforming to their predictions of his behavior. He was not about to act until he had in his possession every scrap of information.

The scenario the president faced was his worst nightmare, for it required him to act, and he did not want to act. He wanted the problem to go away.

Unfortunately, the invasion of Taiwan was a problem that was not going to go away.

THE TAIWANESE marines under Captain Li Biao did all that they could to prepare to meet the gunboat. They loaded their last remaining ammunition into their rifles and pistols and they prepared for a brief and vicious firefight. They had three grenades left and the men with the best throwing arms prepared to lob them at the gunboat when it got close enough.

They hoped that the Chinese would try to take them prisoner. If they did that, they stood a fair chance to fight their way out of this.

But if that machine gun opened fire, they were all dead.

THE ELECTRONIC mail from Taiwan arrived at Secret Service Headquarters in Washington ten minutes after Conrad Haraldsen sent it. His fellow agents were working feverishly to find out the status of those agents who were with the vice president when the Emperor Hotel blew up.

The e-mail was seen almost as soon as it arrived; it was given a cursory glance as the dispatch agent reading it tried to determine its importance in the grand scheme of things.

He did not know who Jennifer Jiang was, or why it was so important to conduct a background investigation of her at this time, or to hold her for questioning. Agents – in many cases longstanding friends – had probably died in the explosion, and there was little to think about at this time which could be more important than contacting families and trying to let them know what was going on.

Jennifer Jiang – whoever she was – would be taken care of when time allowed.

The dispatch agent assigned a code to the task. "Priority three," he wrote, and set it aside for later.

CAPTAIN LI BIAO knew that, if the Chinese gunboat chose to open fire on them, he and his men had but seconds to live; and the boat was now less than one hundred yards away.

The marines held their rifles at level aim, their grenades at the ready.

Suddenly, they could hear something coming up behind them and through the water, nearly at surface level. They turned and saw what seemed like a very fast moving fish, about ten feet long. Whatever it was, it passed almost directly underneath their rubber boat, and headed straight for the Chinese gunboat. In the moonlight, they could see the wake of the "fish" as it moved through the water.

All was quiet for a moment, and then the Chinese gunboat was blown to smithereens in a huge, fiery explosion. A moment later, the *Tiger's Claw* surfaced grandly – less than thirty yards from the rubber boat.

The submarine and the rubber boat joined up and the marines hurriedly began to climb from the small boat to the sub; but they were not yet out of danger. Another gunboat appeared in the distance, and was bearing down. This time there was no luxury for them, for this gunboat had already begun firing its machine gun and the bullets started hitting the water in front of the sub.

The men in the control room of the Tiger's Claw saw the second gunboat and hurriedly sent off a second torpedo.

The marines pulled themselves onto the sub, scampered up the ladder to the top of the sail, and threw themselves into the safety of the vessel.

The last ones to leave the rubber boat were firing the last of their ammunition at the gunboat. The rubber boat, after having done remarkable service, was now riddled with machine gun bullets, and was sinking. The last men into the sub ditched their weapons and scrambled for safety.

The second torpedo struck a glancing blow against the hull of the gunboat, but it would suffice. As the explosion subsided and pieces of the gunboat fell into the water, Chinese sailors were heard shrieking from their hideous wounds as their boat sank into the Sea of Japan.

As soon as the hatch was closed, the sub dived. The commander would resurface later in order to radio Taipei with news of the mission.

In the submarine itself, just below the hatch, there was blood everywhere. Three men had been hit by the bullets from the gunboat attack, and two of the men were dying.

# 54

Jennifer Jiang was ushered into the Oval Office. "You wanted to see me, Mister President?"

"I want you to stand by in case I get through to the president of China," said the chief executive, who was shaking nervously. "I want to get him on the phone and I want him to speak to you in Chinese and I want you to tell me whether he's lying or telling the truth. Now can you do that?"

"I can tell you what he's saying, Mister President, but..."

He gave her a look that said he would brook no discussion.

"Yes, Mister President."

Bill Robinson had come storming into the Oval Office behind Jennifer. "Mister President," he said sternly, "you can't rely on a Chinese national to interpret for you in a situation like this. She could tell you anything she wanted."

"I want someone I can trust."

"How do you know you can trust her?" said the head of the president's security detail. "If she's deliberately misleading you on the intentions of the Chinese government, it could be an international catastrophe."

"I'll take the responsibility," he said.

"Mister President, I insist on having a second interpreter

involved; just to make sure she's got it right. He can listen in on the phone call."

"Fine," said the president. "I'll agree to that. Where is this interpreter of yours?"

"He's on the way."

"On the way? Why isn't he here now? 'On the way' doesn't do any good, now does it?"

The president's secretary walked into the office at that moment. "Mister President, it's the Chinese foreign minister."

"I asked for the president or the premier!"

"I'm afraid they're both unavailable...or so they say."

"I'll just bet they are," he said, taking the phone. "Who is this I'm talking to?"

"Minister Liu," said the secretary. "And he speaks only Chinese."

The president turned to Jennifer. "Well then; looks like you're on."

She picked up the phone and identified herself as the interpreter; then she waited for instructions from the president.

"Tell him I just want to know," Billingsley began, "what his country has to do with all these reports we've been getting."

Jennifer translated the president's words and then listened for the response.

"'Mister President, any reports of the involvement of my government are regrettable lies,'" she quoted verbatim.

"Tell him we have reports of Chinese planes in the air."

She did so. "He says he can confirm that," she said after a moment. "They have a number of observational planes flying very near to Taiwan. He says he's sure that's exactly what your people are seeing."

"Well, tell him to get them the hell away from the island, so we can get a clear picture of what's going on."

She listened further, and then relayed the message. "He says the Chinese will be happy to share with you any information they obtain; although he says his government is very concerned about an attack by the United States upon Chinese coastal cities."

"That's preposterous!" exclaimed Billingsley. "Tell him we have no intentions of attacking his country."

She relayed that message, and then repeated the Chinese minister's comments. "'In a situation such as this, we take nothing for granted. We will be conducting a national defense exercise for the next forty-eight hours. You may see many of our planes over the Taiwan Strait. We hope you will use caution in this situation, Mister President. We urgently request that you move your naval carrier group away from the island.'"

The president shook his head. "First, ask him about these Chinese troops down near Tainan. Is he denying this?"

She asked him, and got back a surprising response. "He says that these are renegade forces."

"Renegade forces? What the hell does that mean?"

She asked for clarification. "'There are some elements of the Chinese military which have taken it upon themselves to restore order to the island,'" she reported back. "'This is not a large body of troops, and they do not have any official support from the government of Beijing.'"

"So there *are* Chinese troops on the island! My god!"

"There's more," she said, and then listened further and reported back. "'Mister President, we have no supply ships offshore. Furthermore, the central government is demanding the immediate return of these troops to the mainland."

"Why didn't he tell us about this before now?"

She queried the minister, and then quoted his response. "'Mister President, I must advise you that the central government regards this as an internal situation. We are tired of the meddling by the United States. We demand that you pull back your carrier group, and that you cease all interference at this time. We need twenty-four hours – forty-eight at the most, in order to gain control of the situation and restore to the people of the island their rightful liberties.'"

"Twenty-four hours?"

She asked him to confirm his demand. Through her, he said, "Mister President, let me remind you that this situation evolved from your own devious actions. I want to warn you, sir, that the sentiment in the Pacific region is that you cannot be trusted. It is most unfortunate that your breaking of faith with the people of Taiwan has served to destabilize their government."

"I did not break faith with the Taiwanese people," said Billingsley angrily. "Tell him I don't want him interfering in this situation. Furthermore, I demand that those troops be pulled off the island immediately."

She relayed the demand, and reported the counterdemand. "'In turn, sir, we demand that you respect our rights of sovereignty or we shall be forced to use all means necessary to protect our interests.'"

"What does that mean?"

She came back a moment later. "'Mister President, the carrier group is within range of our nuclear missiles. I'm sure that you would not want to be responsible for the destruction of thousands of your own men.'"

"Is that a threat?"

She conveyed the question. "'It is certainly not one we would ever wish to carry out,' came the reply. "'Please understand that all we are asking for is time – a day, two at the most – in order to get this situation under control. We are familiar with the personalities. We know the political landscape.'"

"A day or two; and then what?"

Jennifer asked the question. "'We are sure that these renegade forces, without our support, will be forced into retreat.'"

"Twenty-four hours, and you can guarantee that?"

"'Only with your cooperation and your understanding,'" came the reply. "Please do not allow this situation to escalate to the point where the entire world would suffer. Give us time, and we will set things right.'"

The president needed little encouragement to be cautious. It was a characteristic that was deeply ingrained in his DNA. "Fine. Twenty-four hours; and that's all."

The call ended, and the president slumped in his chair. He had just been faced with a nuclear threat, and he had blinked – although, of course, he would say to the historians that he had stepped back from the brink of nuclear war. He had given the Chinese exactly what they had asked for: time. It was a reasonable request, he believed, made even more reasonable by the fact that it accorded with his own desire to buy himself time.

The backup interpreter had made it to the West Wing just after the phone call with the Chinese minister had commenced. The backup advised Bill Robinson that Jennifer had done a superb job of interpreting. She had picked up every nuance of the Chinese minister's words, and had conveyed them with absolute precision.

For her part, Jennifer was worried about the president's state of mind. She was stunned that he had been so cowed by the Chinese that was going to allow them more time to establish themselves on the island. She approached Roy Kelly, the chief-of-staff, and addressed him directly.

"Yes, Miss Jiang?"

"The president is having a very hard time with all of this," she said quietly. "The stress is affecting his judgment."

The official smiled. "He's doing what he gets paid to do, Miss – handle the tough ones. Don't worry; he'll get through it."

"Don't you understand?" she said. "He's going to let Beijing walk all over him. Can't you involve the National Security Council in these discussions and let him get some advice on these matters?"

"Miss, I think you're getting in a bit over your head; now if you'll excuse me." Kelly turned and walked away, but she would not give up.

"Why can't the vice president handle this? He's over there in Taipei right now."

"The vice president has problems of his own," Kelly called over his shoulder.

"What do you mean? Is he alright?"

Kelly turned back and faced her. "Please, Miss Jiang. This is not your concern; but to answer your question, the vice president is doing just fine."

MARK FERGUSON turned to address one of the Secret Service agents assigned to handle communications. "Can you get through to President Liao?"

"We've been trying, sir," came the frustrated reply. "I can't seem to get in touch with any senior official in the Taiwanese government. Something's happened to their communication system."

Ferguson considered the implications of that statement. He turned to Colonel Dow of the Taiwanese army. "Who is the highest ranking officer you think you can get in contact with right away? Someone of unquestioned loyalty."

"That would be General Cheung, sir," replied Dow. "He's very popular with the troops."

"May I make an unofficial recommendation?"

"Of course."

"My recommendation is that General Cheung be considered the head of government until this situation becomes clearer. Let him know that I believe the civilian authorities have been detained or otherwise rendered ineffective and that, should he choose to direct the fighting on his own initiative at this time, I will ask Admiral Townes to feed any intelligence we can provide directly from our carrier group to his HQ."

The colonel nodded. "I'll inform the general right away, sir. By the way, we've just received an announcement from the presidential building. The government has asked all Taiwanese army units to converge at Hsinglung Shan."

"Where the hell is Hsinglung Shan? Do we have a map?"

An aide to the colonel provided a map of the island of Taiwan. "It's right here, sir. Right up next to the Central Mountain Range."

Ferguson shook his head. "That's got to be one of the most isolated areas on the island. That order makes no sense. It proves to me that pro-mainland forces have taken over national communications. This order needs to be countermanded. Do you agree, Colonel?"

"Completely, Admiral. I'll recommend that General Cheung disregard any instructions from the Presidential Building. "

The vice president knew that in a war situation, it was almost impossible to get enough information. There was no way to know exactly what was going on, to have it neatly laid out like a board game.

One had to act, to give commands, to make assumptions, all based on highly incomplete information. One had to be prepared to work without maps, without complete knowledge of the disposition and strength of ones own forces, or that of the enemy. One had to act in spite of disruption of communications, or the loss of key staff, or the uncertainty of where the enemy was or what he was doing.

Battles were won or lost based on factors having precious little to do with textbook strategy. Chance, aggressiveness, daring and intuition – these were the tools that would hold the game together – the only way at times to cut through the fog of war.

A moment later, a fighter escort from the *USS Reagan* came roaring overhead, and it began circling Ferguson's position, guarding against any further attack upon his person. Ten minutes later a squadron of Sea Stallion helicopters landed on Chung Hsiao Road, less than two blocks from the Emperor Hotel.

Navy personnel got all ambulatory personnel aboard within minutes, and the dead Americans – mainly those Secret Service agents whose bodies had been retrieved from the hotel – were carefully placed aboard a separate chopper.

Seated in the lead helicopter, the admiral saw his son for the first time since they had separated earlier in the evening. "Where the hell have you been?"

Nick merely shrugged. "Well, I met this chick in the bar..."

"Never mind."

MAJOR CHI was on full alert in his Washington office, awaiting word as to the fate of young Jin Yi-bo.

Jennifer would want to know as soon as he heard from Taipei. He had insisted that the submarine commander provide information on Jin Yi-bo's status at the earliest possible moment, and that Taipei forward it directly to him.

It would be his task to inform Jennifer of the outcome, good or bad.

And now the call had come, and Jennifer would have to be told.

He sent a message to her by electronic pager, and he waited for her to reply.

THE SECRET SERVICE dispatch agent was being visited by his boss, who was flipping through all the message traffic which had come in during the past several hours.

"What's this?" said the supervisor as he came to the message from Conrad Haraldsen.

The dispatcher glanced at the message. "Oh, that. Says a Jennifer Jiang is to be detained for questioning. Some kind of problem with her background. I gave it a priority three."

"Jennifer Jiang? She's already been picked up."

"She has?"

"She was on a plane out of the country; Agent Buel called me and we had the plane recalled and rerouted to Reagan National. They've already got her in custody."

"I wonder where they were taking her?"

"I don't know; I can find out."

THERE WERE more than a dozen senior officials milling about the Oval Office, waiting for news. The president was pacing nervously, and talking to himself; the stress was clearly showing.

The Oval Office was a beehive of activity as senior officials came and went, and their pagers went off and their cell phones went off, and their aides handed them reports, and they whispered instructions to their aides.

Finally, the president had had enough. "I can't think with everyone talking at once. Now, I want you to start putting together some contingency plans, in the event the Chinese don't get those troops out of there. I want a reasoned-out and rational response. When I want people in here, I'll ask for my national security adviser and the chairman of the Joint Chiefs.

For the time being, nobody else. Now everyone else find a place to work, but not in here."

Just moments before, Jennifer had received a call on her pager. She stepped into a side room off the Oval Office and dialed her cellphone. She called to check her messages.

She had one. It was from Major Chi. Her heart was beating wildly, and she could scarcely breathe. She dialed his number and listened carefully as he spoke.

After the call, she leaned against a wall, closed her eyes, and tried to calm herself. She felt faint, and weak, and lightheaded, and happy beyond belief.

He was out! He was safe. They were aboard the *Tiger Claw*, and they were headed back to Taipei!

All she had to do was to get the next available flight out of Washington, and she would be in Japan within eighteen hours.

And when the situation calmed down, they would meet in Taiwan.

"Mister President. It's Defense Minister Lee of Taiwan."

"Finally!" he exclaimed. "Now we get to talk to somebody in the Taiwanese government. What line is he on?"

"Line One," came the reply from his secretary's office. "By the way, his English is somewhat better than the last one."

"That's good; but I've got my interpreter with me, just in case." He started waving to Jennifer as she emerged from the side room. "It's the defense minister of Taiwan," he advised her. "His English, I understand, is not bad, so I think it would be better if we start out in English – greetings and so forth – and switch to Chinese if necessary."

"Of course, Mister President."

"I want you to listen to every word that he says – and every nuance – and you find out what's going on over there. Got it?"

"Yes, Mister President."

"Put the call through, please."

The president set the phone on speaker mode so that they could both hear what was said.

The line was connected. "Mister President."

Jennifer cocked her head at those words; the voice seemed familiar.

"Yes, Minister Lee."

"Mister President, these reports, I'm afraid are terribly exaggerated," said the minister. "It's rumor, and speculation. Yes, there's been some shooting, and a few foreign troops are rumored to be on our soil, but it's an internal civil matter and quite frankly the origin of it all has not so much to do with China as it does with the most unfortunate actions of the United States."

"I see," the president replied. "That's most encouraging."

Jennifer heard every word, but she knew that something was wrong. There was no doubt the man was speaking not with a Taiwanese accent, but with an unmistakable Beijing accent. Of course, there was no way the president could have been able to tell the difference, but she knew the voice. She knew the voice as well as she knew her own.

It was Song Bei, her uncle.

She waved a hand to get the president's attention.

The president looked quizzically at her. "One moment please." He muted the speaker and turned to her.

"My uncle!" she said quietly.

"What? I don't understand. What are you talking about?"

"That's not the defense minister of Taiwan," she replied. "This man is speaking with a Beijing accent."

"What the devil are you talking about? What do you mean, your uncle?"

"My uncle is in Taiwan, claiming to be the defense minister. Something is clearly wrong. It's not just a renegade force that parachuted in. They've taken over the entire government."

The president was stunned by those words. "Who are you? I'm confused. I'm having a hard enough time making decisions right now, and now you tell me this is your uncle I'm talking to? Your uncle is the defense minister of Taiwan? I thought you were from China. What the hell is going on here?"

"I am Chinese. They've invaded, Mister President. They sent him there; don't you see? This invasion is for real, Mister President! You must stop them!"

"They sent who there? I don't understand. I'm totally confused."

"Mister president, you've got to turn this over to the vice president. Let him handle it."

"No, this doesn't make any sense," he said, as his hands began shaking. Perspiration was dripping from his forehead. "No, no, I don't know who you are, I don't know what you're doing here. I need to sit down."

She could see clearly that the president of the United States was no longer capable of thinking straight.

The Secret Service had finally figured out the fact that Jennifer Jiang had been not been taken into custody for purposes of investigation, but had been taken directly to the Oval Office.

An agent who finally understood the situation rushed up the president's secretary. "Where's Miss Jiang?"

"She's in with the president. Why?"

"Are you people crazy?"

"Why? What's the matter?"

Jennifer knew that she had no choice; there was now only one way to stop the invasion. She grabbed the letter opener from the top of the desk. In one swift movement she grabbed it from the top of the desk, clutched it and plunged it into the president's chest. It tore through the muscle and lodged in his heart.

He gasped loudly, his eyes riveting on hers as he sank from his chair to the floor. "I don't understand…"

The president's secretary pushed open the door to the Oval Office and she took in the stunning scene. The president was lying on the floor beside his desk. Jennifer stood beside him, the bloody weapon in her hand.

"Oh, my god!" the secretary gasped, and then she screamed.

At that, Bill Robinson rushed into the room, with three

more agents on his heels. Their reaction was instinctual; without hesitation, they drew weapons.

She made no effort to protect herself, but stood quietly, her eyes closed, her head bowed. She was hit with a dozen bullets in the space of ten seconds, and she slumped to the floor, her body coming to rest not a foot from the man she had assassinated only moments before.

## 55

The Sea Stallion landed on the deck of the *Ronald Reagan* at eleven p.m. The chopper doors were opened and the vice president was the first one to exit. He was met by a guard of armed sailors, as well as by several senior officers, including the commanders of the carrier as well as of the battle group.

"Admiral Townes," Ferguson said while acknowledging the salutes. "Let me talk to the president."

"That would be yourself, sir," replied Townes. "The president is dead."

Ferguson stopped in mid-stride. "Has that been confirmed?"

"It happened in just the last few minutes, sir. We've got a direct line to the Oval Office open right now. The entire cabinet and the congressional leadership are on the way to the White House. What are your orders, Mister President?"

Ferguson had just been delivered his second huge shock for the day; he looked about and saw the grim looks on the faces of the officers and knew that he had not imagined what he had heard. "Tell me everything we have on the situation up to now," he said as he resumed stride and headed for the ship's tower.

"I think it's for real, sir," said Chuck Townes, as he walked abreast of the president. He led the commander-in-chief into the

## 292 THE SIRENS OF MING HAI

command information center and showed him all of the evidence that pointed to an invasion: the planes were seen to be coming from bases all over Eastern China, and not simply one region.

Ferguson took a look at the radar screen. "It's for real, all right."

"Sir, on our own initiative, we've buzzed those troop carriers," said the admiral. "We've radioed and told them they must turn back."

"And...?"

"No luck, sir. Those paratroopers are falling like rain. I think the only way we're going to turn them back is to shoot a few of them down. I'll need your authorization for that, sir."

"First, warn the Chinese government that we will fire on their troop transport if they don't turn back immediately."

Five minutes later, Admiral Townes was back to Ferguson. "The Chinese refuse to acknowledge our communications."

The president seemed lost in his thoughts. The men in the room were silent as they awaited orders from their new commander-in-chief. "Admiral Townes?" he said at last.

The admiral stepped forward. "Sir."

"Repel the invasion force."

"Repel the invasion force! Aye, aye, sir!"

Within minutes, SA2 missiles began to leave the carrier group's cruisers. They traveled up and headed downrange toward the troop transport planes. Radar showed that every missile found a target, and within minutes two dozen planes had been knocked out of the sky, with all troops aboard presumed killed.

Still, the invasion was on. More planes were loading up on the Chinese airfields, and they were fueled and ready for take off. The loss of a few thousand men meant nothing to the Chinese.

The president was standing on the carrier deck, watching as more missiles sailed downrange. He was approached by the executive officer of the carrier. "Sir, you're going to need to take your oath of office."

Nick was standing nearby, holding a bible.

The officer offered to administer the oath. "Sir, raise your right hand and repeat after me. I, Mark Ferguson, do solemnly swear…"

"I, Mark Ferguson, do solemnly swear…"

"…that I will faithfully execute the office of president of the United States."

"…that I will faithfully execute the office of president of the United States."

"And will, to the best of my ability, preserve, protect and defend the Constitution of the United States."

The oath was interrupted by a senior staff officer, an aide to Admiral Townes. "Excuse me, Mister President. Sir, we just picked up Chinese MIGS heading for the carrier group. It could get a little spicy up on deck; recommend you step belowdecks ASAP."

"How many incoming?" asked the new president.

"Looks like two wings, sir; fully loaded."

"Looks like you're going to have to forget the troop transports for a while."

"Yes, sir. Admiral Townes has already ordered everything we have up in the air."

"Good. I'll be done here in a minute. Sorry about that…Now, where was I?"

"That I will to the best…"

"Right. That I will to the best of my ability, preserve, protect and defend the Constitution of the United States."

"So help you God."

"So help me God."

"Congratulations, Mister President." The captain saluted.

Mark Ferguson turned to his son. "Well, what are you standing around for?"

Nick gave him a puzzled look.

"You still remember how to fly a jet, don't you?"

"I believe I do."

"Very well. I hereby appoint you a lieutenant in the United States Navy, with date of rank restored. Grab some hardware and get up in the air with everybody else." The president then turned to his aide. "And what are you waiting for, Salivator?"

"I'm your aide, sir; my presence by your side is absolutely vital to national security."

"I'll manage without you. Why don't you keep Nick company?"

"Aye, aye, sir."

Within twenty minutes every available fighter aircraft aboard the carrier was up in the air, riding out to meet the MIGs.

THE CHINESE had sent up three waves of MIGs, totaling over one hundred planes. The Americans had launched its F-14 fighter squadron and its F-18 strike fighter squadrons from the *Ronald Reagan*, as well as its marine strike fighter squadron, but the Yanks were nevertheless outnumbered by more than two to one. They would have to rely heavily on their training and their technology: each F-14 Tomcat was equipped with an array of Sidewinder, Sparrow, and Phoenix missiles, and each aircraft had the ability to track as many as twenty-four targets at a time. The Super Hornets were the most sophisticated weapons in the navy arsenal and they carried additional rockets.

Each fighter squadron was led by a navy commander, and each commander was in close contact with the USS Reagan's combat information center. The pilots and their support crews had trained for this contingency for their entire professional careers.

And now it was here.

The Chinese and Americans met in an area approximately twenty miles west of the island, over the Taiwan Straits. The aerial units were still more than five miles apart when the missiles began to fire. The Chinese fired first, and sent a battery of missiles toward the Tomcat squadron. In the nighttime sky, the Americans could easily see the flames from the missiles as they came through the air.

The Tomcats evaded fairly well, while the Super Hornets fired back at the Chinese. Both sides took hits; two Tomcats were blown up in mid-air, but the Chinese lost a squadron of planes to the Super Hornets.

Within less than a minute, their ranks closed, and the dogfights began. Each American had at least two Chinese to contend with, and so they relied heavily on their maneuverability, the accuracy of their radar and weaponry, and teamwork.

For nearly a half-hour they battled it out, each American pilot relying on his navigator to find a target for him. Still, it was impossible to avoid casualties caused by mid-air collisions, the sheer number of planes in the air, and the high probability of being hit by stray missiles.

By the end of the half-hour, half the American planes had been sent into the water, and the rest were running low on fuel. Search and rescue choppers were hovering far below in the darkness, doing their best to pull up the pilots who had been able to eject.

There were still plenty of Chinese in the air, although they had their problems as well. The Americans fought on, acting under individual initiative, with instructions from their commanders to fire every last missile they had and then high-tail it back to the carrier.

There was one final gasp from both sides, as missiles whizzed through the air, planes exploded, parachutes opened, and both sides called it a day.

The president was watching the air battle on the radar screen. He had seen more than twenty little white blips, each representing one American jet, disappear from the screen. He knew quite well that any of those disappearances could well represent the fate of Nick or the Salivator.

Admiral Townes knew what was on the president's mind. "Nick's a damn good fighter pilot, Mark; especially when the heat's turned up. The Salivator too. They'll come out of this OK."

The president watched as another American plane disappeared from the screen. "As long as they do their duty," he said, turning away. "That's what matters."

The president left the CIC and walked to the tower, where he could observe the remnants of the fighter squadrons coming back to base. As he observed the night landings, he was approached by a senior staff officer. "Sir, we have a communication from the Chinese government. The first part of the message is their demand that we pull the carrier group back to within one hundred miles of Japan. Secondly, they have communicated a threat to use nuclear weapons unless we cease our defense of Taiwan."

The president was calm; he continued to scan the horizon with his binoculars.

Thirty seconds later the officer spoke again. "Sir -"

The president had heard all too well. "Commander, I want you to send a message to the Chinese government. Message will consist of two parts. I want you to copy my words exactly. Ready to copy?"

"Yes, Mister President."

"To the Chinese high command. Part One. You are mistaken in who we are. These are combat elements of the United States Navy and we are not in the retreating business."

"'...not in the retreating business.' Go ahead, sir."

"Part Two. You will advise us where you intend to establish a provisional government..."

He scribbled rapidly. "...'provisional government'...Yes, sir, go ahead."

"...after we convert metropolitan Beijing into a blanket of warm, gray powder. End of message."

"'...warm, gray powder.' Yes, sir. I'll send this right out."

A few minutes later the commander was back in touch with the commander-in-chief. "Sir, the Chinese have responded to your message."

"Go ahead..."

"They said they were misunderstood. They have no intention of resorting to nuclear weapons."

Another long pause.

"Right."

MEANWHILE, on land, the Chinese forces found that the road to Taipei was paved with bad intentions. The Taiwanese had long contemplated the possibility of a battle for their survival, and so they had set up prefabricated barriers on all major roads.

Regular troops and local militia converged from every major town and village, and there was spontaneous, spirited, and quite brutal fighting everywhere the two sides met.

President Ferguson was informed of the location of the staging grounds for the Chinese battalions which continued to land, and so he ordered American B-52 bombers to be sent down from Japan and South Korea.

"THE PROBLEM, Mister President," explained Admiral Townes, "is that we can't stop those transport planes. They just keep coming."

Mark Ferguson talked over the next move with his old friend, Chuck Townes. "Admiral, I recommend you get on the horn to the American embassy in Beijing. Locate the Chinese operational command post and get the coordinates to the nearest twenty yards."

"Yes, sir. What is your weapon of choice, Mister President?"

"SLAM."

The American Embassy, Beijing. The message came in the form of a presidential directive. The mission was to figure out where the operational command post for the air invasion was located and to mark it for destruction.

The marine lance corporal on duty ripped the communiqué from the telex and read it aloud to all the men in the room. He turned to the senior enlisted man. "Say, Gunny, where do you think the op center would be?"

The gunnery sergeant had earned his stripes many times over. He leaned back in his chair, picked up a can which he was using as a spittoon, and spat handily into the container. "Well, I'm not sure, Corporal," he said as he resumed his chaw, "but I'll tell you what. At eleven o'clock at night, I'd say look for any government building that has about a thousand bicycles parked outside it."

Over the years, by means both overt and surreptitious, the Americans had come to learn the purpose of nearly all of the governmental buildings in Beijing. As was the case in their own country, those buildings which were least approachable and least identifiable had invariably a military or other defense-related purpose assigned to it.

Furthermore, due primarily to the often unappreciated foresight of the Central Intelligence Agency, the American government knew the latitude and longitude, within ten feet, of every Chinese governmental building in the city; and they kept up-to-date pictures of every building on file.

The assumption was that the operation was being run from one of the two dozen buildings along Chaoyang Road which could reasonably have served the purpose of an operational command center for a massive aerial attack. It was just a matter of figuring out which building was being used for that purpose, and they would already have its location pinpointed and plotted. As an added measure, they carried a transmitter which, if they could succeed in getting it onto the top or otherwise near the target building, could be used to transmit the location of the building via satellite.

The American marines set out for Chaoyang Road within a few minutes of getting their orders. There was no way they were going to get out the front gate of the embassy without being observed and followed, but over the years they had developed other means of egress from the building, most of which involved carefully-constructed tunnel links to nearby buildings.

The marines kept on hand a supply of Chinese peasant outfits for just such an occasion. The loose-fitting garments allowed them to carry a reasonable supply of weapons and ammunition underneath.

When they emerged onto the street about a block away from the embassy, they found that they could move quite easily through the streets. It was a warm night, and there were numerous people moving about the streets. Naturally, all Chinese citizenry were oblivious to any military activities being conducted by their government at that moment.

Chaoyang Road was less than a twenty minute hike from the embassy and when the marines arrived there they saw that the gunnery sergeant was right. There were hundreds of bicycles parked in a lot near a non-descript, windowless, modern-but-drab-looking government building. However, that wasn't the only clue as to the activity being conducted in the building. The roads around the building were blocked off, and there were scores of soldiers from the People's Liberation Army guarding access to it.

Every few seconds a military vehicle or governmental limousine was seen approaching the blockades, and the PLA guards used flashlights to check the identity of the passenger.

Two marines had stayed behind in the embassy, ready to receive and relay any communications regarding exactly which building was to be targeted. The marines double-checked the location of the building against their map and, when they were sure, they radioed back to the embassy and provided the building number. That information was instantly transmitted from the marines in the street to the marines in the embassy to the CVIC – the aircraft carrier intelligence center.

The gunnery sergeant thought that it would be impossible to get the transmitter up onto the top of the building, but the staff sergeant was willing to risk his neck trying. He prepared a sling, and was about to make a run for the building, when the marines noticed that they had company.

They all turned and looked. There were two dozen PLA converging on them with rifles and bayonets.

The gunfight was short, bloody and horrific. When it was over, twelve of the PLA were dead. And all of the marines.

LIEUTENANT D. S. COOKE, one of the most experienced F18-F pilots in the U.S. Navy, was designated to carry out the Standoff Land Attack Missile mission – the SLAM. He was stationed on board the carrier John C. Stennis, which had been on high alert since the beginning of hostilities and which now lay one hundred fifty miles from the China coast, in the East China Sea.

Cooke's plane was quickly outfitted with the special Cruise missiles intended to take out the occupational command post in Beijing.

Lieutenant Cooke left the carrier deck less than five minutes after the location of the OCP had been relayed from the American embassy to the Stennis' CVIC. Cooke headed straight for the Gulf of Chihli, which lay to the east of Beijing.

His instructions were to try to get within fifty miles of the coast, and then fire his missiles. He was lucky and had gotten almost as far as the coastline before he was spotted by Chinese air defense forces and a pair of MIGs was sent up to meet him.

He spotted the MIGs at thirty miles out. The primary mission had to be taken care of first, and so Cooke launched his two Cruise missiles. Their launch jolted his plane, slowing it slightly. The missiles dropped almost to sea level, and made their way toward the Forbidden City.

Rather than making an immediate turn-back toward his carrier, Cooke decided to take on the MIGs. He tracked both and, when he closed to within ten miles, launched two missiles, dived five thousand feet to avoid any return fire, and turned sharply to the east and headed for the carrier.

The carrier was able to pick up the air battle, and the CIC let him know that both MIGs had disappeared from the radar.

Cooke was well past the Shandong Peninsula when his television screen came on and showed him exactly what his Cruise missiles were seeing with the infrared cameras mounted on their noses. They had just then arrived over Beijing.

Despite the night, the infrared cameras could make out the eerie blue-white tints of the government buildings along Chaoyang Street, where the marines had battled it out only a short time before and now lay dead.

Cooke got his first glimpse of the OCP when the missiles were less than three miles away. The marines had communicated the presence of the distinctive radar and communications tower of the building, and Cooke had little trouble being certain of his target.

The first Cruise missile was a half-mile ahead of the second, but it was off course very slightly. Using signaling equipment aboard his F18, the pilot was able to steer the lead missile so that it headed directly for the windows on the second floor of the building. The missile complied with the electronic command, and entered the OCP less than twenty minutes after leaving the F18. The explosion inside the building could be seen from the camera of the second missile, and it showed a fifty foot section of roof being blown away, with massive shuddering of the building and clouds of dust spewing out.

A few seconds later, the second Cruise followed its companion into what remained of the building.

## 56

When the center of a centralized government will not hold, everything comes to a halt. And so it was when the OCP was knocked out: all aircraft takeoffs from the mainland ceased. And thus it was that a combination of factors led to the quick cessation of hostilities on the island: the loss of the command center, the ceaseless bombing of the Chinese troops by the B-52s, the spirited fighting of the Taiwanese, and the presence of Mark Ferguson at the top of the American chain-of-command.

By noon the next day, the commanders of the Chinese paratrooper regiments knew what the score was, and they began surrendering what was left of their units.

At the same time, the new president of the United States was walking through the corridors of the American naval hospital in Yokusuka, Japan, where the U. S. Seventh Fleet was headquartered. He was accompanied by several officers of the headquarters staff, as well as by his own staff; and Nick.

The president moved slowly among the wards, stopping to check on the condition of every pilot who had been brought back from the waters off the coast of Taiwan.

Finally he came to one whose face was bandaged heavily, but who was still somewhat recognizable. "Who's he?" asked Ferguson.

"Lieutenant Russell J. DiSalvo, sir," said the attending physician.

"How bad?"

"Several broken bones, shrapnel in the shoulder and face. Some internal bleeding. Severe concussion. Comatose."

"Prognosis?"

"Stable, but too early to tell, Mister President."

"I want you to take good care of this one."

The president walked into a large ward where several pilots, wearing casts or walking on crutches, came up to shake his hand. Others, who were conscious but not ambulatory, lifted their heads from their pillows in order to see the president.

"When will you boys be going home?" asked the commander-in-chief.

"They tell us they'll have a plane ready by next week, sir," said one lieutenant.

"I suppose you'd like to go home today, if you could," said Ferguson.

"Yes, sir; the sooner the better."

The president turned to a military aide. "Put 'em on my plane; I got room." Air Force One had arrived from Washington that morning.

A staff officer approached the president and whispered quietly. "Sir, some of these guys are a bloody mess."

The president halted sharply and gave the officer a withering stare. "I really don't like to repeat myself, Commander."

An hour later a dozen pilots, some on crutches, some on gurneys, made their way toward the president's plane. They were helped up and into the well-appointed presidential plane, accompanied by several doctors and nurses.

Numerous coffins were placed aboard the plane, carrying the bodies of a half dozen pilots and several agents of the Secret Service.

Shortly thereafter, Air Force One lifted from the runway and headed across the Pacific. And so, like a modern-day Arthur, Mark Ferguson gathered his broken and weary knights around him – and mindful of the heroic dead, whom he brought with him – he led his men home.

# Epilogue

The Salivator recovered fully, and went on to serve the president as a trusted aide for the balance of the Ferguson Administration. His son grew up to hear time and again the stories of his and Nick's exploits in the air and on the seas; needless to say, they were brilliantly exaggerated.

When Nick arrived at Andrews Air Force Base on the flight from Japan, he was pleased to be met in the waiting area by Ellen Conley and Gregory. After a renewed courtship of several months, Nick and Ellen were married. No one could have been more overjoyed upon the occasion than young Gregory "Ace" Conley, whose idol and father were now one and the same.

A naval investigation board concluded that there was sufficient evidence of a mechanical failure within the avionics of the Super Hornet to cause the plane to spin out of control, and Nick was fully exonerated.

President Mark Ferguson served with great distinction for the remainder of his predecessor's term, and his own reelection was a mere formality. He extended the hand of friendship to China at every turn on their long and difficult road to democracy.

His death, six years after leaving office, was universally mourned, in every land and clime where heroic action in the defense of liberty is still prized. And in no case was his death more deeply mourned than on the island of Taiwan, which, due to his calm, deliberate and resolute actions, retained its sovereign status.

It retains it to this day.

THE BODY of Jiang Ou was placed in a metal casket and was flown to San Francisco and from there to Hawaii, where it was met by an unofficial contingent from Taiwan. There, Jin Yi-bo claimed the body, showing proof of having wed her in a secret Buddhist ceremony some years before. In order that their marriage not come to the attention of her parents, they had not registered their nuptials with the Chinese government. The bride had been seventeen and the groom nineteen, and within a year she had been told the false story of her husband's death in the lao gai.

In the wake of the assassination, the political situation was awkward from every point of view. The murder of an American president – even one who had not been elected and who had never been terribly popular – was a horrendous shock to the American public. Any politically–motivated injury to a government official was a grave affront to their democratic system, and the assassination was viewed as nothing less than a capital crime.

However, if there were to be any tempering of sentiment in the matter, it lay in the knowledge that, had Billingsley not been assassinated, a free and democratic nation of twenty-six million would have been subjugated.

It was further tempered by the knowledge that President Mark Ferguson had acted with supreme confidence and that the American navy had covered itself with glory in a noble cause.

The Chinese, of course, protested, with intense anger and threats, the interference in the invasion, but their anger could not but be muted by the world's knowledge that it was one of their own citizens – a niece of the highly-placed Song Bei – who had played a critical role in foiling it.

The Taiwanese were immensely grateful to the American government for its role. However, due to the death of the American president, the Taiwanese government could not be seen to be taking part in any burial honors given to Jiang Ou.

Thus, no military officer or government official was part of the funerary procession, although the public had been given permission to observe the procession along Su Wei Road and to commemorate her passage through the city. Three million Taiwanese citizens – or one out of nine out of that country's population – were to line the processional route.

Upon its arrival in Taipei, the body of Jiang Ou had been removed from the metal casket and placed in a wooden one, which was in turn placed upon a simple wooden cart. The cart was to be drawn through the city by six men: two former prisoners of the lao gai, including Bao Luan; two Taiwanese fishermen; and two farmers from outlying villages. Jin Yi-bo limped behind, aided by a crutch.

As the procession passed through the streets, there was no sound to be heard except for that of the wheels of the little cart rolling along on the pavement.

On the outskirts of Taipei, the body was cremated and the ashes placed in a small wooden container. By means of a motorcade, Jin Yi-bo accompanied the container to the western coast of Taiwan. The motorcade arrived just before dusk at the tiny village of Ming Hai, the fishing village where the Chinese planes had entered Taiwanese airspace.

At a point just south of the village, he and Bao Luan stepped into a small boat and set the container of ashes in the boat.

From every part of the island nation of Taiwan they had been coming all day: firetrucks – scores, hundreds, perhaps a thousand firetrucks from every part of the island nation. As Jin Yi-bo plied his way along the coast, he passed the firetrucks lining the road which ran beside the sea. One by one, they turned their sirens on as he passed below in his boat. He began taking small handfuls of the ashes and sprinkling them in the sea.

By the time he had traveled a half-mile, there were hundreds of sirens wailing. By the time he had gone two miles, there were a thousand. And just in case the sirens of Ming Hai could not be heard across the Straits of Taiwan, numerous radio stations had come to that village and were broadcasting the strange, thunderous sounds so that they could be heard in homes up and down the coast of China.

As Jin Yi-bo cast the last handful of ashes into the sea, a solitary seagull swooped down, hovered over the boat for a moment, and then flew up and into the twilight sky.

After all of the ashes had been consigned to the waters, the little boat continued up the coast, out of sight of the village of Ming Hai. Still, the sirens raged on.

The sun set over the Straits of Taiwan, and the sea grew dark. Still, the sirens raged on, high-pitched voices and low rumbling basses. The moon came out and cast an eerie glow on the beach and the cliffs and the sea. Still, the sirens went on, rising and falling.

They went on long, long into the night, roaring defiance.

308 The Sirens of Ming Hai

# Afterword:
# The Lao Gai

The following information comes from an article "The Lao Gai Archipelago", originally published in The Weekly Standard, excerpted with permission. The author is veteran war correspondent David Aikman.

The term *lao gai* stands for *laodong gaizao*, or "reform through labor." The lao gai is a vast system of camps, detention centers, reeducation-through-labor institutions, and prison factories throughout China. There are an estimated 1,100 of these institutions in which prisoners are compelled to work under conditions, essentially, of slave labor. Over five decades about 50 million Chinese have been through the lao gai and the current population of the lao gai is estimated to be 6-8 million.

Much of our knowledge of the lao gai is due to the work of Wu Hongda, or Harry Wu, as he likes to be called in the United States. "Lao gai," says Wu, "is not simply a prison system, it is a political tool for maintaining the Communist Party's totalitarian rule."

The system was set up by the communists in the early 1950s, primarily to deal with the millions of real and suspected opponents of China's newly established regime. It had two main objectives. One was identical to that of the Soviet gulag: the use of coerced labor for ambitious state projects for which ordinary workers could never have been found. In the 1950s much of Manchuria was reclaimed for agriculture and industry by the labor of lao gai inmates, and in other parts of the nation coal mines were developed, canals dug, and railroads carved out of mountainsides by whole brigades and divisions of lao gai workers.

The essence of the lao gai system is obviously not the mere fact that prisoners are required to work, a phenomenon that occurs in prison systems throughout the world. It is that the lao gai from the very beginning of communist rule in China has been a hideous, ruthless instrument for keeping in power a regime that no one elected, for propping up by force a 19th-century philosophical myth that nobody believes in, and for frightening into silence any individual inclined to speak the truth about these things or anything else that has happened during China's last five decades.

The second objective of these prisons, often cited by the communist authorities as more crucial than the first, was actually far more sinister. It was not enough, the Chinese communists believed, for a prisoner to admit his guilt. He had to be morally and spiritually broken down through "thought" reform (often referred to as "brainwashing")—sessions of relentless interrogation, orchestrated emotional bullying by fellow-inmates, and sometimes the torture of sleep deprivation.

One prisoner spoke of being suspended in the air and having icy water thrown on his body, being beaten repeatedly, being shackled for months at a time in leg irons, being burned with boiling water and given shocks by that unique creation of Chinese communist technology, the electrified police baton. (This implement is sometimes misleadingly labeled a cattle prod, but it was designed solely to inflict pain on human beings and is unobtainable in China for non-police use.) This prisoner survived starvation largely by being able to catch and eat frogs, snakes, and rats.

In Mao Zedong's increasingly paranoid hunt for political oppositionists within China during the 1950s and '60s, one cruel political campaign followed another - against "counterrevolutionaries" or "rightists" much of the time. Probably the most dramatic increase in the lao gai population came between 1958 and 1960, when hundreds of thousands of suspected rightists, sometimes simply students who had criticized something the Russians had done, were rounded up and subjected to "thought reform," then to the nightmare without end that constituted the lao gai system. Many of them simply perished in the camps, part of a lao gai death toll that by Wu's calculations may have reached 15 million since 1949. Others survived, but remained in legal limbo for the rest of their lives.

Unlike [Soviet] gulag inmates, most of whom were permitted to go free if they survived their terms, many lao gai survivors never actually go home. Until Deng Xiaoping came to power in 1978, about 90 percent of all lao gai inmates who completed their terms were compelled to work for the rest of their lives in locations and at jobs assigned to them by the authorities.

Wu confirms what others had long suspected: Chinese corporations, in their lust to break into the lucrative U.S. market, were often contracting directly with lao gai labor to produce export products. Working at times with a BBC crew and with hidden cameras, Wu documented on-the record admissions of slave-labor export from Chinese traders and officials.